MW01047134

Other Books by Alain Gunn

Tale of Two Planets
Red Exodus
If Pigs Could Cry

Writing as A K Gunn

The Honey Bee
The Death of Aloha

Collections

Mystery in Paradise:13 Tales of Suspense by 13 Masters of the Genre
Dark Paradise: Mysteries in the Land of Aloha

Fire at the Bottom of the Sea

Library of Congress Control Number: 2017917964
CreateSpace Independent Publishing Platform, North Charleston, SC

Dedication

This book is dedicated to the brave men and women of the United States Navy Submarine Force, who protect our freedoms while forgoing their own, risking their lives on a daily basis while confined in submarines operating in the depths of our planet's oceans

Fire at the Bottom of the Sea

by Alain Gunn

Prelude
11 March 2011

2:46 p.m., Miyako, Japan

Before the Tohoku earthquake, the floating dock in Miyako was popular with commercial fishing boats that tied to it when not in the Pacific gathering food for the homeland and money for the owners and crew. When the earthquake hit, many of the twenty-six boats that normally tied to the dock were away, but seven were tied up, their crews either on the dock off-loading their catches, on board preparing their boats for the next voyage, or in nearby saloons drinking beer or sake.

The crews had little warning. After the earthquake hit, they barely had time to contemplate its cataclysmic consequences before the resulting tsunami rolled into Miyako Bay and over the harbor. Some drowned when the thirty-foot wave broke over their boats, while others perished when the flood destroyed the sake bars they patronized. Others were killed in their cars when the water picked them up, rolled them, and smashed them into the pavement. A few lucky ones escaped and came back days later to a scene of utter devastation.

The dock itself broke in half when the first wave smashed onto it. Attached cables and hawsers tore ragged pieces from the fishing boats moored to it when they were ripped away to be rolled and sunk. The larger section of the dock, with all its attached hawsers and cables, was dragged nearly a mile inland before being swept out to sea as the second wave receded. There it began an eighteen-thousand-mile voyage, accompanied by a million tons of other tsunami debris spread over an area of ocean the size of Texas. The debris floated northeast, carried by the great Coriolis current that circulates water around the North Pacific. It tickled the coasts of the Aleutian Islands before turning south, passing Alaska, British Columbia, Washington, Oregon, and California in the Alaskan current, then headed out to sea again, having joined the same westerly current in the northern tropics that Thor Heyerdahl captured on the raft Kon-Tiki when he tried to prove that Polynesia was settled by migrants from South America.

The dock made a second loop around the northern Pacific and a third before it finally came to a position northeast of the Big Island of Hawaii nine years after it left Japan.

In the years it wallowed in the ocean, the floating dock changed its character, becoming almost unrecognizable as an object made by man. The long cables and hawsers that hung from its stanchions, torn away from their vessels when the boats were demolished by Neptune's fury, became encrusted with barnacles. Their dangling ends corroded to spear points. Coral polyps set up home in the crevices and spread to the dock itself. The structure gained weight as the polyps built homes of calcium, until the dock barely broke the surface. It attracted schools of small fish that hid in its recesses and ate the plant and animal life that clung to its surfaces. These, in turn attracted larger predators. By the time the dock neared Hawaii, it had transformed into a floating island that hosted all manner of sea life, including schools of bait fish surrounded by numerous pelagic predators.

Its many cables hung a hundred feet below it like the toxic tentacles of a box jellyfish awaiting the brush of unwary prey. A constant school of small fish and the predators that ate them surrounded and camouflaged the structure. The dock thus became the centerpiece of its own little ecosystem, a fisherman's dream, except that it was untethered and uncharted, almost invisible from the surface of the ocean. From afar, only the sea birds circling in the sky above it provided a hint of its existence.

Chapter 1

21 January 2020

6:23 a.m., Submarine Base, Pearl Harbor, Hawaii

"I'll miss you guys," Commander Daniel Farriott said, breathing in his wife's fragrance while he held her in his arms.

Ellen Farriott kissed her husband good-bye. "I'll miss you, too," she said. "We all will."

"At least we're not going to war. It's just training. We'll be back in two or three months."

"It's hard, though." She released him so he could hug Steven and Penny.

He knelt to their level and held them both together. "You take care of your mom and your sister," he told Steven. Then he turned to Penny. "You be nice to your brother, you rascal," he said. He kissed each on the forehead.

Daniel released the kids, stood, gave Ellen a wry smile, shrugged, and said, "Duty calls."

"Be safe," she said. "We'll be okay. We're used to it."

He turned, went up the ramp, saluted Mike Polanski, the Chief of Boat (COB), and asked, "Crew accounted for?

"All aboard, sir. Ready to push off," Polanski answered.

"Good. Let's get moving." He descended into the submarine, giving a final wave and a smile to his family before his head disappeared into the hatch. Polanski stayed topside to supervise their embarkation, a communication bud in his left ear. Two sailors, one at the bow and another at the stern, awaited the order to cast off.

Daniel went first to his stateroom, where he stowed his personal gear. Not much of that was needed on a submarine, and storage space was almost nonexistent. Sharing was encouraged. He put his gear in a single drawer, then left for the bridge.

A half-dozen individuals awaited Daniel in the crowded bridge. The area was only twelve feet long and a little more than eight feet wide. Three helmsmen were in their seats, and various officers waited to report to him. Daniel first greeted his new executive officer (XO),

Lieutenant Commander Wendy Peyton, then got to work. They had a checklist to run through before embarkation. Among the one hundred twenty-eight items on the checklist were myriad details critical to the functioning of the submarine. They'd be underwater for nearly three months, and the checklist covered everything from the reactor status to the number of frozen hamburgers on board.

He and Peyton checked with every one of his fourteen officers and eighteen petty officers, each in charge of a key portion of the boat's functioning; radiation control, communications, engineering, navigation, weapons, supplies, etc. Finally satisfied, Daniel logged in the results of his checklist review.

"Start her up, Chief," he ordered, communicating with the reactor room.

"Aye, aye, sir."

A whirring sound commenced, accompanied by a familiar, unpleasant vibration they would have to live with for the next few months.

"Prepare to cast off," he ordered, his voice broadcasting over all the common links so the entire crew could hear, including the COB topside.

After a moment, he ordered, "Cast off."

"Hawsers free," he heard Polanski say a moment later.

"Ahead slow. Fifteen degrees' port rudder," Farriott ordered. "COB, guide us into the center of the channel." Farriott could feel the submarine begin to move in response to his command, turning subtly to port.

"We'll be central in five seconds, skipper," Polanski reported.

"Rudder fifteen degrees starboard, Farriott ordered"

"We're centered, skipper," Polanski stated a moment later.

"Set course for one hundred eighty degrees. COB, stay up there until we're out of the channel. Keep a lookout."

"Aye, aye, sir. We're centered nicely. No obstacles I can see ahead. We've got the channel to ourselves."

"Very good. Come down when we're past the first buoy."

While Daniel was thrilled to be underway, he often felt a profound sense of responsibility and inadequacy at the beginning of a voyage. Submarines these days were technical and complex. He knew he could never remember every detail he was expected to know. Fortunately, he had a dedicated team with him. Together, they had the answers to just about any question of importance. The crew of the JPC were highly selected, and he was proud of them all. He felt privileged to command them.

Some, of course, were new and unproven. He'd know soon if there were any bad apples among them. Good or bad, he was stuck with them, at least until they returned to Pearl Harbor. *Not to worry,* he thought, with a smile. His talented non-commissioned officers (NCO's) were expert at handling potential troublemakers. Any slackers would be shown the light in very short measure. He didn't always want to know just how his NCO's engineered their epiphanies. Whatever method they used, it was effective. Over time, only a few sailors had not acquired wisdom. Those were now on other boats or out of the Navy.

He was also proud of his submarine. It was the most recent addition to Pearl Harbor and one of the first of a new class of submarine, much more versatile than the prior boomers and attack submarines that still made up the bulk of American submarines around the world.

The John P. Craven had been named after the legendary chief scientist of the Polaris Missile submarine project. The crew laughed about the name of their boat. They couldn't call it the "Craven" since that signified cowardice, nor could they call it the "John," even though toilets were called "heads" on a boat. Even the P in the middle name was unfortunate, as it stood for "Piña," a little too close to the word for a portion of male anatomy. So, they called her the JPC, pronouncing it "Jaypek."

Of course, since it was so new, its limitations were still being defined. Only with the experience of running it could the built-in problems that plague all new, technically-sophisticated machines be brought to light. It was Farriott's job to discover these problems, hopefully before they became dangerous. Better to find and fix fatal faults in a controlled environment than in the heat of battle.

In their first two voyages, the JPC had performed flawlessly, but in the first running, he'd been restricted to a series of basic maneuvers handed to him by the engineers. They had stressed the submarine, but not in ways that reflected the reality of combat conditions. He was given more leeway in testing during the second voyage but was still on a tether. During this third voyage, he was no longer bound by the engineers, and he planned to really push her, to test the limits of his submarine and the competence of his crew.

He wondered what would go wrong. Something would. In a boat with this much technology aboard, there had to be flaws somewhere, and Daniel was duty-bound to find them before they became critical problems. He could only hope that the flaws he discovered would not be fatal ones.

6:33 a.m., Submarine Base, Pearl Harbor, Hawaii

Ellen stood at the dock for a moment longer than she wanted. Mike Polanski was watching her, and she knew it wouldn't look good if she charged right off. She had to show a little reluctance to part. After a suitable time, she gathered the kids and said, in a loud voice, for Polanski's benefit more than for the kids, "We've got to get you to school." They turned away from the sub and walked back to their van. She latched them into their car seats, got into the driver's seat, and drove off.

"When's daddy coming back?" Penny asked.

"Can't say. When the mission's done," she answered, in her South Carolina twang. "A couple months. Maybe three"

"I miss him already," Penny said

"Me, too, honey." In some ways she would miss him, she thought. He was a good man. He was making rank and would be a captain soon, and then it would be only a few years more until he would be an admiral. But she had more freedom when he was gone.

She looked in the rear-view mirror at Steven. He looked like a rag-head, with curly cowlicks standing up like the hair on a kewpie doll that's been mauled by a dog. Daniel liked to cut Steven's hair himself when he was home, and it looked like a home job to Ellen. Too short and military-looking. She usually took Steven to the barber soon after Daniel left. Not that it made a lot of difference. He never combed it, and he had curly hair, so it never looked very good.

He wiggled in his seat, earphones in his ears, tapping out the rhythm of whatever he was listening to. What was it about kids that made music so important after a certain age? He was only eleven. The hormones hadn't kicked in yet. But he was practically dancing in his seat. Was it an omen, an indication of what was to come as he matured? Her son had become mysterious to her, developing in directions that she found surprising. She had no adult experience with adolescent boys. What she knew about them was derived from her own experiences as a teenager, with no brothers and no boys in her all-girl preparatory school. It was a wonder that she knew anything.

She dropped them off at Makalapa Elementary School and hesitated only a moment before driving off. She'd taken them to school with plenty of time to spare.

When she got to Salt Lake Boulevard, she had a choice to make. Should she turn right and head into Foster Village, where they lived, or should she turn left toward the freeway that would take her toward downtown? She knew what she should do, but she didn't head home. She turned left, then right, then right again at the freeway entrance. She grumbled, caught in bumper-to-bumper rush-hour traffic over Red Hill and all the way to the Pali Highway exit. She had already expended thirty minutes before she exited on the Pali Highway, and another half-hour passed before she was in Kailua.

She knew that what she was doing wasn't right. She wondered how she'd come to this and where it would go. She hoped it wouldn't blow up in her face, destroy her and her family. When she halted at the stop light at Kalaheo, she almost turned around and went home, but then her imagination took over. She felt herself dampen below. Instead of turning, she drove straight ahead, then pulled into a mall's parking lot, stopped, and took out her phone. She called. "He's gone," she said, when Victor answered the phone.

"Wonderful. Are you available for an interior decoration consultation?" he asked her, a welcoming chuckle in his voice.

"I'm five minutes away."

"I'll be expecting you."

She hung up, drove down Honeawa street, turned right, and then pulled into the visitor parking of a luxury condominium. She had to sign in at the front desk–something that always made her uncomfortable, even though she had a legitimate business excuse to be there. She was, after all, an interior designer, and Victor was an architect. In fact, he had designed the building in which she stood, and she had done the interior design work for his apartment.

He opened immediately when she knocked on his door. He wore a silk bathrobe and a big smile when she entered, and he kissed her on both cheeks in the European way once the door was closed. "Would you like some coffee before the consultation?" he asked her.

"No. I'm hungry, very hungry," she answered.

He nodded, nuzzled her neck, and then began to unbutton her blouse. His bathrobe fell open, and her breath caught in her throat. He was already erect. She sighed, her heart beating a mile a minute as he unsnapped her bra and let it fall to the floor. He took her nipple in his mouth, and she gasped, but then stopped him. "In there," she whispered, pointing to the bedroom.

She finished undressing slowly while he watched her from the bed. She took her time, letting the tension build. By the time she finally straddled him, her nipples were hard and hypersensitive, her heart was racing and she was panting from anticipation. A short time later, she erupted, overwhelmed by the strongest, most satisfying orgasm she'd had in the last three months.

Before they stopped for brunch, she had two more.

7:20 a.m., Pacific Ocean, southeast of Oahu, aboard the JPC

Farriott yielded command to his executive officer (XO), Lieutenant Commander Peyton, after the submarine exited Pearl Harbor. He wasn't sure of Peyton yet. He'd never had a female officer before, and he wasn't convinced she had what it took. From her records, the woman seemed technically competent, but tales of her dealings with past crews worried Farriott. The scuttlebutt was that she was officious, disdainful, and insulting. Was she a "kiss up, kick down" woman? If so, that would be a problem. Good officers had to treat their crew with respect while still maintaining discipline.

The other possibility, of course, was that the problem was with her past crews, who weren't used to being commanded by a woman. He'd noticed during the preparation for the voyage that his COB, Mike Polanski, for example, seemed to bypass her and come to him every time he got a chance rather than using the chain of command. That was okay when the boat was ashore but wouldn't be possible when the boat was at sea. It was a pattern of behavior that Daniel would have to fix. It would be better, however, if LC Peyton fixed the problem herself. Overcoming bias was basic in command. All new commanders went through a period where their new crew questioned their competence, and being one of the first female XO's in the Navy certainly would increase her challenges in establishing her credibility. The only way to overcome insubordination was to demonstrate leadership. Daniel intended to give her the chance. If she failed, of course, he'd step in.

Having never seen her on duty at sea, he could not vouch for her technical competence. She'd made grade ahead of her peers, so she must have had at least acceptable skills, but Daniel knew that making grade involved a combination of competence and politics. She was a woman breaking a glass ceiling, and the politics were not ignorable.

The only way to assess his new XO was to watch her while she was doing her job. That meant starting her on simple tasks, then gradually watching her do more and more complex tasks. Eventually, she'd make a mistake and Daniel would intervene. Daniel wanted that mistake to happen while they were performing routine maneuvers, not in a crisis. By the end of their three-month tour, he'd know Peyton well and they'd either have a great working relationship or a real problem. Either way, Daniel was probably going to work with her for a long time.

They ran on the surface until they were clear of Pearl Harbor. Peyton didn't try to set the boat's final course until they were submerged, over a nautical mile from shore. At that point, Peyton asked, "What's the heading, Skipper?"

"Keep it at one-eighty for now," Daniel answered. "Let's do a sonar check first."

"Yes sir," answered Peyton. She got on the intercom. "COB, set up a passive sonar screen," she said.

A few minutes later, Mike Polanski's voice came back on the intercom. "Sonar's clear, ma'am. Commercial boat traffic only, and nothing within a mile of us."

"Acknowledged," Wendy answered. She glanced at Daniel, raising her eyebrows in an unstated question.

"Set course for one hundred ten degrees. We'll work off the south point of the Big Island for a while. Take her down to four hundred feet." Daniel waited until they were at depth and on course, then stood up. She'd made one small mistake. If he hadn't intervened, she would have set course before she checked the sonar for surveillance submarines. He'd talk to her later about it, in private. It was no big deal in peacetime, but it could be a fatal mistake in time of war.

Daniel had picked up foreign submarines before. Both Chinese and Russian subs liked to monitor Pearl Harbor. If they picked up an American sub's course, they'd try to follow. The result was a cat-and-mouse game. Most of the time, Daniel had found the alien subs easy to outmaneuver. Some, though, seemed to have CO's with unusual skill and intuition, and their submarines had technical sophistication that almost matched the U.S. boats. One boat had followed for half a day before Daniel was able to shake him. Today was easy, though. The aliens had gone back to Vladivostok or wherever they'd come from. The next few hours would be a straight shot to the southern tip of the Big Island. The excitement wouldn't begin until they were in the deep ocean. That's when they'd really find out what this new boat could do.

"You've got the bridge," he said. "I'll walk the length, then be in my stateroom."

He climbed down the ladder to the main deck, and walked aft, past his own quarters and the crew quarters, ending at the reactor. He watched each crew member work, seeing the sideways glances and light touches of one crewman to another to spread the word that the CO was present. He exchanged small talk with the technical crew, paying particular attention to new crew members. The JPC had a crew of a hundred and twenty-eight, with fourteen officers. This cruise, six new crew members and two new officers had to be assimilated. He had to get to know them, their limitations as well as their strengths. By the end of the cruise he'd know them as well as he knew his best friends. There were very few secrets on a submarine. For now, though, the new crew members were a mystery and had to be considered a potential danger.

He sniffed the air. Every submarine had its own smell, a combination of grease, body odors, acrid effluents from the electronics, and the salt smell of the sea. This one still smelled new, like a well-oiled machine, but that would change after a full year under the sea.

He walked forward, past the crew's quarters, the kitchen, mess hall, and sonar room, stopping to talk to Mike Polanski, the COB, who was working with a new sonar man.

"Everything good, Chief?" he asked.

"We got the usual bunch of bullshit, Skipper," Polanski answered. "Number three sonar just started acting up. Wouldn't pick up a turd in a head. The other four are okay, though. I think we'll have this one fixed in an hour or so.

"We got some new crew, too. One female sonar tech, she seems to know her stuff. Takes no shit from any of the guys. I got her hot-bedding in a bunk with Celia Hutchinson. They'll get along fine.

"Two of the other guys look competent. Three guys don't know shit, but they're trainable. You don't got to worry about them. I'll whip them in shape right quick. We don't want none of them calling for mama when the shit comes down."

"I'm sure you will. We're going to shake them up pretty well tomorrow. Deep dives and pop-ups."

"I'll have the barf bags ready. Thanks for the warning."

Farriott sniffed. "Smells pretty good in here now. Try to keep it that way."

Polanski laughed. "Seems to me you got a couple newbies in the officers' quarters, too. You better watch out where you're standing, Sir. Them nice brown shoes you got won't look so good if they get splattered."

"I'll be careful, COB. Good advice."

"I aims to please, Sir."

Farriott smiled at Polanski's salty language as he walked away. The man was a gem, a top-notch COB. As with all military units, the JPC had two parallel lines of authority. The first went from Farriott to his subordinate officers, through their respective petty officers, and to the crew. The second went from Farriott through the COB straight to the petty officers and crew. Both lines were important, one providing a check and balance on the other. Farriott regarded Polanski as the most important man on the submarine. It was his job to "cut through the crap" and communicate command decisions to each member of the crew. To do that, he had to use their language, which wasn't the king's English. But his vocabulary belied his intelligence. Mike Polanski was one of the smartest men Farriott had met, a pragmatic thinker with uncommon common sense.

He walked back past the torpedo room and stopped at the cruise missile tubes.

Like the Ohio class submarines, the JPC had been built for stealth, with an advanced and silent propulsion system and an ability to hide in the deep ocean. The hull was carbon-fiber, lighter and stronger than steel, and less echogenic. The JPC would be super-hard for enemy submarines to find once it was away from port.

Instead of ballistic missiles, however, the JPC fired cruise missiles, similar to the old Tomahawks, but much more versatile. These could be fitted with a variety of warheads, including tactical nukes and the newer blockbusters that packed almost as much power as a tactical nuke and could destroy facilities that were deep underground. They could be fired from seventy-meters keel depth, and could target "intermediate" distances, up to two thousand miles away, with pinpoint accuracy. Very few places in the world were more than two thousand miles away from an ocean.

Like the attack submarines, their power-train was powerful enough to attain speeds above forty-five knots, beyond that of most surface ships, and their maneuverability was far in advance of any prior class of submarine. In Daniel's view, the Cowrie class was truly today's solution for enforcing world peace, and he was proud to be the skipper of one. She had a full complement of fifty cruise missiles. On this training mission, however, only five missiles had blockbuster warheads, and only one was nuclear.

As he walked back to his quarters, he reflected on his last two shakedown cruises with the JPC. The boat was a technical marvel, to be sure. She could run deeper and faster than any vessel he'd ever seen. Each time he went out in her, he pushed her and his crew just a little bit harder, and after six months total at sea, he still didn't think she'd come near to her limits.

Well, tomorrow, off the Big Island, he'd push them all hard.

When he got back to his quarters, he sat at his desk and plotted the next day's activity. When he finished, he looked at the picture on his desk of Ellen and the kids. He smiled, then took the picture and put it in the drawer. It was better if he kept his mind on the task at hand. He wasn't going to see his wife and kids for months. He could not communicate with them. Submarines had no telephones, and they could only contact their base when they came near the surface and deployed a communication buoy. This was done very rarely, as the maneuver risked revealing the submarine's position. Most voyages, they never came within two hundred feet of the surface.

For the next three months, it was better if he pretended he had no family.

6 a.m., Submarine Base, Pearl Harbor, Hawaii

Marisa Polanski dropped off her husband, Mike, at the JPC at 0600. She kissed him good-bye, then drove back to her quarters in Aliamanu Navy housing. She served a quick breakfast to her daughter, Yvonne (Missy), and her son, Rudy. She drove them both to Maryknoll Schools, where Yvonne was an eighth-grader and Rudy was a high school senior. From there, she drove to Tripler Medical Centeer, where she worked as a receptionist in the dental clinic. By the time she pulled into the *makai* parking lot just before eight, she'd already been up more than three hours, and she'd been in rush-hour traffic for half that time. She was glad to be off the road.

She liked her job. It paid well, and the civil service benefits were outstanding. The hours were convenient for her, and she had a lot of job security. She liked the clientele she served and the dentists themselves. Dental surgeons weren't as serious and morbid as medical surgeons.

She'd been a dental technician for decades before she switched to the front desk. She'd liked the technician job, but the long hours of bending over while cleaning teeth had put a strain on her back, so when the time was right, she'd made the switch. Technician's work hadn't been the best job for a woman as well-endowed as she was, though it had been fun when she was younger.

Now it was different, though. She was happy the sailors who came into the office still seemed to appreciate her appearance, even though she was in her forties. She let them look, no harm in that. But she responded to flirting with a stony glare. Marisa was a devout Catholic–hence, her kids being enrolled in Catholic schools–and she didn't fool around. No one else came near her. Mike treated her with kindness and respect, and she rewarded him with her fidelity.

Marisa was known in the clinic as a "strong woman." She didn't tolerate misbehavior, either on the part of fellow staff or of patients, and she had the strength of character to enforce her will. Not surprisingly, her clinic ran with much better efficiency than the norm for governmental operations. She saw that the patients in pain were seen quickly and that misunderstandings were resolved before patients left. Complaints were few.

She was also the one who most frequently brought cookies to the clinic. Known for her raucous laughter and her uninhibited sense of humor during lunch and coffee breaks, she always had a story to tell, frequently an off-color one. As a result, she was one of the most popular people in the clinic.

She worked until twelve-thirty, when the last morning patient left, then was off until one. She went first to the bank branch within the hospital. She took out $100 from her own account. Every so often, it was nice to have extra money in her hand. It gave her a sense of freedom she wouldn't have otherwise.

She and Mike had an arrangement. What she made on the job was hers, and what he made was theirs. So, she had her own account, and she also had joint use of his, since she had to pay all the bills when he was gone. She was careful not to abuse the privilege. All her personal items came out of her own account.

Marisa routinely skipped lunch. By doing that, and by weighing herself every day and exercising away any excess, she had been able to keep her 36/24/34 figure. "They ain't bigger," she told Mike when they made love, "But they hang a little lower now." He didn't seem to mind. When he got off the boat, he always made up for lost time love-making. Every night for the first week, then every other until he left again two or three months later.

Their eldest son was in the Navy, of course, and had been for eight years. He was only two stripes in rank below Mike. Soon, he'd outrank his father. Their second son had gone to Cal Tech, and was in the Atlantic somewhere working on his PhD in oceanography. A middle child and younger son, he had chosen a different path than the family tradition, but at least he wasn't a landlubber.

Rudy Polanski was in high school, a football and baseball player, brash and uncontrollable. She smiled as she thought of him. He was almost a duplicate of his father, a lovable rascal. He'd make some girl very happy in a couple years. Then there was Yvonne (who they called Missy at home), as sweet a girl as Marisa had ever known, and a beautiful ballerina. She hadn't blossomed yet, and Marisa hoped she hadn't inherited the physique she had. If so, that would kill her ballet prospects. Missy had incredible talent and an insatiable love of dance. It would be a shame if she had to give that up.

Marisa returned to the clinic promptly at one. and checked in the first afternoon patient five minutes later. After the clinic, she went straight home, arriving an hour after Yvonne, who was in the dinette doing her homework. Yvonne had a surprise for Marisa. A boy sat on the other side of the table, also doing homework.

"Hi mom," Yvonne said. Then, a few seconds later, "This is Todd. Todd, this is my mom."

"Hi," said Todd.

"Hi," Marisa said. "Do you go to school with Yvonne?"

"Yeah. We take algebra together. I'm helping her out."

"Oh. Well, that's good. Can I get you kids anything?"

"I'll take a guava juice," Marisa said. "Todd, you want anything to drink? We have all kinds of juice."

"How about lilikoi. You have that?"

"Sure. Just a minute."

Marisa was in the kitchen popping the tabs on the juice cans when Yvonne came in. "Todd seems nice," Marisa said.

"He is. He's a dancer, really strong, and he's smart, too. He can lift me up with one hand."

"Sounds like a great kid to know. Should I be worried?"

"Mom. Come on. He's just a friend. Besides, I think he's gay."

"Oh. Okay."

Yvonne smiled, a twinkle in her eye. "One of these days, I'll bring home a hunk, you know. Maybe next year. Maybe next month."

Marisa rolled her eyes. "Lord, save me. Do it when your father's home, please. And make sure your father's not surprised. Otherwise, there'll be trouble. And wait about six years."

"Mom. I'm fourteen."

"Right. When you're twenty."

They both laughed. Then Yvonne went back to study algebra, and Marisa went to her bedroom, lay on the bed, and thought, *I hope to God she doesn't do the things I did when I was fourteen.*

Chapter 2
22 January 2020

3:22 p.m., Pacific Ocean, East of Island of Hawaii

The JPC cruised at a keel depth of forty feet and a speed of only six knots, its sail thirty feet below the surface. "Let's take a surface check," Daniel said, pressing a button to deploy one of their two photonic masts.

The JPC didn't have a periscope. Periscopes were obsolete. Instead it had photonic masts with an array of specialized digital cameras at the top. By extending the masts upward, they could get a full 360-degree view of the ocean surface and zoom in on anything interesting, angle the lens upward to check the sky, switch to telephoto or panorama at the touch of a button, or take a video for perusal later at the touch of another button.

A moment later, a crystal-clear color image appeared on the LED screen. A toggle lever allowed Daniel to control the main camera. He did a quick 360-degree sweep, then another, more slowly. He focused in on anything that looked the least bit unusual but saw nothing of interest. The sea surface was choppy, with five-foot swells from the tropical storm south of the islands. He was glad they were below the surface activity. The deeper they were, the less surge they felt.

"Nothing visible, but there's heavy seas. A small vessel could be hidden by the waves." he said. "Let's get a sonar check. Deploy the VDS."

The type of training activity they planned to do could be dangerous if vessels were nearby. A few years before, a fellow submarine doing precisely what they were about to do had come up under a Japanese fishing vessel, sinking it. The freak accident was a disaster for everyone concerned, and one that Daniel didn't want to repeat. He knew that visual observation wasn't enough, particularly in heavy seas.

The VDS was an array of hydrophones towed kilometers behind the submarine to limit interference from the sub's own noise and designed to detect noise made by ocean vessels many miles away. Even more impressive was its ability to detect return echoes from low frequency pings emitted from their active sonar. These low frequency sound waves would travel through the ocean, strike any object in the vicinity, and bounce back to the VDS. Like radar–which was useless underwater–active sonar could be used to estimate distance, direction, and size of any ship within fifty miles. A good sonar operator could even distinguish the type of vessel by detecting variations in amplitude, resonance characteristics, and distortions of the sound that returned. The JPC's active and passive sonar had recently been upgraded, and with the modern software, they could detect vessels up to two hundred miles away.

Use of active sonar in close combat was discouraged because the pings could be picked up by enemy vessels who could then use them to track the sub that emitted them. But use of active sonar during training exercises ensured knowledge about any ships surrounding them, giving them a remarkable extra level of safety.

Daniel held depth, direction, and speed while the VDS was deployed. Then, they took readings while gliding in a lazy circle a mile in diameter. Within fifteen minutes, they had an abundance of information regarding any hazards around them.

"Cap, we got no vessels anywhere near," Ferguson, his sonar Chief, said. "Picked up a pod of whales a few clicks to the northeast, but they're migrating away from us. The only thing anywhere near us is something that looks like a bait ball about eighteen miles to the south-southwest. One of those monster schools of bait fish."

"Bait ball? How deep does it go?"

"It's fuzzy on the margins. Hard to tell. Maybe sixty feet."

"Big fish around it?"

"Looks like it. One looks like a ten-footer. Marlin, or maybe a shark. I wouldn't be able to see a marlin's bill at this distance. The bait ball's got something solid and irregular on the surface above it, too. Maybe a big log or something. Hard to tell. Must be thousands of fish in the ball. They block the pings from everything behind them."

"Okay. That fits. Bait balls tend to collect around floating logs. Let's pull in the array." *If we stay below eighty feet, we'll be fine*, Daniel thought. The bait ball wasn't a big problem, but he had no great desire to mulch a school of innocent fish. The JPC didn't have propellers. Instead, it had pump-jet propulsors, like a jet ski. These were much more silent than propellers, because cavitation was minimized. As a result, the sub was very difficult to detect by passive sonar.

The intake of the pump-jet propulsor was screened, of course, but because clogging of the screen was a potential problem, the screening was loose enough that the powerful suction the propulsor produced could suck small fish through the screen into the mechanism, where they would be sliced and diced and then ejected. Bait fish, to submarine commanders, were the marine equivalent of birds to jet pilots. Small ones just got chopped up and ejected, but they always left a little bit of residue behind, inside the pumps. A fascinating variety of junk was routinely found in sub propulsors on routine maintenance, performed after every voyage.

The sub descended to a depth of five hundred feet. They could go a lot deeper, but this was sufficient for what they had to do now. "All ahead full," Daniel said. He listened for the whining of the propulsors. When the frequency maximized, indicating top speed, he said, "Helmsman, thirty degrees ascending."

"Aye, aye, sir"

A moment later, with the submarine at a thirty-degree tilt, he said, "Hit the chicken switch. Blow the hull." By this time, he could already hear clanging as improperly-secured objects slid to the deck.

"Aye, aye, sir."

The submarine shot upward, with every unsecured object, including people, clattering to the floor. He smiled. Sometimes, teaching the hard way was the only way to teach at all.

"Level off at eighty feet," he said, when the depth indicator was at a hundred and fifty feet. He watched as his crew tried to level off. He knew they would overshoot. A submarine at high speed has tremendous momentum. It doesn't stop on a dime, turn on a dime, or stabilize depth on a dime, and a sub with a fully-inflated hull needs to have the air released before it can be stable at low depth. It shot well past eighty feet, finally stabilizing at thirty feet.

"Take it back down to four hundred feet and try it again. Helmsman, set it to thirty degrees downward. Release the air in the hull. We want to go down as fast as we went up."

They sped down to four hundred feet and stabilized there, then adjusted their buoyancy by blowing more air between the twin hulls, then moving the air's position slightly forward so that the boat was level. He was pleased that his helmsman did this with very little vertical wobble. Of course, it was easier at depth, where neutral buoyancy was more stable.

He called the Chief of Boat on the intercom. "COB, let 'em know that any unsecured objects will mean double duty for the next week. I'll give them fifteen minutes to get the boat secured."

The PA blared, and the COB's voice came on. The language was a good deal saltier than Daniel would have used. Every third word, it seemed, began with F. He smiled. Polanski definitely got the message across, more effectively than Daniel could ever do himself.

He waited fifteen minutes.

"Full speed ahead," he barked. Once again, when the frequency stabilized, he ordered. "Thirty-degree ascent."

He listened but heard only silence. No clatter of falling objects. *They learned,* he thought. "Blow the hull," he ordered. He heard the whistling of air into the ballast area between the twin hulls as the compressed air forced water out of the area, making them more buoyant. They flew upward. No clanging sounds. "Level off at eighty feet." This time, they overshot only a couple of feet.

"Better, but not good enough." he said. "Let's do it again."

This time, we'll add a twist, he thought. He ordered them to descend to depth once more, but before they'd leveled off, he ordered "Left full rudder."

He watched with satisfaction as one new seaman slid off his chair.

After they were stabilized, he called the COB again. 'How many barfers do we have down there?" he asked.

"Three so far. Gonna be a few more before we're done. Give us some time to clean up."

"You got it. We'll hold steady for ten minutes." *About par*, he thought. Being on a submarine ascending and descending was like being on a high-speed roller coaster that jerked you to the side as well as up and down, except that you had no bar to lock you into your seat and no visual cues to tell you what direction you were going. Not too many new recruits were ready for it, despite their training in simulators. Even experienced seamen could have motion sickness for the first week or two.

The JPC ascended, this time to cruise at three hundred feet. Daniel's crew needed some variety. In a combat launch scenario, they wouldn't be able to predict the starting depth of their launching run. Daniel planned to make three or four runs from this depth. In the last two, he planned to do a mock firing sequence as well. That would double the trouble, he knew. It was hard enough popping up to shallow depth without having to worry about launching a missile as soon as you got there.

On the other hand, that was why they had vertical launch tubes on the sub. In a war, launching their cruise missiles might be their most important mission. They had to be proficient at doing it correctly, with minimal risk of detection before and after launch. With a launch at the same time, the whole crew would be stressed, both mentally and physically. If the time came–and he hoped it never would–he wanted their actions to be so well-practiced that they were almost automatic.

The first ascent went reasonably well, but they leveled off twenty feet below their targeted depth. They returned to three hundred feet and tried again. This time, they were right on. Daniel brought them down to four hundred feet, and then contacted the COB. "We're going to add a mock launch sequence on the next run," he said. "Let me know when you're set up for it."

The problem with mock launch sequences was that they had to be as near to the real thing as possible, except that when they pushed the launch button, no missiles would be fired. To make sure it could be done safely, the electrical pathway between the missiles and the launch controls had to be interrupted. A large throw switch had to be opened, and both the COB and the XO or CO had to personally see the thrown switch. In addition, a red light would glow on the bridge, confirming that the switch was open and the launch system disabled.

Daniel turned to Wendy Peyton. "XO, please go down and help the COB with that switch. Confirm with me when we're ready to go."

"Aye, aye, Sir."

A few minutes later, the red light came on, and the intercom buzzed. "Circuit is open," the COB stated. "I confirm that circuit is open," said Peyton.

"Thank you. XO, return to bridge."

"We'll launch at my command," Daniel announced. "Number five tube. Target number six three." Target six three was in mid-ocean, in the landing zone of the Pacific Missile Range in the Marshall Islands. Even in a mock drill, they would never aim toward a populated area.

"All ahead full," Daniel commanded. When the whining of the propulsors stabilized, he ordered, "Thirty-degree ascent." A moment later, when they passed the two-hundred-fifty-foot mark, he ordered, "Blow the hull. When they passed the one hundred fifty-foot mark, he barked, "Open number five tube." A few seconds later, as they passed one hundred feet, he ordered, "Level off at eighty feet. Arm number five missile."

As he expected they might, they leveled off fifteen feet above the intended depth. It took about twenty seconds before they were at eighty feet. He timed the event, then began a countdown. "Five, four, three, two, one, fire." As the light came on indicating firing, he checked his stopwatch.

"Thirty-two seconds," he said. "We can do better. Let's try it again. Close number five tube and disarm the missile. Empty the hull and descend to three hundred feet."

He heard the bubbling noise of the air leaving the twin hulls and felt the sub begin to descend. Then he heard what he afterward described as the most God-awful racket he'd ever heard, a grinding thrashing sound followed by a weird silence punctuated by a loud buzzing sound. Something slammed against the outside of the sub, and warning lights came on all over the instrument panel.

Something was very wrong. They'd have to sort it out on the surface. "Pull the chicken switch," he ordered. That should have resulted in a rapid ascent as compressed air blew into the ballast tanks, but though he heard the whine of air entering the twin hulls, he did not feel the sub ascending. They should have been buoyant, but they weren't. When he ordered the sub to a twenty-degree ascent, the helmsman said, "I'm trying, Sir, but something's pulling us down. We're at a hundred twenty feet, and we don't have any power."

The silence, he realized, was due to the absence of the propulsors. Their whining had been replaced by a buzzing sound like the sound of a stuck garbage disposal, except it was a hundred times louder. "Reverse thrust," he said.

The sound momentarily stopped, and then resumed.

He turned to Peyton. "Have sparks launch a communication buoy so we can send a mayday," he ordered. Then, to the engine room, "Try the forward thrusters again." The buzzing resumed. "All engines stop," he said. *We'll burn something up if we continue to push the engines,* he thought.

He began to visualize what would happen during the next few minutes. A gradual descent into one of the deepest parts of the ocean, eight or nine thousand feet below them. Somewhere below five thousand feet, the hull would collapse and the men inside would be subjected to a hundred and fifty atmospheres of pressure. They would be crushed before they had a chance to drown. No one aboard would be alive to witness their settling on the bottom of the ocean. The whole process might take less than an hour. Was that the length of his remaining life?

"Helmsman, try to keep us as level as possible," he ordered. Over the intercom, he said, "COB, return to the bridge." He needed Polanski's input.

3:27 p.m., Pacific Ocean, East of Hawaii Island

Daniel's thoughts were interrupted by Wendy Peyton on the intercom. "Cap, I'm with LT Carter in propulsion," Peyton said. "Carter thinks something got sucked into our propulsors. From the sound of it, he thinks it was something metallic. Both propulsors are jammed. Won't go forward. Won't go back. He can't fix it. We've shut them down and diverted the steam around them. We must have hit something, but the COB and I can't figure out what the hell it was. He's on his way to the bridge. Should I come, too?"

"Yes. But first, make sure the communication buoy is deployed. We're going to need help. We've got to send an SOS before we get too deep for the buoy to reach the surface and still be connected to us. Get that thing deployed ASAP."

"Aye, sir. We're working on it. It's deployed but hasn't hit the surface yet."

"Get back here as soon as it does. You and I need to figure out a course."

"A course? With no power? Not sure I know what you mean."

"I'll explain when you get here." He turned to the helmsmen. "Turn us to 270 degrees. Angle us bow down one degree."

He got on the intercom to sonar. "Chief, get me a three-hundred-and-sixty-degree image of the bottom. What do you see? How deep is it below us?"

"I'll have it in a minute, skipper." He was true to his word. A minute later, he came back on line.

"Skipper, we've got about eight thousand feet under the bow. We're going slowly down, but as of now, that makes it eight thousand two hundred feet bottom depth directly below us. Looking around, there's a seamount about eleven miles northwest of us, with a depth there of about three thousand feet."

"What's the direction to the top of it?"

"I'd say about two hundred eighty-two degrees to the highest point I see."

"Okay, great. Calculate an exact range for me, please. Let me know if you see anything else interesting."

"Helmsman, set course for two hundred eighty-two degrees," he ordered. He turned to the COB, who had just come on the bridge, and asked, "What do you think?"

"We ran into something big. Must have been whatever was in that bait ball. There's nothing else around us. Whatever we hit was floating, but it ain't anymore. Now, it's sunk and pulling us down."

"But we should have been below that bait ball, and a vessel, even a derelict, wouldn't get sucked into our propulsors," Farriott answered.

"Cables might, if they were just the right size and hanging down far enough. They'd foul up the propulsors for sure. Then, whatever was attached to them got pulled underwater by our momentum and lost its buoyancy. Now it's just dead weight. Nothing else makes sense," Polanski said.

"So where do you see this going?"

"We're sinking, sir. We're going to the bottom unless we can figure out how to get rid of whatever's pulling us down."

Wendy Peyton entered the command area behind the COB.

He turned to her. "Just in time," Daniel said. "Figure for me the arc-tangent of twenty-eight hundred feet divided by eleven miles"

Peyton used the calculator on the navigation computer and had the answer a minute later.

"It's 2.76 degrees," she said.

"Good. Now tell me what 2800 divided by the tangent of 2.0 degrees is."

"80181 feet. About fifteen miles."

"Okay. That should give us some leeway."

"What's this all about, skipper? I don't quite follow."

"We're sinking. Right? Nothing we can do about it."

Beads of sweat appeared on Peyton's brow and her eyes widened. "I guess that's true. Unless we can figure out what happened, anyway."

"If we sink to the bottom, eight thousand feet below us, we'll be crushed, right? No survivors."

Peyton couldn't bring herself to answer, but she nodded.

"So, we're setting a course for Loihi Seamount. It's a little less than three thousand feet deep there. It's below our operational depth, but if we can land on the top of it, we have a chance of surviving. The calculations you made just told me that if we drift down at a two-degree angle, we'll be able to make the Seamount with four miles to spare. That's if we don't encounter any currents, of course. If we do, we'll have to recalculate.

"XO, COB, do you see any value in abandoning the JPC or trying to get some of the crew off her?" Farriott asked.

"No, sir," Polanski ordered. "We got no time. Before we can get the first people ready to go, we'll already be too deep. I think your plan for going to Loihi's our best bet."

"I agree," Peyton said, after a moment. "We have to concentrate on getting the JPC to that seamount. Trying to evacuate would be a useless distraction."

"Okay. XO, please compose and transmit a terse message to COMSUBPAC letting him know what's going on. Tell him where we are, where we're going, that we have no power and are negatively buoyant. We've got to get that message out before we're too deep to communicate."

Peyton's face turned white and beads of sweat appeared on her brow. "I've got to sit down," she murmured. She looked around for a vacant chair, and seeing none, collapsed to the deck.

Ignoring Peyton, Daniel turned to the COB. "Mike, get an SOS out to COMSUBPAC. Tell him we're sinking. Powertrain's out, we're negatively buoyant, and we're heading to the top of Loihi Seamount. Request emergency assistance."

"I'm on it, skipper." He glanced at Peyton. "Want me to do anything for the XO?"

"She'll be okay in a minute. Get that message off. That's critical."

Daniel watched the COB disappear down the ladder. *Just what I need,* he thought. *An executive officer who's useless in an emergency.*

3:42 p.m., COMSUBPAC, Bldg. 619, Pearl Harbor

The message made its way across two hundred miles of ocean where it was decoded at the Headquarters of the Submarine Fleet, Pacific. The communication specialist who decoded it brought it to his Commanding Officer. "Sir, you need to read this one ASAP.".

The CO read the message in silence, swore under his breath, and said, "Not a word of this to anyone."

He then sealed the message, stamped it Top Secret, and personally hand-carried it to the office of Rear Admiral Jacob R. Green, Commander, Submarine Force, U.S. Pacific Fleet.

"Emergent transmission for Admiral Green," he said to Lily Tanaka, the G-7 civilian who served as Green's secretary. "Top Secret."

Lily pushed the intercom button. "Admiral Green, you have an officer here with an emergent Top-Secret message."

"Send him in," Green responded.

The CO entered, saluted, and handed the message to Admiral Green. "We received this about five minutes ago. I thought you'd want to see it ASAP," he said.

Green opened and read the message. "Who else knows about this?" he asked.

"Just you, me, and the communications specialist who transcribed it."

"Good. Let's keep it that way. Thank you for carrying it over."

"Is it real? It could be a hacker."

"I can't say. We'll find out, though." Admiral Green rose, signaling the discussion was ended.

The CO left Admiral Green's office. He was vaguely unsatisfied. He'd hoped to learn more. He returned to his own office. He sought out the transcriber of the message. "We're not sure the message is real," he said. "Could be a hacker. Forget you ever saw it."

3:52 p.m. COMSUBPAC, Bldg. 619, Pearl Harbor

Admiral Jacob Green read the message over once more. He'd been in the Navy over thirty years and this was a message he'd never wanted to see. He'd thought that he never would. After all, they were in peacetime, and he was due to retire soon. As he read it again, he scratched his head.

To: Commander, Submarine Force Pacific

From: CDR Daniel Farriott, Commanding Officer, SSGN John Pina Craven (SSGN927)

Time: 061843Z 23 January 2020

Priority: Emergency

Security: Top Secret

USS John Pina Craven (SSGN927) drive train crippled by collision with unknown object in open ocean. We are negatively buoyant and have no propulsion. Setting drifting course toward Loihi Seamount with hope of settling on bottom at depth of approximately 500 fathoms. Current position 155.08W 18.52 N. Hull intact. No personnel injured. Request assistance.

It was complete and yet it wasn't. He wanted to know more, needed to know a lot more. Was the JPC still in existence? Was its crew still alive? They were living as of the time the message was sent, but they were sinking. The JPC might be able to survive a depth of three thousand feet, but they couldn't survive a depth of eight thousand feet. If they didn't reach Loihi, they'd die. He searched the syntax for a clue, but he didn't find one.

They were planning to settle at a depth of three thousand feet, five hundred fathoms. It was deeper than the JPC's working depth limit, but the JPC's hull should be able to handle it. But would they be able to reach the seamount? Presumably, they had some control, so their rudder and dive planes must be working all right. They were negatively buoyant and had presumably inflated ballast tanks with air, so either there was an air leak from the ballast chamber or whatever they hit was dragging them downward. They would use their dive planes to try to control the rate of descent, and the planes would also convert any gravitational pull downward into forward motion. They were like an airborne glider, except that they couldn't expect much help from updrafts, except possibly near Loihi, where the currents might hit the seamount and veer upward. If they planned it right and executed their plan properly, they might be able to reach the seamount. It was eleven miles away from their stated position, however, and whatever currents were present might screw up their calculations.

Okay, he thought. *We have to be optimistic and assume they made it. If so, we'll need to find a way to get in touch with them. We have to precisely locate them first, then determine whether they're still alive. No sense planning a rescue if there are no survivors.*

What if they are still alive? Jesus. We'll need help. A lot of it. We can't do much from here.

He pushed the intercom button, "Lily, get me COMPACFLT on a secure line." He had to go through the chain of command, of course, but he knew this one would go all the way to the Navy Chief of Staff. After all, a billion-dollar submarine was jeopardized, as were a hundred and twenty-eight crew members. And the submarine was filled with dangerous weapons that needed to be secured.

It was a nightmare. The navy had never performed a rescue of this sort before. Could it be done? Probably. But could it be done in time? Green forced his doubts out of his mind.

6:33 p.m., Pacific Ocean, East of Island of Hawaii

The silence was un-nerving as they drifted to the bottom. The white noise of the air conditioners was constant, but no propulsor noises were present as they coasted slowly deeper. Occasionally Daniel could hear a dull thud that seemed to emanate from outside. *Something's rattling our cage*, he thought, and wondered what it was.

He could do nothing except aim for the shallowest water and hope for the best. They'd sent an

SOS, but they were now too deep to hear a reply. They'd set their course and were committed to it. He didn't have to rely solely upon basic navigation to tell where they were. GPS wasn't useful at this depth, but sonar-derived bottom topography estimates told them a great deal, particularly as the boat's command computer was loaded with bottom maps. The computer could match what sonar sensed below them with these maps and derive an estimated position. He was happy that the JPC was not only the fastest, most maneuverable, quietest, strongest, and deepest sub in the fleet. It was also the smartest. He suspected they would need every neuron in the JPC's brain before this little setback was over.

"What do you think we hit?" he asked Peyton. Her fainting spell had been short-lived, lasting less than a minute. She was back on duty and seemed fine, now. Whatever had freaked her out didn't seem to be a continuing problem.

"I've been thinking about it," Peyton answered. "I think Polanski's right. We sucked in some cables, and they're hooked to something floating. But it wasn't a boat. We would have seen it on our visual screen or detected it by sonar. It must be something lying flat on the ocean. It could be something that fell off a container ship, or fishing equipment, or trash swept away during a hurricane. There's a lot of junk floating around from that Japanese tsunami. Maybe we hit some of that."

"I think you're right," he said. He considered her words. "My bet is it's a goddamn floating dock we ran into. It's the only explanation," he told Peyton. "Cable hawsers were probably hanging from it and got pulled into the propulsors, putting them out of commission. Then the floats imploded when we dragged the thing down to depth. Now, the dock's pulling our bow down, dragging us right down to the bottom, and there's not a damn thing we can do about it except try to glide down to the top of an undersea mountain, where we might just be able to survive."

"Okay. What's the plan?"

" Simple. We go sit on top of Loihi and wait for someone to come rescue us. No way we can get to the surface without help."

"Loihi? Isn't that a volcano?"

"Right. But it's not erupting right now."

"When did it last erupt?" Peyton asked.

"I can't remember. A few years ago."

Peyton was silent, thinking. "And when's the next eruption expected?"

"I have no idea. Any time now, I expect."

"Oh, great. Just what I wanted to hear."

The intercom boomed out. "Skipper, I'm watching our sonar. We're coming up hard on the Seamount now," the COB said.

"What's our speed and distance from the bottom? Our depth, too."

"Speed's slow. About three knots. Keel is 97 feet from the bottom. Depth is 2923 feet."

"Anything in front of us?" Peyton asked

"No. It's pretty level for the next thousand feet or so."

"Set planes at two degrees upward. I want our bottom speed at less than one knot. Give me a running readout of bottom distance."

"Right. We're still going down. Now at ninety-five feet from the bottom," Polanski said.

"We don't want to settle on whatever is hanging on our bow. That could damage the hull," Daniel said. "Here's the plan. I want us to back onto the Seamount. We'll set the planes to go upward. We'll slow to a stop when we do that, and then we'll reverse. Whatever is dragging us down will hit the Seamount first. We'll back away from it and then settle down. With good luck, once it's on the ground, we'll be buoyant enough that we'll never hit bottom. It'll be like we're anchored there, just floating three thousand feet below the surface."

"We're going up again," Polanski said. "A hundred and two feet to the bottom. Speed's almost stopped. Less than one mile an hour."

Daniel acknowledged. *So far so good,* he thought.

"We're gaining depth again, very slowly, Polanski said. No motion forward or backward. Just drifting down. Now at ninety-six feet."

"We need to be going backward," Farriott said. He turned to the helmsman. "Set bow planes to ten degrees upward," he ordered.

"Slow motion backward now," Polanski reported. "Bottom's ninety feet below us."

"Continue. No changes."

"Eighty feet," Polanski said. "About twenty feet per minute now."

"Let me know if we drop more than thirty feet per minute."

"Sixty feet. Jesus. There's a hell of a racket out there. Something's hit the bottom and sounds like it's sliding, crashing into stuff."

Daniel felt a minute change in their motion, like the slow braking of a car. "Whatever's stuck on us is on the bottom. What's it look like under us?"

"Sonar shows it's ragged. Lots of big rubble. Depth variation maxes out at about nine feet."

"Okay. Keep me informed." A moment later, he heard a scraping sound from the hull, He felt a mild jerk as the sub's backward motion stopped and the sub began to tilt slightly, bow downward.

"We're stalled, skipper. Thirty-two feet from the bottom at the bow. No backward movement."

"Thank you. Let me know of any change." He turned to Peyton. "Looks like we're safely down."

"Now what?" Peyton asked.

"Now we wait. Hope somebody comes to rescue us."

"How long, do you think?"

"Who knows? It'll take a while. I'll be happy if we're topside in two months."

A moment later, Daniel felt a dull, soundless rumbling, like the shaking of ground from a passing train. A look of alarm passed across Peyton's face. "What the hell was that?" she asked.

"Earthquake," he said. "No problem. That one was small. We're on a volcano, though. Who knows about the next one?"

"Sir. What happened above. I apologize. It won't happen again."

"We'll talk about it later, in private. For now, I'll just say that you have something to prove, to me and to the crew. You'll have to convince them that you're a dependable leader in a crisis."

"I am, but I don't blame you, or them, for doubting that."

"I expect you'll get the chance to prove yourself before we get back to Pearl Harbor. I can't be everywhere. I need you to be my extra eyes and ears and my voice, and you'll have to convey to the crew your absolute conviction that if we work together, we'll all go home, even if you don't believe it yourself. If you do that, you'll do fine."

Chapter 3

24 January 2020

3:27 a.m., Loihi Seamount

We're in a fucking coffin, pure and simple, a hundred and twenty-eight souls buried a half-mile deep in the ocean, none of us quite dead yet, Mike Polanski thought, as he made his way aft. The narrow corridor was only three feet wide, and heavy equipment encroached on either side. He walked on a grating over more heavy equipment, and the grating above him was only six inches from his head. He'd been in submarines for his whole navy career. He was used to these cramped quarters, but somehow, the JPC felt more cramped than usual as they drifted with the current, barely off the ground, anchored by whatever had dragged them downward.

When the boat was underway, everyone not sleeping had something to do. A third of the crew would sleep, another third would be on duty, and the rest would either be doing mandatory training or be on leisure time out of the sack. Most of the jobs were both physically and mentally demanding. A good commander and COB made sure they were. Inactive sailors tended toward trouble. Keeping them busy kept morale up.

Now, when they were just waiting, jobs that were often boring became monumentally so. Helmsmen sat in their designated seats and did nothing at all for hours on end. Some of them read books or listened to music while sitting there, activities that would never have been tolerated while they were underway. Sonar operators listened for hours without hearing anything interesting. The towed active sonar arrays were retracted and stowed. There was nothing much for the sonar operators to do except listen to the cracking of crabs and the white noise of currents flowing around them. They kept awake by making games of the noises or by making wisecracks whenever they heard anything that even approached the sounds of sexual activity.

The radiation officer, Lt. Bartlett "Buzz" Henderson, and his crew were the only busy people on the sub. The nuclear reactor's only function was to provide heated water, turning it to steam. The steam then powered generators that produced electricity for many functions, including lighting and propulsion. In addition, it provided heat that kept the JPC warm in the very cold ocean water that normally surrounded it at depth.

Normally, the reactor provided more heat than was necessary, and the submarine needed air conditioning to dissipate this extra heat. Blowers circulated air through filters to remove dust and noxious odors, then pushed the air through scrubbers to remove excess carbon dioxide produced by the respirations of the crew. Heat from the air was then extracted by passing the air through a cold-water bath. This water, in turn, was cooled by passing through tubes adjacent to the hull. The net effect was to transfer the excess heat to the cold ocean outside the submarine, thereby keeping the interior at an optimal temperature of seventy-two degrees Fahrenheit.

When the sub was not moving, the reactor could be partially shut down by the simple expedient of inserting control rods into the nuclear pile. These absorbed radiated particles, slowing the nuclear reaction, resulting in less power and less heat. While they were stuck at the bottom, the reactor ran at a minimum, just providing the power necessary to keep the lights on and the interior warm. The entire process could be computer-controlled. Buzz and his crew should have been relaxing.

Since they'd settled, however, the temperature had been unstable, sometimes far too cold, and at other times uncomfortably hot. Sometimes it was hot at the bow of the boat and frigid at the rear at the same time. Other times, the stern became uncomfortably hot and the bow cooled. As a result, the radiation control section had to constantly fine-tune reactor output to match what seemed to be a random and unpredictable need for heat.

Seaman Jake Rooney, one of their nine helmsmen, provided the clue that led them to discover what was going on. One day, while he was sitting at the helm doing nothing, he said, "They're going to be bitching in about five minutes."

"What'd you say?" asked the Officer of the Deck. "Who's going to be bitching?"

"The guys in the stern. About two minutes from now, we'll get a call that they're too damn hot."

Puzzled, the Officer frowned, "Why do you think that?"

"Because we've been hanging at an orientation of 165 degrees for the last few minutes. Every time we do that, we get complaints from the folks in the stern."

A moment later, the first complaint was registered, just as Rooney had predicted.

The OD was impressed enough to call the skipper. He told Farriott what Rooney had told him. "I thought it might be important, though I don't understand why our orientation would make a difference," he said.

Farriott was silent for a moment, then gave an audible sigh. "I got it," he said. "We're floating, right? Tethered around whatever we hit on the surface. The junk's lying on the bottom, and cables from it are tangled in our drive train. We circle around that tether like a bobber in a river, going wherever the current pushes us. When we get oriented at 165 degrees, our stern must be positioned over a steam vent. That's the problem. We can't cool the sub properly then, because we're floating in superheated water. The stern gets hot as hell, but the rest of the JPC is still in cold water, so it's cool everywhere else. Steam vents are like undersea geysers. The water could be 300 degrees or even higher around us."

"Wouldn't it boil if the temperature got beyond 212 degrees?" the OD asked. "Wouldn't the sonar people hear the bubbling?"

"Not at this depth. Because of the pressure, water temperature can go way above surface boiling temperature without boiling, even to 600 degrees. Water boils at lower temperatures on top of mountains, where there's less atmospheric pressure, and at a much higher temperature when you're deep in the ocean. Of course, we keep the pressure inside the sub to surface pressure, so the pressure outside doesn't affect us, but it does affect any water outside our hull."

The OD took a minute to appreciate the implications. "So, if we stayed at that orientation, the temperature inside could just keep rising, and we could all be cooked like turkeys in an oven."

"Exactly. The steam vent must not be very large or we would have been cooked a long time ago."

"So, what do we do about it?"

"Damned if I know. For now, we just hope the current changes quickly enough to give us time to come up with a solution before we get cooked. In the meantime, we can evacuate and isolate areas that get too hot."

Evacuating the stern, though, wasn't as easy as it sounded. Some of the men, even drifting, had critical jobs to do. They just had to sweat it out. If it got too hot, they could put on a hazmat suit. The rest had nowhere else to go. Crew quarters were already occupied, and the mess hall was in constant use and limited in size.

As Polanski made his rounds, he pushed past seamen sitting in the corridors because they had nowhere else to go. *This can't last,* he thought. *We need a better solution.*

He felt like he was sitting on a powder keg. He knew very well that idle crew members tended to misbehave. They would get on each other's nerves soon. Some of them were already beginning to irritate him.

Their situation had all the criteria for a social disaster–overcrowding, a sense of helplessness, isolation from loved ones, and a constant unspoken fear that permeated the consciousness of every man and woman aboard the submarine, whether they expressed it or not. The only thing that kept it all together was the crew's indoctrination and their acceptance of the command structure that ruled them. If they lost their *esprit de corps,* the results could be devastating.

Then the real shaking started. Mike hung on to the rail while one pressure wave after another slammed into the JPC. The earthquake lasted a full minute. In the middle of it, the JPC must have hit ground, because Mike was knocked right off his feet. He grabbed hold of the railing to his side, holding on for dear life. He thought he was going to be tossed into the hot machinery around him at any moment. When it was over, he knew what its effect would be on the rest of the crew. They'd be terrified. He'd have to calm them down, or someone would go nuts.

He put a big smile on his face before he encountered the next group of sailors he had to supervise. If he could make it into a laughing matter, he could embarrass them into doing it, too. "Wasn't that a ride?" he asked. "Reminded me of the roller coaster at Cedar Point when I was a kid. Great fun." He glared at them as he walked past, and said, "You guys look like you just came out of one of them horror movies. All pale and chicken-like. I got a great idea. How about getting your lazy asses back to work?"

He felt their eyes on him as he went forward to the next group of sailors. But he also noticed that they dragged their butts off the deck and back to their posts.

Chapter 4

25 January 2020

3:20 a.m., Loihi Seamount

Wendy Peyton was inspecting the weapons systems when the earthquake struck. She and the weapons crew held on like mussels on a rock in the surf zone as they were jerked back and forth in a sort of macabre dance.

When it ended, she was one of the first to recover, and she knew what she had to do. "Damn. For a minute there, I thought I was back in California," she said, laughing out loud.

Scotty McLean, the weapons officer stared at her in disbelief for a moment before his face also lit up. "I thought I was in one of those old submarine movies, where the depth charges are exploding all around them. I imagine that's a lot worse than this. Right?"

"Right. This sub's built about a hundred times better than the ones in the movies. A little shaking like that isn't going to hurt us.

"Let's continue where we left off," she went on. "You were telling me what steps you were going to take if the balloon went up and you had to fire Big Bertha here. Show me what the sequence is."

"First, we get the word via ELF transmissions. The code will have to be authenticated by both the CO and XO, right? One of you then hand-delivers the first code to us."

"Correct."

"We then enter in that code here," he said, flipping up a cover, revealing a number pad. "We have three tries to get it right. If we don't, the mechanism locks. The proper code allows us to open the cover to the switch to activate the missiles."

"You were a little slow in our last drill. Why was that?"

"The cover was stuck. We had to jiggle it. Probably because we hadn't opened it in a while."

"And you've fixed that now, right?"

"Right. A little lubricant. Not a problem now. Then we get a second fire command code from the CO. We enter it here and push the button. When the button turns green, indicating it's active, we push it again and the missile fires. All this presupposes that the appropriate missile is in the tube, of course."

"And you've already checked that, right? By matching the serial number with our checklist. For all five tubes. In the presence of the CO, before we ever left port."

"Right. Strategic missiles just stay in their tubes until they're fired. Then they're replaced by the same type, unless we've run out. Only the torpedoes routinely get loaded en route. And the loading of missiles is done very formally. By the numbers."

"Have you memorized what missiles are in what tubes?

"I have, but I don't rely on my memory. The computer knows. It'll tell us just what missile we're preparing to fire, and what the target is set for. Computer memory's more accurate than human memory. At least, we hope it is."

"We do, and it is. Unless we get hit with a lethal blast of radiation. Radiation tends to fry computers. Fortunately, sea water protects us from radiation. Even gamma rays get absorbed by a couple dozen feet of water.

"That's enough for today," she added. "I'm convinced you know what to do. Practice with your crew. Plenty of time now that we're stuck here."

"Aye, aye, sir...uh...ma'am."

"Carry on."

She checked out the sonar next, put on the earphones and tried to make sense of what she was hearing. She did her best, then had to ask. "What's that crackling sound?"

"Don't know, Ma'am. Sounds like crabs popping, but this deep down, I'm not sure I can answer that. The noise is lower-pitched than the clicks crabs make nearer the surface. Do they have crabs this deep? If so, they must be huge, judging from the sound."

"Yes, they do. Very large ones, I understand. Particularly near steam vents or lava tubes, where there's a lot of energy in the water."

"Sounds like here."

"Exactly right. Carry on."

She walked aft, stopping for a cup of hot, black java, and thought over the day before. She'd fainted, pure and simple. What a stupid thing to do. Now, her new crew thought she was a wimp, undependable in the clutch.

She'd overheard the usual arguments about the dependability of women enough times to know that a lot of the crew had doubts about her before she ever got aboard. The rhetoric always went something like, "The navy wants to put pussies on subs, so they'll find some bitch and stick her where she don't belong, no matter what her qualifications. It's all politics." The point of it was that they expected her to fail. So, she had to prove them wrong. And when she'd fainted, she'd caused a lot of the crew to think that they'd been proven correct.

So why had she fainted? She knew herself, but she didn't understand it. Probably it had something to do with her skipping breakfast–she hadn't wanted to barf during the maneuvers she knew they would do, so she left her stomach empty. And, yes, it was her time of the month. And without question, she had felt anxiety about sinking. But she knew that those three problems, even together, weren't enough to make her faint. She was stronger than that and had more self-control.

She reviewed the events in her mind, searching for whatever had triggered her fainting. It was like searching for a pen you'd laid down somewhere. You weren't going to find it unless you remembered every insignificant detail about what you did before you lost it. So, she closed her eyes and went over the scene again, searching for the key.

She almost had it once. An idea flashed into her mind, giving her a momentary blast of anxiety, but the thought flitted away without registering in her consciousness, leaving her tantalized but unsatisfied.

She chugged her coffee, forcing her thoughts elsewhere. She couldn't indulge herself. She had work to do.

5:52 a.m., Makiki district, Honolulu

Susan Cho jogged out of the elevator at her condo in Makiki before dawn, just as a portion of the sky turned azure in the earliest morning dusk. By the time she jogged down Wilder Avenue to Punahou Street, the sky was already bright on the eastern horizon, and when she reached University Street, the sun had just reached the horizon and was lighting the tops of palm trees and monkey pods. She reached the School of Oceanography, Earth Sciences, and Technology a minute later. There, she checked her watch. *Not bad,* she thought. She'd averaged seven minutes, forty-two seconds per mile for the two-plus mile run, and she'd barely broken a sweat.

Her speed didn't come close to what she'd been able to attain at Punahou School in her teens or during her undergraduate days at Manoa University. Back then, though, she didn't work a sixty-hour week, and she didn't spend half her time in or on the ocean. Scuba diving and paddling used different muscles than she needed for running. Doing both, as she did now, ensured she was in top shape both above and below the waist, and she did great in tin-man triathlons, even though she'd lost some of her running speed and wasn't a super-fast swimmer either.

She rinsed her face and torso in the lady's room, changed into the lab clothes she kept in her locker, and was ready for work. She reached her cubicle, hung her backpack behind the door, and turned on her computer. She was alone on the floor, which suited her well.

She began by reviewing the fascinating metabolism of organisms living around deep sea volcanic vents, like those of Loihi. The living creatures had adapted in ways she found to be marvelous, but in truth, she (and everyone else) knew so little about them that they could have lived on another planet. Many of these organisms relied upon sulfur more than oxygen for their generation of energy for the sustenance of life. Heat from the steam vents, not the sun, provided their base source of energy at depths to which no sunlight penetrated. Sediment that fell from above provided a food source. And they thrived. The bottom was anything but dead. To her, it was a minor miracle.

She reviewed one article after another, both those that were on the internet and those in print journals like Science, Nature, and the Journal of Marine Biology, taking notes and comparing the results of other authors to the work she herself was compiling. The problem she saw in her field was that, with the improved technology, particularly submersibles that could go miles deep in the ocean, data was pouring in faster than researchers could analyze it, so she (and everyone else in the field) had a huge and growing backlog to plow through.

Susan was so engrossed by her research that she didn't notice as the floor filled with people, their voices clearly audible around her if she had been listening at all. Phones rang, secretaries laughed, computers beeped, but she heard nothing until Herman Elliott poked his head in the door and, in his booming bass, announced, "The Navy wants some information about Loihi. The secretary for some admiral called and wants one of us to call him ASAP. I volunteered you to help."

Susan wasn't happy. Just as she was getting her project organized, here was an interruption. "Can't you find someone else?" she asked. "I'm right in the middle of something."

"Tough. We're all busy, too. Suck it up and call him back. It probably won't take that long. Then you can get back to your precious research." He handed her a telephone number written on a post-it note and left.

Susan flipped a middle finger at his broad back as he left, organized her research papers so she'd know where she'd left off when she got back to them, and called the number on the post-it note.

"Admiral Green's office," she heard.

"This is Dr. Susan Cho at Manoa University Oceanography Department. I was told to call this number."

"Thank you for returning our call," the secretary replied. "I'll connect you to Admiral Green."

A moment later, Admiral Green came on the line. "Dr. Cho, we have a pressing problem I need to discuss with you," he said. "I can't talk with you about it over the telephone, but I can assure you it's very important. Can you come to my office as soon as possible?"

She looked at her schedule on her cellular telephone. "I could spare an hour or so on Wednesday morning, say at ten. Is that okay?"

"I'm afraid it's more urgent than that. We'd really like to see you this morning."

"I can't do that. I teach a class at ten."

"I think you'll find that this discussion we're going to have is more important than your class. Do you have a teaching assistant who can cover for you?"

The nerve of this man, Susan thought. "Admiral, I'm sure it's important to you, but my class and students are important to me. I'm not willing to drop everything just because you have a pressing need. Your problem is not suddenly my emergency, and I don't work for the Navy. I work for Manoa University."

"Doctor Cho, I assure you that we wouldn't bother you in this way unless it were very important. Please give me the chance to explain it in person. If you come now, you can still make your class at ten, if you wish. But I think that when you hear what I have to say, you'll understand the urgency."

Susan was ready to hang up, but thought that if she did, the Admiral would just call her boss, Elliott, and raise hell. She would be fighting the inevitable. She sighed and said, "I jogged to the campus. I don't have a car here."

"I'll send a staff car to pick you up. He should be there in twenty minutes. Is that okay?"

"I guess. Do you want me to bring anything with me?"

"Just your expertise. Thank you for agreeing to see me." The line clicked dead.

"Shit," she said. Her day had barely started, and it was already ruined.

The car arrived eighteen minutes later. She made the driver wait ten minutes, on general principles, while she finished the article she was reading.

9:15 a.m., Navy Commissary, Pearl Harbor

Ellen chose her groceries carefully. Produce at the Commissary was very cheap, but you had to be selective. It wasn't always as fresh as she would have liked. Not that the kids cared. When Daniel was gone, their menus became very basic. The kids weren't gourmets, nor were they vegetarians. If she wanted to eat high quality food, she had to wait until Daniel came home. Then it was also worthwhile to get a babysitter and go out.

As she sorted through the green beans, rejecting the asparagus and broccoli because the kids wouldn't eat them, she thought back to the early days, when she'd been Daniel's high-school sweetheart. She'd respected his Navy career dreams then, particularly after meeting his father, Rear Admiral Farriott. Navy admirals were well-respected in Charleston, and Admiral Farriott was the very picture of a modern Navy admiral. A distinguished-appearing man whether in his bright white uniform or his casual civilian wear, he was an honored member of Charleston's high society, of which Ellen's parents were proud representatives.

She had met Daniel the summer before he went to the Naval Academy at Annapolis and she went to Converse College in Spartanburg, South Carolina to study interior design. She'd thought of her time with him as summer fun, a fling in celebration of her graduation from high school, but Daniel had other ideas. He'd proposed to her before the summer ended. She'd declined, of course. She was only eighteen, and her parents would never have consented, nor would his. Besides, it didn't make sense for them to be engaged when they were going to be a thousand miles away from each other.

But each time he returned to Charleston, he called her, and they went out and had a good time and (eventually) made passionate love. Daniel seemed to have no doubt they would be together forever. His self-assurance was one of his most admirable traits. When he went back to the Naval Academy, he left her with sweet memories and uncertainty.

It was his confidence that attracted her. He also looked great in his Navy uniform, and all her friends were envious. Besides, he was always polite and thoughtful when he was with her, and he made her laugh. He was definitely a great catch, so she hadn't discouraged him, though she hadn't said yes either. She didn't want any attachments right then, because she liked being free to date anyone she wanted. But then again, she hadn't met anyone she liked better, despite an active dating life.

Finally, the time came when she had to make a decision. He graduated from the Naval Academy. She got her BFA from Converse. He received orders for San Diego. He wanted to set a date for the wedding, and she knew that if he left without her promise, he wouldn't come back. She thought it over for a week and then accepted his proposal.

The wedding was one of these huge Charleston affairs attended by everyone who mattered. She was beautiful, he was handsome in his Naval uniform, the Country Club was a beautiful venue, and the wedding dinner was as large and picture-perfect as Ellen's well-to-do parents could afford, with over three hundred of Charleston's finest citizens attending.

Two weeks later, the honeymoon in the Bahamas her parents financed ended and the real world intervened. They drove across country to San Diego, where they checked into Spartan junior officer's quarters. She quickly discovered that ensigns don't make very much money. Fortunately, she was able to use her interior design training to get a job in a high-end furniture store. The job helped to supplement his naval salary, and also got her out of the house during the long periods when he was at sea, saving her from utter boredom. She began to realize that being a Navy wife was not as romantic as she had pictured. In fact, it was very difficult and sometimes very lonely.

She told herself that it wouldn't always be this way. He was bound to be promoted quickly. In a decade or two, she'd be an Admiral's wife, he'd be mostly on shore duty, and they'd be living the good life together. She just had to be patient.

Then Steven and Penny came, and life really changed for her. She could no longer balance her career and motherhood. She was busy with the kids all the time and began to feel she had no time for herself, particularly when Daniel was out at sea and she was, in practice, a single parent.

The first few years were a flurry of activity interspersed with obligatory command get-togethers with other wives facing the same challenges, "little bitch sessions" she called them. They served a function, but she came to think of the other wives as "little bitches" when she witnessed the back-stabbing some of them would do in their jockeying for power in support of their husbands. Navy wives were expected to fight for their husbands' careers as fiercely behind the lines as their husbands did on their ships and boats. Alliances were made and broken. Rumors were spread about other wives, other husbands. Sometimes, the rumors were true, but often they were not. It made no difference. Regardless of truth, the rumors often broke marriages apart. Once trust was gone, the marriage was gone too, and the Navy career of the husband dwindled with it.

When they received orders for Honolulu, she was elated. She was glad to leave the political minefields of San Diego, and she'd heard a lot about Honolulu, how beautiful it was, and Daniel was excited to be assigned to one of the largest submarine facilities in the world. He was sure the move was good for his career.

The first year in Honolulu was wonderful. They found housing off post, and she began to form friendships with people who were not associated with the Navy. She took painting lessons at the Honolulu Museum of Art and began to volunteer with community groups, particularly those that were art-related.

She put her interior design career on hold until the kids were in school. Then, when she had a little more free time, she began to do some consulting. She started with military clients, particularly those with higher rank who appreciated furniture and lighting that couldn't be found in the Navy Exchange. Eventually, her work became known to people who were not military, including many she knew from the artistic community. These people referred clients to her or became clients themselves. She became a full patron of the Honolulu Museum of Art and met other patrons, one of whom was Victor Villanueva.

They met at a cocktail party to introduce a new exhibit at the museum. She was alone at the party because Daniel was out to sea. Victor was there with another woman, a friend and fellow volunteer. Ellen could tell he was interested. Once they met, he paid more attention to her than to the woman he was escorting, creating a situation that Ellen found mildly uncomfortable but flattering.

A few days later, he invited her to lunch, ostensibly to discuss her contributing interior design to a demonstration suite at a new condominium he had just built. At the luncheon, he hired her. Several other jobs followed. Their collaboration was mutually beneficial. Ellen was happy with the jobs and appreciated the extra money.

Then, one day, in the privacy of an unoccupied flat she had just furnished, the European peck on both cheeks he always gave her in greeting became a full kiss on the lips, and the light hug that always accompanied the peck on the cheeks became a full caress. Daniel had been gone for nearly two months, and the result took her breath away. Her heart started to pound, she became wet between her legs, and her desire was overwhelming. Alarmed at her own reaction, she forced herself to push him away.

He smiled at her. "I can wait," he said. "When you're ready, we will make beautiful music together." He kissed her hand and left, leaving her breathless and wanting more.

During the next week, she could think of nothing else. At night, in her bed alone, her fantasies turned to thoughts of Victor. Two weeks later, when Daniel returned, they made love as usual, but another man intruded himself into her mind when she closed her eyes during their most intimate moments.

She did not see Victor while Daniel was on shore leave, but a month after Daniel's next deployment began, she called Victor. She told herself that she wanted work, that the reason she called him was professional. After all, their collaboration had put a lot of money in her pocket, and she didn't want to let their collaboration die because of a silly misunderstanding. "Do you have any need for an interior decorator consultation?" she asked him.

"I do, indeed," he said, with a light laugh. He gave her an address. "Could we meet there in an hour?"

She agreed to meet him, and she was not really surprised to find that the address he'd given her was his own. He greeted her with a glass of red wine followed by a kiss on her cheek that drifted to her neck and then to her lips. Then he took the wine glass from her hand, set it on a side table, and began unbuttoning her blouse. She didn't stop him. He undressed her slowly, brushing her nipples with his lips as she stood before him. Each place his hands touched, his lips followed. By the time he joined her on his bed, she was ready to explode, and explode she did, several times.

Now, as she lingered over the produce, she felt ashamed. She knew she had to end it. Otherwise, the affair would blow up in her face, destroying everything important to her–her family, her reputation, her husband's career. Every time she left Victor's, she resolved to end the affair, but somehow, she hadn't been strong enough to do it. Eventually, her need overwhelmed her and she decided to have one more liaison, a last one. And after each "last" liaison, her sense of guilt became more overwhelming until, like today, she felt like dirt. Tears were rolling down her face, and a woman next to her asked, "Are you all right, honey?"

She nodded. "I just miss my husband, that's all," she said. "He's in submarines."

The woman nodded back. "I understand. We all feel like that at times. It's hard when they're away."

"Thank you," she said, flashing the woman a quick smile. Then she hurried away, her face burning with shame, tears still flowing.

She parked her cart and hid in the ladies' room until she could get control of herself. Still, when she went through checkout, she had a feeling that the clerk and the people behind her in line were looking askance at her.

8:40 a.m., COMSUBPAC, Bldg. 619, Pearl Harbor

Admiral Green had a measured sense of accomplishment. The JPC problem wasn't close to being solved, but things were at least starting to come together. An untold number of local calls, thirty calls to the Pentagon, and several video conference calls involving COMPACFLT, the Pentagon, and Norfolk Naval Base had resulted in constructive emergency action. With luck, they'd be able to attempt a rescue of the JPC's crew within the next two weeks. Right now, though, they needed more information, and the fastest way to get that was by using Manoa University's submersibles, and he'd taken the first step in making that a reality.

The Navy had no submersibles in Hawaii. Since Hawaii has no continental shelf, the potential need for submersibles there was minimal. The nearest Navy submersible was in San Diego, but its operators had no experience in Hawaiian waters. It was cheaper and more effective to collaborate with Manoa University, which did have submersibles and skilled personnel to run them. The Navy had built up a mutually beneficial collaboration over the years, utilizing the University's equipment and expertise on the rare occasions when they needed to.

In front of him in his office was Susan Cho, PhD, a marine biologist and an expert on Loihi. She already had top secret clearance and had been briefed on the plight of the JPC.

"We know the crew's alive," he told her. "Sonar shows us that the sub is drifting a few meters off the bottom, apparently anchored there by some unknown heavy object. We can hear some rumblings, probably from the volcano. "We had a brief, encoded talk with the skipper via Gertrude, our underwater telephone, and he tells us he's having trouble controlling temperatures, probably because of hot water venting. The crew of the JPC has no good way to inspect the area surrounding it, so we're not sure of the terrain, nor can the crew see the outer surface of its own hull. We need better information before we can mount a rescue."

"So, you want our submersible to go down and explore, inspect the hull, and maybe even contact the crew? Is that it?" she asked.

"Right. We want to know what shape the sub's in and what we need to do to bring it up. We still don't know what's holding it down."

"Okay. One of our mini-subs is being repaired, but the *Hululua o Maui* is available. It can take a crew of two down there, but it's also configured for robotic use, controlled from the surface by a Gertrude data system. We can take a look. I'd suggest using it robotically to start. If we need to, we can look in person later, but for a quick survey, it's safer and easier to do it robotically."

"What's it like down there?"

"Loihi's an active volcano. It varies from day to day. Sometimes, there'll be lava flowing, but that's variable in location, and it's not always present. It's been dormant for the last couple of years, but it seems to be coming awake lately. Steam venting is constant, though it can vary in both location and intensity. Of course, nothing boils at that depth, so it's not really steam, just superheated water.

"Fortunately, the vents are fairly easy to see. The hot water diffracts light differently, so you get a shimmering, like you see when you're boiling water on your stove. Otherwise, the vents could be much more dangerous for us. The water above them can be hot enough to cook our instruments if we go directly over a vent.

"There's a lot of life down there, particularly around the steam vents. All sorts of tube-worms, jellyfish, crabs, and some weird fish. A lot of the fish are photo-luminescent, so you can see them in the dark. Some of the plants and invertebrates are luminescent, too. Otherwise, it's pitch black except for our lights. When lava's flowing, there's a red glow, but red light doesn't travel far in water, so you have to be pretty close to see it.

"What are the capabilities of the Gertrude on your submersible?"

"It's equipped for data transmission, navigation and control, not speech. Why would you need it? You said you'd already talked to the submarine from the surface?"

"Yes, we have. But when we use Gertrude from the surface, the sound waves travel for miles in the ocean. What we say is encrypted, so we're not worried that someone might be listening in, but if we talk repeatedly, some foreign listening post, a ship or a submarine, will eventually figure out that something is happening in that location. They'll come sneaking around to see what's going on. We want to minimize the chance that others will interfere as much as we can. If we had a Gertrude right next to the JPC, we could turn down the volume enough so that only ships or subs within a few hundred meters could hear it."

"We could configure the *Hululua* for speech, I suppose, but you'd have to run a cable from the surface if you wanted to keep it confidential. The alternative would be to make the run with a human pilot aboard.

That would be me, I suppose. Normally, though, we do a survey run first, to find out where the vents are before we risk a pilot."

Green glowered and pursed his lips. "We can run a cable down and attach a Gertrude to the outside. I don't want to put you or anyone else at any more risk than necessary.

"The *Groton III*, a Submarine Rescue Diving Recompression System (SRDRS) vessel is already on its way to Hawaii," he said. "This vessel is capable of rescuing sailors from a submarine at depth. It's never been used in rescuing sailors from three thousand feet–thank God, there's been no need–but it has been successful in repeated rescues from a submarine intentionally sunk three hundred feet deep in the Atlantic in training exercises. We think it can do the trick."

"How about the sub itself? Can you bring that up after the crew is rescued?"

"Good question. We'll know more about that after we've seen what the real problem is. The *Groton III* can maneuver and grab fragments of a non-intact submarine for analysis but would only be able to bring up an intact submarine if it were buoyant. I guess the real answer is, we've never tried it, but I think we'll need much more sophisticated equipment than the *Groton III.* Have you heard of the Glomar Explorer?"

"I remember it vaguely. Tell me about it."

"It was built to recover a sunken Soviet submarine in a clandestine CIA operation in the 1970's. It tried to bring up the submarine from depth, but the sub broke in half as it neared the surface. One half fell back to the bottom and was never recovered."

"Not a good outcome."

"No. We'd like to do better with the JPC. No, that's wrong. We *must* do better. But we learned a lot from the Glomar Explorer experience. I'd like to think we're much more sophisticated now."

"Why the urgency?"

"It's a pretty special boat. It's new, and it cost more than a billion dollars. Plus, it has some unique attributes."

Susan caught the drift of what he was saying, and was silent for a moment, thinking. Finally, she had to ask. "Could some of those unique attributes be weapons?"

Green didn't answer.

Susan continued, "Because if you're worried about an explosion down there, you might want to talk to a volcanologist. A large explosion on top of an undersea volcano might give you more bang than you figured on."

Green didn't answer right away. He drummed his fingers on his desk, thinking. Finally, he sighed and asked, "Who would you recommend?"

"Russell Wilkes. We've collaborated on Loihi many times. He knows Hawaiian volcanoes-including Loihi-better than anyone. He's been down to see it with me several times."

"Can you give me his contact information?"

"It's probably better if I call him. He can be a little edgy. Hard to deal with."

"Please talk to him," he said. "Don't tell him more than you have to. He doesn't have a security clearance. Try to get him to come to see me ASAP. You can set up an appointment with my secretary. Anytime. I'll make myself available."

"He's British. Will that make a difference?"

Green thought hard before answering. "It does. We won't have time to run a proper security clearance on him. We'll have to be very careful of what we tell him. It would probably be better if you and I went together to see him, at his place instead of mine. Can you set it up?"

"Sure. He's on the Big Island, at Kilauea. We'll have to fly there."

He frowned. "I hate to leave Oahu with all that's going on, but I don't see any alternative, and it will only be three or four hours if we fly on military aircraft. Yes. It's okay. Try to set it up tomorrow if you can."

"How about today? Can we do it this afternoon?"

"Why not? Sure. Give it a try." He paused. "I thought you had a class to teach."

Susan took a deep breath, then admitted, "You were right. I think this is a lot more important. I guess I'm committed now."

Green smiled. "I thought you'd see the light," he said. He was delighted, of course, but he also knew that this young woman had just committed herself to a task that was going to be much more difficult–and dangerous–than she could have imagined.

10:42 a.m., Kilauea Volcano Observatory, Island of Hawaii

Russell Wilkes pored over the seismograph data and rubbed his chin. *What the heck is going on?* he wondered. He saw the familiar pattern of magma flow deep below the surface, but it was too subtle to be at Kilauea. Where was it? His thoughts were interrupted by the phone ringing. Irritated, he picked up the phone, pushed the answer button and then hung up. A minute later, just as he was about to piece it all together, the phone rang again. He let it ring, but after the eighth ring, he could tell that the person on the other end wasn't going to give up. He pushed the answer button and then hung up again.

When the phone started ringing the third time, he got angry. He picked up the phone and–without checking the caller ID–said, "How many times do I have to hang up on you before you get the point that I don't want to be disturbed right now?"

The woman on the other end laughed and said, "It's Susan, you jerk. Having a bad day?"

He smiled, his anger gone. "Yes. Something's going on. Magma's flowing but I'm not sure where it is. It may be way deep. It's pretty faint, wherever it is. What's with you?"

"Something big. I want to meet with you ASAP. Can you spare me an hour or two this afternoon?"

"I can probably fit you in. Are you here on the Big Island?"

"Not yet, but I will be. How about three o'clock?"

"Okay. Would you be staying for dinner?"

"Not this time. It's work. I'll be bringing a friend."

"Oh. Too bad," he said.

"So, I'll let you get back to your work. See you at three."

"Okay. Bye."

After he hung up, he decided to get some tea before going back to the seismographs. He walked to the kitchen, poured himself a cup, and ran his hands through his long, brown hair. It was shoulder-length. Sometimes he tied it in a ponytail, but most of the time, he let it hang free, as it was now. He sifted some powdered cream in his tea and sipped the hot brew gingerly.

He decided to go home at lunch time and put on another shirt before she came. He'd also brush his hair and. maybe trim his beard a bit. It was a little unruly.

When he went back to his seismographs, it took a moment before his mind shifted from Susan Cho to the work at hand. Then, the seismographs recaptured his attention and he forgot all about her. He forgot about lunch, too, and never got home to change his shirt or adjust his personal appearance.

11:10 a.m., Loihi Seamount

It was the utter silence that made it particularly frightening. At first, Daniel Farriott just felt a little unstable on his feet. Then he noticed the expressions on the faces of his crew. It wasn't just him. They all felt unstable. Then, the submarine jerked sharply upward and sideways and they all crashed to the deck. When the submarine reversed direction, they all rolled on the deck in the same direction unless they had something to hold onto.

At first, he thought it was just a sudden current that had caught them, but submariners are used to currents. This was something entirely different. A jerking back and forth and upward and downward unlike anything he had ever felt before, except once, and that had been on land.

There was nothing to do but ride it out. He grabbed a handrail and held on for what seemed an eternity. Finally, the jerking stopped, but not before the odor of vomit swept over him. Someone nearby had succumbed to motion sickness. He bet there were plenty more around the boat.

He pulled himself upward and grabbed the intercom. "Gentlemen, that was just another undersea earthquake, more severe than we're used to, but probably not dangerous. All section leaders inspect your areas and give me damage reports ASAP."

He turned to Wendy Peyton. Peyton was a bit wild-eyed, but at least she hadn't been one of those who vomited. "You okay, XO?" Farriott asked.

"Shaken a bit but fine, sir," Peyton answered.

"In that case, go forward and check out munitions. Make sure nothing got tossed loose. Let me know if they need any help."

"Aye, aye, sir." Peyton proceeded down the ladder leading forward, Farriott's eyes following her every step.

"Where's my COB?" Farriott asked. He looked aft and saw Polanski standing and shaking himself, blood flowing from a gash on his head. "Somebody give the Chief something to push against the cut on his head. He's soiling the deck."

One of the helmsmen gave the chief a cloth he used for wiping the dials. Polanski used it to wipe his face and then pushed it against his head, wincing from the pain.

"You okay, Chief?" Farriott asked.

"It's nothing, Skipper," Polanski answered. "Just hit my head on a bolt on the way down. I got a hard head. I'm fine now." He glanced at the bolt and smiled. "Bolt seems okay, too."

"Glad to hear it. I want you to do a full assessment of the boat. Start aft and work your way forward. Make a list of anything that's fallen. We need to make sure everything's secured, so we can be ready for the next earthquake. Check out the men, too. Some of them may need some emotional help. Make a list of those who were scared shitless."

Polanski smiled. "I'll put myself at the top of that list," he said. "I almost peed my pants."

"I have a hunch laundry detail is going to be extra heavy today. Your list is going to include a lot of the crew," Farriott answered. "Have the medic patch your head, too."

"Aye, sir. I'll let you know if anything's goofy," Polanski left, heading aft.

Farriott paced, so far as he was able in the confines of the bridge. The jerk that knocked them all down had been different from the rest. They had slammed forward, not just swayed back and forth. A sudden stopping. They'd come to the end of their tether and couldn't move any further. They'd been lucky that the tether hadn't pulled something loose, maybe even torn a hole in the hull. They might not be so lucky If it happened again.

The solution came to him suddenly. They could solve two problems at once by blowing the tanks and setting the JPC solidly on the bottom. That would remove the risk of a sudden, fatal jerk and at the same time ensure they wouldn't drift over volcano vents anymore. The down side, of course, was that they'd lose buoyancy, probably permanently. He doubted they had spare air enough to inflate the ballast tanks again. Not at a hundred atmospheres of pressure. Because the air in the ballast tanks would be compressed a hundred times by the pressure, they would need a hundred times more than what they would need to inflate at the surface. They didn't have that much anymore.

He called sonar. "Give me a read on the bottom underneath us. Where's the smoothest portion. What orientation would be best for us to sit down on?"

A few minutes later, he had the answer. "It's a pretty smooth bottom at eighty-five degrees. Not as smooth as at a hundred and fifty degrees, but at that orientation, you've got a steam vent nearby. Wouldn't want to drop on that, I would guess."

"Right. Out." He hung the intercom on its hook and addressed the helmsman. "Let me know as soon as we drift to an orientation of eighty-five degrees. We'll open the ballast tanks and set the sub on the bottom."

He waited, wondering if he'd made a fatal error. Subs weren't made for sitting on rocky bottoms. What if the stresses were too high and the sub split in half? What if letting the air out of the ballast tanks made a subsequent rescue attempt impossible?

He sighed. It was the nature of command to make decisions that could have fatal consequences. It was also natural to second-guess these decisions after they'd been made. He felt a sudden recognition of the responsibility that lay upon him. He'd wanted command, fought for it, and now wondered if he'd be sorry he'd been granted his wish.

They swung to eighty-five degrees two hours later and he released the air from the hull. They settled to the bottom. It wasn't quite flat where they settled. The decks were tilted ten degrees to starboard, the bow was ten feet higher than the stern, and a lot of their extra air was gone, but whatever the result, they were stuck with it.

"XO, have all the officers meet me in the wardrobe in two hours. I want reports from all their sections. COB, run the boat. Make a list of concerns from the crew. We're going to be stuck here for a long time. I need the crew to accept it and buy into our strategy."

1:10 p.m., Hilo International Airport, Big Island of Hawaii

The military chopper carrying Susan Cho and Admiral Green landed at the Hilo Airport on the Big Island. The nearest military vehicles were hours away, at Puhakuloa Training Area in the saddle between Mauna Kea and Mauna Loa, so their best alternative was to rent a car. Automobile rental took fifteen minutes, and the drive to Kilauea took another hour. They arrived at the Hawaii Volcano Observatory twenty-five minutes before their intended meeting time.

Admiral Green followed Susan, who seemed very familiar with the Observatory. They walked down a short corridor to an unmarked white door. She knocked on it, then opened it without waiting for a response.

Inside the room was a desk piled with papers a foot high, a large computer monitor with a lot of wavy lines on its screen, and a wiry man with a beard and a ponytail, wearing rimless glasses and a black polo shirt. The man's smile turned to a frown when he saw Green's uniform.

"Hi," Susan said. She turned to Admiral Green. "This is my friend Admiral Green. He needs your help. Admiral Green, this is Russell Wilkes."

"You didn't choose to mention that your friend was a militarist, did you," said Wilkes.

"You wouldn't have agreed to a meeting if I had. I'm helping Admiral Green with a project, and we need your help."

Wilkes drummed his fingers on his desk. "Okay. I'm listening." He turned to Admiral Green. "You may have guessed that I'm a bit anti-military. A pacifist, actually. I don't offer my services to the military. Not to my own British military. Not the Americans."

"Will you agree to keep what I am about to tell you confidential?" Admiral Green asked.

"It depends. If you tell me of some plan of yours that's immoral, I might tell the whole world. Otherwise, I'll agree to keep quiet."

"Okay. Susan tells me you're an expert on Loihi. Is that true?"

"Righto. My favorite volcano. Why?"

"Because one of my submarines has sunk and landed on top of it."

"Tough. Crew all dead?"

"No. All alive, and we hope to rescue them."

"So, what do you want with me?"

"We want to know if there are any geologic problems that could have an impact on our rescue action."

The fingers of Wilkes' right hand drummed against the desk and his foot tapped, irritating Admiral Green while Wilkes considered the question. Finally, he sighed and said, "You're not going to like this answer. Loihi's probably going to become active again soon. It's showing all the seismic indicators of pre-eruptive activity, minor earthquakes centered there, magma flow under the surface just this morning that might be coming from there. Besides, volcanoes are cyclical and it's time for its eruption. It will happen, probably soon. I'd say the sooner you get those guys out of there, the better."

"We're already moving as fast as we can on that. Do we have to worry about any special circumstances?"

"I'm not sure what you mean by 'special circumstances,' but whatever method you use to rescue your people, you'll also have to worry about steam vents. If your rescue craft is above one of them, the heat might cook your instruments, or even the people in the craft.

"Lava may be flowing soon, too. It could appear at the top, in the caldera, or vent out the side of the volcano. It could ooze out–that's the norm–or it could explode out. I don't know what your ship is made of, but my guess is it won't stand up to the heat of molten lava. Of course, by the time the lava breaches the hull, your sailors might be beyond knowing about it. They'd be in an oven, you see. So, I'd get them out of there rather quickly if I were you."

"When do you think this eruption might occur?" Green asked.

"Don't know. Could be tomorrow, could be a month, but it's coming, that's for sure."

"Any other considerations?"

"Your submarine–it's nuclear, right?"

"It is."

"Weapons aboard? Any chance of an explosion if the heat were high enough?"

Admiral Green didn't answer.

"Because if there's an explosion, then you might have a lot bigger problem than you think you have."

"Tell me."

"Kilauea Volcano's been pushing out lava for the last thirty years, a half-million cubic yards of the stuff more or less every day. Much of that lava flowed into the sea and accumulated on the undersea slopes off the Big Island. It's formed a big pimple on a steep slope. It's not stable there. It's mostly particles with very little adherence, sort of like sand. If there were to be a large enough explosion nearby, the shock wave might trigger an undersea landslide." He paused, and the fingers drummed harder.

"So?"

"We've talked about this for years. Sooner or later, it's bound to happen. But we never considered that a man-made explosion might set it off. Anyway, if it all started to slide at once, that landslide could result in the biggest damned tsunami you've ever seen or heard of."

"How big a tsunami are you talking about?"

"Wilkes shrugged. "Don't know. It'd depend on the size of the explosion and how much sliding it induced. It could be as high as a thousand feet. You wouldn't have much warning, either. It would hit the Big Island almost immediately and Honolulu within a half hour."

Admiral Green was silent for a moment, absorbing this. Then he stood up, pulled his card from his pocket, and gave it to Wilkes. "Thank you for your time," he said. "If you can think of anything else that might help us to meet this crisis, please give me a call. In the meantime, please keep this to yourself. A panic wouldn't help anyone."

"Righto. I'll keep it quiet. I'll also monitor the seismographs and tell you if there's any change. But if there's an explosion...., well then, all bets are off, aren't they? We'll just have to accept what happens, because there won't be a damn thing we can do about it."

"Yes. That's an event that we have to prevent," Green answered. "Thank you for your help."

Admiral Green stepped out. As Susan followed, Wilkes put his arm over her shoulder and whispered directly into her ear. "Susan, if I were you, I'd stay away from the ocean until this thing's resolved," he said. "I wouldn't want you to get hurt."

"Me neither," she said. "Thanks for the concern, but I think I'm in this one up to my neck. I'm going to dive the *Hululua* on that submarine soon. At least you'll be okay. You'll be up here, three thousand feet above sea level, whatever happens."

"Small consolation. Can't you stay with me tonight?"

"Thanks. I'd like to, but I've got a big job to do." She flashed him a smile and blew him a kiss as she followed Admiral Green back to the rental car.

Chapter 5

26 January 2020

11:15 a.m., Loihi Seamount

Food was good on the JPC. In their present straits, the normality of eating good food on a regular basis somehow took the stress off the men. The only problem was that the mess hall was too warm, and the kitchen was worse. The men ate and sweated, and the cooks became dehydrated and chugged desalinated ocean water by the gallon.

A couple degrees of increased warmth was all it took to make it uncomfortable on the JPC. Henderson and his men had done everything they could to lower the temperatures, even going to far as to dim the lights, so that the reactor would produce as little heat as possible. Nevertheless, the heat had been a constant irritant, particularly in the aft portions of the submarine, ever since they'd laid the submarine on the bottom. They didn't have the variations in temperature anymore, but cooling it was more difficult.

Mike Polanski picked at his food. He made a point of grumbling only to himself and not to others. He knew that his appearance affected the morale of everyone on the boat. If he seemed anxious, so was everyone else. So, he kept his emotions to himself. Sometimes, the strain of doing that was hard to bear.

ETC Terry Butler, Reactor Controls Leading Chief Petty Officer (LCPO), sat across from him and shoveled in corn dogs. They ate in silence, enjoying the food and making the meal time a break from work. A half-dozen other enlisted personnel sat in the Mess Hall at their own table, giving wide birth to the table reserved for the Chief Petty Officers.

Only when they had finished eating and were sipping a cup of Joe did Butler say a word. He was a naturally quiet man, diffident, technical, and competent. Mike had learned that when Butler spoke, he should listen.

"This constant shaking is driving my guys nuts," Butler said. "I know you can't do a damn thing about it, but I thought you should know. Everybody's afraid something's going to get knocked loose and we'll lose control of the reactor. Then, we'll really be up the creek without a paddle."

"Not likely," Mike replied. "That reactor's built to last. It's built for combat. Depth charges and all that. A little earthquake isn't going to hurt it.

"I told them the same thing. But one of the guys–I think it was Hanson–piped up and said the sub's made for dealing with one-time events, like explosions, not recurrent shaking. He's afraid of metal fatigue."

Mike shook his head. "I think we're okay. The JPC is still new. I'd worry a lot more about fatigue in a sub that was twenty or thirty years old."

"Good point. But no sub's built to be whipped back and forth like a squirrel in the mouth of a hound dog."

Mike had to laugh. "Point taken," he said, smiling as he pictured what had happened the first (and last) time he'd brought home a stuffed toy model of a submarine for his son. Rupert, their golden retriever, had reduced it to a pile of stuffing in a matter of hours. "A little exaggerated, though. We're not...." He never got to finish his sentence.

From somewhere outside the mess hall, Mike heard screaming. He jumped up. "Stay here," he ordered the other men in the mess hall. He ran to the corridor and followed the screaming aft, climbed down a short ladder to the lower level. He hadn't gone fifteen feet before he knew what the problem was. The air he ran through was hot and moist. *Ruptured steam pipe*, he thought. He continued aft but with due care. Somewhere close, steam was escaping, blowing a stream of superheated vapor that had apparently already scalded at least one person. Mike didn't want to be the second one. He advanced another step and realized the ambient heat was going to be higher than he could bear. He was about to run back to get a Hazmat suit when someone tapped him on the shoulder. "We got it covered, COB," said a man already in a Hazmat suit. "See if you can find a valve to turn the damned steam off." The man advanced past him.

Alarms blared, he heard orders barking from the intercom, and he knew where he had to go. His place was in the command center with the CO. He dashed up the stairs to the upper level and ran toward the sail amidships. When he got there, the CO and XO already had charts of the steam pipes out and were making plans.

You couldn't just randomly close valves in this situation. It had to be the right valve, leading to the right pipe, and you had to know where the pipe led, because when you closed it off, whatever it ran wasn't going to work anymore. Moreover, the reactor had to be slowed or stopped to avoid sudden overheating. Mike generally knew where most of the valves were and which pipes led to what. Most of the pipes in that location led from their electricity generators to the heat exchangers in the outer hull. They were redundant, so that closing off any one pipe would not appreciably affect the functioning of the generator they came from.

Before he checked the pipe charts himself, he called MMC Sternberg, LCPO of machinery. "Get one of your men in a Hazmat suit. We've got a pipe rupture. He'll need to isolate the ruptured line by closing the valves in front of it and behind it so we can patch it. I'll let you know which pipes ASAP. Have him ready to go on my command."

He looked over the shoulders of the CO and pointed when he found the pipes he needed. "It's one of these four, Skipper," he said. "I've just been down there. Too damned hot for me to get close enough to know which of the four pipes it is, though. A guy in a Hazmat's already there, hopefully dragging the wounded man out. A machinist's mate is putting another suit on and can turn the valves off when we're ready."

"Good work, COB. Tell the reactor guys to cut power by twenty-five percent. Do that and we should be able to isolate and patch the pipe without anything else going haywire. Know anything about who's hurt?"

"I don't know. I think it's only one guy, but there may be others who aren't as vocal. He sounded like he got hurt bad. He was screaming bloody murder, but I couldn't get close enough to see him. Hotter than hell down there."

Commander Farriott looked up from the charts. "Like you say, it could be one of four pipes that ruptured. No way to tell which one from here. Have the machinist mate turn off valves 46 and 47. Valve 46 is on the inflow side. Make sure he turns that one before he turns off 47. That's the outflow. We'll see if that does the trick. If not, we'll try another pair."

"Aye, aye, sir," Polanski answered. He relayed the order to the Machinery LCPO, then stayed on the line.

A minute later, he said, "Skipper, he's closed both valves. Still blowing steam."

"Right. Open them up again and close 48 and 49, 48 first."

"Aye, aye, sir." He relayed the results to Farriott a moment later. "Steam's stopped blowing. Seems to have done the trick. They'll need to air the place out before they can get a crew in to fix the pipe, though"

"Tell the repair crew to be careful. Have Hazmat suits ready for all of them, and do as much as they can while wearing them. Have them call me when they're ready to open the valves again." Farriott said, then added, "After you talk to them, head down to sick bay and give me a personal report on the injured."

"Will do," Polanski answered. He relayed Farriott's orders to the Machinery LCPO, then headed down to sick bay. It was a small dual-purpose room tended by a Hospital Corpsman, HM Jose Gomes. They were lucky to have him. Most submarines had no medical personnel and no sick bay, although the officers wardrobe had emergency supplies and lighting and could be used to tend injured personnel in an emergency. Gomes, a short man of Filipino background, had already started an IV on his patient, who was squirming and moaning on the single cot in the room. The IV fluids were pouring in.

"Who's hurt, Doc?" Mike asked.

"ET2 Dennis Lozano. He's got scald burns to the face and left arm. The pipe must have blown just as he was walking by. It sprayed steam directly at him. He's got first and second degree burns on the face and at least second degree burns on his arm from his shoulder to his wrist. The whole arm is blistered, and it's really swelling up. The way he was screaming, it must hurt like hell.

"He probably also breathed in some steam," Gomes continued, "but his lips and mouth aren't burned and he's breathing okay so far, so I think his lungs are going to be okay. He's pretty hysterical, though. Hard to get him to say anything rational. I just slammed him with some morphine to stop the screaming. He's calmed down a bit now."

Mike knew Lozano. He was a brash young Italian kid from New York City. He'd gotten into some sort of trouble, and the judge had given him a choice between jail and the armed forces. He'd chosen the Navy, where he'd been turned into a better than average electrical technician. "He going to be okay?"

"Too early to stay. He's got serious injuries. I'd be calling for air-evac if we weren't stuck in this hellhole. His arm is a mess. I'll smear it with a silver compound, then dress it. That'll help to prevent infection when the blisters burst. It'll take away some of the pain, too. He'll need a lot of fluids. We're pouring it into him via the IV, because we can't depend upon his drinking anything. He's going to be laid up for a while. It's going to hurt like hell for a few days, and he likes to thrash around, so we'll keep him high with morphine until he comes around."

"Nobody else hurt? Is he the only one?" Polanski asked.

"So far. One's too many. We don't have good facilities even for him."

"He likes to mouth off. He's a good man, but I think he'll be a tough patient for you."

"The noisy ones don't bother me," Gomes said. "At least they tell me what's going on with them. Of course, a lot of the city kids have drug problems in their past. I have to watch how much morphine I give them, and if they start screaming for more drugs than I want to give them, I just cut 'em off and let 'em scream."

"Keep me informed, Doc. With good luck, he'll be the only one hurt here, but you can't depend on that. The crew is stressed out. Someone's going to go whacko if we're stuck down here much longer. Save some meds for the next guy. And keep your eyes and ears open."

"Lozano thinks he's going to die down here. Actually, I'd guess most of us do. What's our chances of a rescue during the next few days?"

Polanski shook his head. "We're going to get out of here, but it isn't going to be right away. Maybe in a month or two. But you tell your buddies we're going to make it. Lozano, too. He'll be the first one to the surface."

He said it, but he wasn't sure he really believed it.

11:42 p.m., Loihi Seamount

Wendy Peyton awoke with a start. She found herself on the floor of her wardroom next to her bed, disoriented and very afraid. At first, she couldn't remember the nightmare she'd just had, but then it all came back and she realized it was not a nightmare but a flashback that had awakened her, a memory of another time long ago that was the most horrifying experience she'd ever had. Even now, thirty-plus years later, it still horrified her.

She'd suppressed it, never brought it to consciousness, for decades. And now, it had forced itself upon her mind and horrified her once again. Now, she understood why she'd fainted.

She remembered that day so long ago, the worst day of her life, the agony that still made her heart pump in uncontrolled fear and brought tears flooding from her eyes.

She saw it through the eyes of a four-year-old child who had no understanding of what was really happening around her. She was watching a white box slide down a ramp into the sea and then disappear below the waves, and in that box was her father, and in her mind, he was still alive, and she could not understand why everyone just stood around and watched him disappear without doing anything to save him. She could hear her own voice screaming and feel her legs kicking her mother as she tried to pick her up and restrain her.

She kicked loose and ran to the railing, needing to do something, anything, to bring her daddy back, but when she looked over, there was only the deep blue of the sea. She screamed with horror and frustration, then with anger as arms grabbed her and held her immobile. The terror continued until someone put a needle in her arm and she lost consciousness.

She didn't remember what happened afterward, only that she'd been very angry with her mother for a long time. What she did remember, though, was the flashback of the same scene right before she felt dizzy on the bridge of the JPC and the thought that flashed through her mind–*I'm going to be buried alive at sea, just like I thought daddy was*–and the overwhelming fear it caused, until she escaped into unconsciousness.

She lifted herself from the deck, sat on her bunk, sobbed, and--for the first time-- understood. Her family and friends had all wondered why she'd chosen to go into submarine duty. When they'd asked, she'd been unable to give them an answer. "It's challenging and hard. By doing it, I'm advancing women everywhere," she told herself and them. "It's the last bastion of male privilege." But she knew even then that what she said hadn't been the whole reason. She hadn't understood it back then. Now, she knew it for what it was, the strange attempt of a little girl, now grown up, to reconnect with her daddy, lost a long time ago. If he was below the sea, then she would be also.

She took a deep breath and stopped sobbing. *Daddy*, she thought, *I'm with you on the bottom of the sea.* And in response, she thought she heard him say, "Yes. But I have to stay here, and you need to go back to the surface and live." And it was suddenly all right.

She stood up, smiled, rinsed her face, put on her blouse on, and went to work, confident it was all going to work out. *Thanks, Dad*, she thought.

Chapter 6

27 January 2020

7:00 a.m., Pacific Ocean, above Loihi Seamount

The *Hululua o Maui* was one of two deep semi-robotic submersible vehicles owned by Manoa University. The virtual experience couldn't quite match the thrill of actually descending with the *Hululua o Maui* and watching marine life forms live through the front viewing ports, but Susan Cho had spent many pleasant hours over the years exploring Loihi from the research stateroom of the *Iwi*, the Manoa University surface research vessel that was the *Hululua*'s mother ship.

The foreword hull of the submersible had two manipulation arms that could be used to take specimens. Hence the name *Hululua*, or "two-barbed fishhook" in Hawaiian. Two video cameras on either side of the prow had separate feeds for the left and right eye of the operator, allowing a three-dimensional image to be formed by the virtual reality goggles that the operator wore. With her extensive experience, Susan could feel she was right there, on the spot, while never really leaving the *Iwi.*

She leaned forward in her seat on the *Iwi*, the *Hululua*'s controls on her lap, and the goggles stabilized in front of her eyes by a head strap that circled her cranium and crisscrossed over her scalp. The *Hululua*'s depth, latitude, and longitude appeared in a red printout at the periphery of her goggles, along with the temperature, battery status, and speed. She kept the submersible's floodlights off to conserve battery power, and as a result, the screen was pitch black, except for occasional flashes as luminescent marine life passed before the lenses. She kept the focus set to twenty feet, except when she focused in temporarily on unusual life forms that passed before her, including a curious luminescent angler fish which took a tentative nip at the protruding floodlight arm and then swam away.

She kept the lights off until the *Hululua* passed the nine-hundred-fifty-meter mark (3,115 feet). When she turned them on, the top of Loihi was still twenty-five meters below the *Hululua*, and the JPC was expected to be another fifty meters deeper, on the East flank of the volcano. The *Hululua*'s lights did not carry far in the water, which had more suspended sediment than she had anticipated. She could barely see a faint reflection from the ocean bottom beneath her. She circled the

Hululua until it was hovering five meters above the seamount and then navigated toward the expected position of the submarine.

Beneath the submersible was an active landscape spotted with an abundance of life. Ten-foot-wide clusters of red tube worms grew, particularly close to sites where heated water rippled as it rose above steam vents. Each tube could be three or four inches in diameter and several feet long. Though the tube worms were animals, their clusters looked like spiky red bushes. They filtered micro-organisms for nutrition. The micro-organisms, in turn, derived energy for growth and reproduction from the hot water that exuded from the steam vents.

Susan knew that the water above the vents might be well above the boiling point of water at sea level. While piloting robotically, she couldn't feel changes of interior temperature as well as she could if she were within the submersible, so she kept a very close watch on the temperature readouts that appeared on the periphery of her goggles.

As always, she was amazed at the bounty of life in this area of her world that the sun never penetrated. An eight-foot-long six-gilled shark swam below her, and giant, multi-legged crabs fed on the tube worms and small fish that congregated around the bottom growth.

It took her a half-hour to find the submarine. She first saw a tangle of ropes and cables reaching upward, with what appeared to be pieces of a floating dock at the lower end. Then, as she cleared a small hummock, the lights on her submersible caught the outlines of the submarine. She didn't want to get hung up in the debris herself, so she circled the JPC at a distance of twenty meters before approaching any closer. The submarine was lying on its belly, canted about ten degrees to starboard. She looked for bubbles and saw none. The hull appeared intact.

She hovered near the bow intake tubes, snapping multiple photographs of the cables tangled in the propulsion system. With the starboard robotic claw, she grasped a cable running into the port intake and reversed, attempting to dislodge it. The cable didn't budge. She repeated the process on the starboard intake with the same results, then took many pictures of the hull, particularly around the escape hatch. She saw no damage that would preclude a rescue vehicle from attaching to the hull, except for some cables flapping in the current that tended to drape over and block access to the escape port. She made a mental note that these would need to be secured when the time for rescue came.

The *Hululua* was fitted for this dive with a Gertrude undersea telephone that was capable of voice transmission. For security, it was connected to the surface through a direct cable, so that she could talk to the submarine from a very short distance away and not have to transmit through three thousand feet of open water. As a result, only those within a thousand feet would be able to intercept her speech. The conversation would not even be heard on the surface, except by her. The cable presented some added difficulties, however.

She had to worry about it getting caught on objects protruding above the *Hululua,* so it added one more risk to the submersible. So far, though, it had not been a problem. She hovered ten meters from the sail of the JPC, well away from the debris, turned on the Gertrude, said, "Aloha, JPC," and waited for a reply. She heard no answer. She tried again and was rewarded by a response from inside the submarine.

"Aloha. Who are you?"

"UH submersible *Hululua o Maui,* Susan Cho from Manoa University piloting. Admiral Green asked me to do a reconnaissance and contact you. Who am I talking to?"

"Commander Daniel Farriott, Commanding Officer. Our sonar people picked you up a half hour ago. We were wondering what was going on."

"I was circling your submarine, taking some pictures for Admiral Green. Are you OK?"

"We have one man who was burned on the face and arm who will need attention ASAP. He's stable but in a lot of pain. A steam pipe blew and he was scalded. The rest of the crew is uninjured. What do you see around us?"

"Your hull looks intact. A lot of junk is lying on the bottom beside you. It looks like a floating dock. The floats have imploded, so it's dead weight now. The whole structure is encrusted with barnacles and some coral. Steel cables from it have been sucked into both of your intakes. I tried to loosen the cables by pulling on them, but they're stuck tight."

"We had to blow our buoyancy tanks and lay the sub down because we were drifting over hot water vents," Farriott said. "We don't have enough air remaining to get buoyant again at this depth, even if those cables were cut. Is help on the way?"

"A rescue vehicle is coming from San Diego. We'll get you out of there."

"When?"

"Can't say. A few days, I'd guess. What's your situation inside?"

"It's hot in here," Farriott answered. "The volcano is heating up the water around us, making it hard for us to eliminate heat. Our air conditioners are maxed out. Earthquakes are shaking up the crew. Plus, there's the injured sailor. He needs medical attention."

"Noted. I'll convey all that to Admiral Green. What's the sailor's name?" Susan asked.

"ET1 Dennis Lozano, an electrical technician. Say Hi. Let our families know everyone's OK."

"Will do. I need to get the *Hululua* back up," Susan said. "Batteries are low. We'll be in touch again soon. Anything else you want to say before I bring her back up?"

"Thanks. It's great to make contact," Farriott said. "It's going to add a lot to the crew's morale. Come back soon."

Susan smiled. "I'll be back when the rescue vehicle arrives. Maybe before," she answered.

She brought the *Hululua* to the surface, held it stable until the cranes and belt loops had secured it, and then removed her virtual goggles and went to the deck to see it hoisted aboard. She blinked from the bright light and put on sunglasses to protect her eyes. She reveled in the ocean breeze that wafted through her long black hair. It felt so good, particularly after having her head confined by the virtual reality goggles for several hours. Using the goggles was like wearing a dive mask, but heavier. She never minded them when they were on–she was too engrossed in what she was doing–but she was always glad to take them off.

A seaman came down a ladder and caught her attention. "Ma'am," he said. "Admiral Green is calling on the bridge. He'd like to talk to you."

"I'd like to talk to him, too," she said, following the seaman up the ladder to the bridge.

When she got to the bridge, the skipper of the *Iwi* handed her a cellular phone. "This is a coded, secure line. He wants to talk to you privately. Go into the head and lock it. That should give you the privacy you need," he said, holding his hand over the phone and pointing to a door behind them. "The admiral's concerned."

"He's got good reason to be," she said. She accepted the phone, put it to her ear, locked herself in the head, and said, "This is Susan Cho."

"What can you tell me?" Admiral Green asked.

"The drive train is hopelessly tangled with steel cables attached to an imploded floating dock. They've blown their air, so they can't become buoyant even if the cables are cut. I'm afraid they're stuck there until you can get them out."

"Injuries?'

"Only one, an electrical technician named Dennis Lozano. He has scald burns to the arm and face. But they say it's hot. I'd guess they're parked near a thermal vent. They say the AC is being stressed. They've had a lot of earthquakes, too, as we already know, and those are freaking out the crew."

"The *Groton III*, our SRDRS, is on its way. It should be here in a couple days. With good luck, we can attempt a rescue in about five days. You think they can hold out that long?"

"They seem to be pretty stable, but they're on top of an active volcano, so the situation is fluid. I'd try to get them out of there ASAP."

"Noted. I agree."

"One more thing. Commander Farriott asked me to tell his wife and the crew's families that they're all okay."

Green didn't answer immediately. "We can't do that," he said finally. "I don't want any of this getting out. Keep your mouth zipped. One word, and the press will put it in the newspaper on the front page. Next thing we know, the rescue site could be infested with Russian and Chinese submarines."

"Understood. When you get ready, you'll need to pull some cables out of the way so your SRDRS can hook up."

"You should know. We need to get the crew out of there, but we also have to bring that submarine up. Because of what Wilkes told us. That's going to be a lot more difficult. We'll need your assistance again, I'm sure, so please don't go anywhere."

"I figured as much. I'll make myself available until this rescue's finished. I think it's reassuring to the crew to have regular contact with someone on the surface. I'd suggest we take the *Hululua* down every day or two to exchange information until they're rescued."

"Agreed. We'll call your superiors at the University and arrange for an extension of your services. The *Iwi* and *Hululua*, too. Your submersible is perfect for this task, and you have an edge over any crew we could get from the mainland, since you already know the terrain. Thanks for your help. Can you put the captain of the *Iwi* on again?"

She exited the head, handed the phone to the captain, and said, "He wants to talk to you."

As she left the bridge, the implications of what he had said about needing to salvage the JPC struck her, and a chill went through her. *Mother of Jesus*, she thought. *They must have nukes aboard.*

12:33 p.m., COMSUBPAC, Bldg. 619, Pearl Harbor

Admiral Green was frustrated. Things weren't moving as fast as they should. He doodled impatiently with his right hand while his left hand held the phone to his ear, on a terminal hold once again.

After what seemed an eternity, he finally heard a human voice. "Sorry for the hold, Jake. I was on a call to the Pentagon." Admiral Ted Rosen, Commander in Charge, Pacific Fleet (COMPACFLT) said. "What can I do for you."

"It's about the JPC, the submarine that's stuck at the bottom on Loihi. I can't seem to get the message through to the Pentagon that salvage of that boat is an emergent priority. They're giving me estimates of one or two months to figure out a salvage plan. We just don't have that long."

"Really? I was told that the *Groton III* is already on its way. It should be on site tomorrow or the next day. With good luck, we should have your men off the boat within a week."

"You're correct, Sir. The *Groton III* should be on site late tomorrow. But it's not just the men that concern me right now. It's the submarine itself."

"Why is that such a high priority?" Rosen asked. "Once the men are off it, we should have all the time in the world."

"That's just it. Loihi's getting ready to erupt. It could happen at any time. We have to get the boat off it before it erupts."

"I appreciate your concern," Admiral Rosen said. "But submarine salvage from that depth has never been done successfully before. We need to plan very carefully on how to do it or it could break apart, like that Russian sub did in the '70's, the K-129."

"I understand the difficulty," Admiral Green said. "But the JPC is a billion-dollar boat and it has a nuke aboard, some block-busters, and a mass of other conventional explosives. If those blow, the results could be catastrophic. It could result in a landslide at Kilauea and a resulting tsunami that could wipe out Honolulu."

Admiral Rosen laughed. "Jake, that's very unlikely. As you know, the nukes have fail-safe protections that prevent their being accidentally detonated. Unless the CO enters a launch code transmitted to him by us via ELF, the nuke can't fire. I think you're wildly exaggerating the danger."

"I know. It's disarmed. As I understand, the conventional explosives in a nuke form a ring around the fissionable material. They all have to explode at exactly the same time in order to compress the fissionable material to a critical mass and cause a chain reaction leading to a nuclear explosion. The code that we give the CO, when entered, sets up the electrical system so that the explosives all go off simultaneously. Right?"

"That's oversimplified but true," Rosen answered.

"Okay. Imagine this scenario. Lava overflows the bow, where all the weapons are. The hull becomes red hot and everything within the sub heats up until the heat eventually rises to the point where one of the conventional warheads blows. That sets off all the other explosives, because they're all at the same temperature and only need a tiny nudge to get them to explode. Can you say for sure that the explosives in the nuke won't all go off at the same time and compress the nuclear fuel in that scenario?"

Admiral Rosen took his time to answer. "I can't say for sure. Not in that scenario," he finally replied. "But even if they did, it would be a localized problem. The bubble from a nuclear explosion at that depth would probably never even break the surface."

"True, but the shock wave of it would travel until it hit the nearest land, right? It's not the explosion itself that worries me. It's what the shock wave would do when it hit the lava fields in the ocean off Kilauea. Our volcanologist tells me that those fields are unstable. According to him, a shock wave hitting them could cause a massive landslide that would, in turn, trigger a tsunami that might be a thousand feet high and would hit Honolulu in less than a half hour."

Admiral Rosen was again quiet for a while. "Okay. You got my attention. Maybe we'll have to pull all the stops on this one. Any suggestions?"

"I've been digging through our archives, and It's all been worked out before. It just hasn't been put into practice yet. I've also reviewed this with our shipyard engineers. They know the specifications of the JPC better than anyone else. The best option, to me, is to lift it up with cables from the surface. Using pontoons can make it safer by minimizing the effects of surface chop. To do that, we'll need to get two lift boats on the way here ASAP, with at least sixteen pontoons and four lift cables, each about seven thousand feet long. The cables will need to be strong enough to lift about a hundred tons each"

"It'll take a few days, but I can start the ball rolling," Admiral Rosen said. "How far have you thought this through? Any more details?"

"We lift it off the bottom by putting the cables underneath its bow and stern and attaching these to a set of four pontoons, say fifty feet below the surface. When we inflate these pontoons, they pull the sub off the bottom. That will allow us to get two more sets of cables under the sub, making it a lot safer. All the cables can then be attached to a second set of pontoons, say a hundred feet deeper than the first set. When we pump air into those, they'll lift the sub up another hundred feet. Then we attach eight more pontoons to the cables another hundred feet deeper. We just keep doing this until the boat's about two hundred feet from the surface. At that point, divers can cut the cables holding it to that collapsed dock, and we can inflate the JPC's onboard ballast tanks from the surface. Then we just tow it home."

"Sounds like a good plan. It'll need refinement, though. How do you plan to get the first two cables under the sub? Divers can't go that deep."

"I'm hoping we can use the UH submersible for that. I haven't worked out the details yet. We'll really need to go over the videos from their next dive on the area. That's set for tomorrow."

"I have a better idea, but I can't tell you about it over the phone," Rosen said. "We've been working on something that might help."

4:35 p.m., Kilauea Volcano Observatory

Russel Wilkes pored over the latest twenty-four hours of seismographs. He loved seismographs. To him, they were the brain waves of the earth. Small intermittent tremors, usually at random intervals, combined with longer, more harmonic patterns to make complex arrays that might look like meaningless scribbles to the uninitiated, but carried tremendous information to him. Just as a neurologist reading an electroencephalogram can gain insight into the well-being and future of his patient, Russell could discern the physical health and immediate future of the earth by looking at the periodicity of its movements and its variations from the norms as depicted by seismographs. He didn't need a computer. He recognized patterns that predicted certain events. By comparing seismographs from multiple locations, he could also determine the point of origin of the earth movement he was seeing and make a good guess as to where future events might occur.

As he studied the graphs, his phone rang. He frowned. He hated interruptions, but he picked up the phone anyway. It was Susan.

"Hi," he said. "I was just about to call you."

"Good news, I hope."

"Not really. I'm getting clear seismic evidence that Loihi's getting ready to blow. Magma's moving, and we're seeing clusters of small earthquakes originating from there. That's just what we see prior to an eruption. I think it's going to be a large one. Your admiral needs to get that submarine out of there."

"Christ. That's why I called," Susan said. "We sent the *Hululua* down to Loihi yesterday, and the crew told me that earthquakes were a big problem for them, I wanted your insight on that. When do you expect it to happen?"

"Can't say exactly. Sometimes these things peter out without our ever knowing why. But my best guess is lava's going to start flowing sometime during the next three to four days."

"I'm assuming you can't tell yet how much flow or where it'll break the surface."

"I'm afraid I can't. It could be on the other side of the seamount from where the submarine's sitting or right on top of it."

"What if we do a dive down there? Could you get any clues from seeing Loihi?

"I might well. It would certainly be worth a try."

"Okay. I'll talk to our Navy friend and get back to you. Keep your schedule open. We may send the *Hululua* down again, and I might want you with me when we do."

"Righto. Will do."

After the click, he rocked back in his seat and smiled with satisfaction. *Maybe I can get her to stay over this time.* It was only then that he noticed his fellow volcanologist, Ellen Chang, in the doorway of his office.

"Jesus. What was that all about?" Ellen asked. "Is there some submarine stuck on top of Loihi? That would be scary, for sure."

"Close the door," he said.

She complied.

"What you overheard, it's a secret. You can't tell anyone about it. Okay?"

She shrugged. "Okay. You think Loihi's going to blow?"

"It's likely. Yes."

"And there's this submarine sitting on top of it. Is its crew still alive? Wow. I wouldn't want to be one of them."

"Nor would I. But we should keep this quiet. It's classified. I can't talk about it. You mustn't either."

"Sure. I get it." She winked at him, then left.

Susan called him a half-hour later. "We're making a dive tomorrow. You're invited. Be at Hilo Harbor at six a.m. We'll pick you up, motor out to Loihi, and make a dive in the afternoon."

"I'll be there." He raised a fist in triumph. *Yes!* he thought.

"It's going to be rough water. If you have waterproof gear, bring it."

"Oh, great," he said. "I'm prone to seasickness."

"Get a couple of those patches. They help a lot. See you tomorrow." She clicked off.

Suddenly, this didn't seem to be so much fun anymore. Once, he'd studied Surtsey, an undersea volcano that broke the surface of the ocean in Iceland in 1963 and grew to be an island over five hundred feet tall and a square mile in area. The vessel he was on had been caught in heavy cross-chop as they'd circled the island. By the time they returned to Reykjavik, he was so dehydrated from vomiting that he needed intravenous fluids. It had taken him three days to recover. He wasn't anxious to repeat the experience.

Surtsey had been his first experience with undersea volcanoes, and it was a wonder to him that, after such a negative experience, he'd become so fascinated by them. There was something remarkable to him about the creation of new land. The birth of a new island out of the center of the ocean was a wonderful thing to Russell. He was a member of a very small coterie of people who understood them. He'd found his academic niche. Every paper he published gave answers that no one else in the world knew, to questions that few in the world had the expertise to ask.

"I'm a geologic neonatalogist," he once told his mother in Manchester, England. "I'm interested in the birth and infancy of volcanoes. I've seen them just after birth, and that's great, but what I really love is seeing them while they're still fetal, before they've popped out of the womb of the sea."

A side benefit of working on Loihi was that he got to work with Susan Cho. They clicked, miracle of miracles. He enjoyed being with her. He'd always considered himself to be a loner, a person who worked better by himself. But then he'd stumbled into this interesting collaboration, a partnership between two intelligent people with very different knowledge, skills, and thought processes, and he'd found it to be great fun.

Chapter 7

28 January 2020

9:20 a.m., Pacific Ocean, above Loihi Seamount

The virtual dive Susan Cho and Russell Wilkes made together on the JPC site was quite different from the one she had made the day before. Rolling from persistent northeast swells made launching of the *Hululua o Maui* difficult and dangerous. The deck crew had to time the launch perfectly to keep the *Hululua* from slamming into the side of the *Iwi* while hanging from its launching davits. A transient gale with driving rain added to their problems. Despite their weather gear, Susan and a very green-appearing Russell were soaked by the time they sat in the *Hululua* command cabin and put on their virtual reality goggles. Unfortunately, the goggles then accentuated Russell's seasickness–what he was seeing didn't match the motion he was feeling–and he had to run to the rail almost immediately.

The *Hululua* sank rapidly under Susan's remote control, with Russell intermittently running to the *Iwi*'s rail to vomit during the first half of the dive. It was only when Susan turned on the floodlights, revealing the landscape of Loihi, that Russell became fascinated enough that he could focus despite the motion around him. He leaned forward in his seat, as though to get a better view, though his position had no effect on the images he was seeing.

In the floodlights, the near landscape tended to be red or gray, while more distant objects shown with a greenish hue due to the ocean's absorption of red light from the floodlights with distance. Large colonies of tube worms waved in the currents and bizarre-looking fish and spindly crabs were everywhere. Russell noticed a glimmer off to the left "Watch out," he said. "There's a large vent to the left."

"I see it."

"There's more activity than there was the last time I was down here," he said. "How far are we from the main caldera?"

"It's behind us, maybe a hundred yards away. The local denizens do seem to be more active. Like they're on steroids."

"How about the water temperature? Is that up from last time?"

"Look in the upper right corner of your goggles. It's shown there, in Centigrade. I've been following it since I turned the lights on, and it varies, but I think the average is a couple degrees warmer," Susan said.

"That's probably because of increased volcanic activity. Maybe that's why there's so much marine activity, too. The organisms are soaking up energy from the volcano.

"We're headed toward the submarine," Susan said. "It should be about a hundred feet in front of us,"

"Can we take a little detour before we go to the submarine?" Russell asked. "I'd like to see what the caldera looks like."

"We don't have that much time. Probably better if we check out the caldera afterward. They need videos of the sub to plan a salvage."

Russell frowned. "Okay. Let's be sure to do that, though. It's important."

"Duly noted. There's the sub," she answered.

"I don't see it. Wait. There it is. I see it now. It's bigger than I expected."

The stern was five or six feet above the reef, and there appeared to be some open space directly under the sail. Susan manipulated the *Hululua* so that it was almost on the bottom and its lights could shine directly on the area. "I can't see if there's a clear channel all the way under. I hope so. Putting a cable on the stern would be no problem, but there's no other place I can see to put a cable under the bow."

They made one more pass around the JPC, as close to it as Susan dared. She avoided the cables from the floating dock and made sure her video included the entire dock as well as the submarine. "I think we're done here," she said. "Let's turn on the Gertrude and talk to the people inside while we go check out the caldera."

She flipped a switch on the console and said, "Ahoy, JPC. *Hululua* here. We've been circling you, videotaping to assist planning for a rescue and salvage. How are you guys holding up?"

"This is Commander Farriott speaking. Who am I talking to?"

"Susan Cho. Same as before. I'm piloting the *Hululua* from above. Do you have any messages for Admiral Green?"

"Please tell him our injured man needs help. He's in a lot of pain. He's not critical, but the sooner he's brought to the surface, the better."

"Can you give me some more details about the nature of the injury? Anything that would prevent normal transport? Can he walk?"

"He has severe burns on his face and one arm. The burn on his arm seems to be third degree over a two inch by five-inch patch. The skin there has turned black. Our medic thinks the dead skin's going to have to be removed or it'll get infected. Legs are okay, but he can't climb ladders with his bum arm."

"Roger. I'll relay the message," she said.

"When can we get out of here?"

"I'm not privy to the details of that, but I'm told that the SRDRS rescue vehicle is expected to arrive tomorrow. They might need a day or two to set things up after that."

"Thanks for the info. Yours is the only communication we've had," Farriott said.

"They don't want to use the Gertrude from the surface any more than necessary. Even with the encryption, it could broadcast your plight all over the Pacific. You never know who's listening in. We're on a secure cable to above."

"Understood. We need the contact, though. It helps a lot with morale."

"I'll probably be working down here pretty often during the next few days," Susan said.

"Good. Keep us informed."

"Will do. How's your AC operating now? Temperature all right?"

"Hotter than we like but stable, so far. Earthquakes are a real problem."

"We're going to check out the caldera before going up," Susan said. I'll have to break off now."

"Roger. Out."

"Out."

"I wouldn't want to be where they are," Russell said.

"Me neither. It must be a nightmare down there. That ridge in front of us is probably the caldera edge."

"I see it. Be careful going over it. The water may be hot."

"It is," she answered. "We're still twenty feet away and the temperature's gone up ten degrees." She raised the *Hululua* remotely ten feet and pointed the video cameras and lights downward, so they could look over the edge without being over the edge themselves. "I don't see anything except the shimmering," she said.

"Let's see what it looks like without the lights," Russell said.

"Okay." She killed the lights, and they waited, letting their eyes adapt to the dark. Russell saw it first. About a quarter of the caldera floor glowed with a dull red color.

"The caldera's filling up," he said. "The surface is at least thirty feet higher than it was in November, the last time you and I looked at it together. It's only a matter of time before lava starts flowing downhill. When the caldera gets full, it'll flow through that low area of the edge over there. Then it'll meander, like a stream. No telling where it'll go from there."

Susan turned on the lights. The terrain below the lowest edge of the caldera was irregular, but from their vantage point, it looked like the JPC was downhill and a hundred feet to the right of the lowest point of the caldera edge. The lava lake in the caldera was about twenty feet below the edge.

"I'd guess the flow will miss them, but it'll be close," Russell said.

"Let's get the *Hululua* up and report," she said. She noticed the movement then. As they watched, rock outcroppings broke off and rolled downhill. The temperature gauge rose a couple of degrees. And when they looked back at the caldera, a jagged crack ran across its middle, and red lava could be seen below it, even with the lights on. The water shimmered above it, looking like a transparent curtain cutting across the ocean above the crater.

"That water has to be super-hot. Let's get out of here before we get cooked," she said. She veered the *Hululua* away from the caldera and headed it steeply upward.

6:00 p.m., Family Housing, Pearl Harbor, Oahu

Marisa Polanski's kids had the television on while she cooked dinner. Yvonne (Missy, to her family) and Rudy watched it while doing their homework. Marisa didn't mind. Both kids were straight A students. She didn't care how they studied. Whatever worked.

She was chopping cabbage when Missy called from the living room. "Mom, the announcer just said there's a submarine sunk on top of a volcano off the Big Island. Do you think that might be the one Dad's on?"

"That doesn't sound right," Marisa called back. "Are you sure you heard him correctly?"

"Yeah. That's what he said. Rudy, you heard it too, didn't you?"

"I wasn't listening," Rudy said. "I'm cramming for an exam tomorrow."

"So, what exactly did he say?" Marisa asked.

"He said they had an 'unconfirmed report' that a submarine was stuck right on top of some undersea volcano off the Big Island. They tried to confirm the report with the Navy but weren't able to reach anyone who would confirm or deny it."

"Strange," Marisa said. "If it were true, the Navy would notify the families before they released information to the news media. So, I can't imagine how the TV station would hear about it before we did. I wouldn't worry about it much." She went back to preparing dinner.

A half-hour later, while they were eating a meal of pork sausage, potatoes, and boiled cabbage, the telephone rang. "I'll get it," Missy said. She ran to her bedroom to pick up the phone.

"She's got a boyfriend," Rudy said, smiling.

"She better not," Marisa said. "Eighth graders don't have boyfriends. Not in my house."

A moment later, Missy returned, carrying the phone. She handed it to her mother. "It's for you," she said, disappointment in her voice.

Marisa took the phone. "Hello."

"This is Becky Morton. You probably don't remember me, but my husband is on the JPC. I'm sorry to bother you, but I just heard a really disturbing news report on the six o'clock news. They say a submarine is sunk off the Big Island. I figured the COB's wife would know if it involves the JPC. Have you heard anything?"

"No. My daughter heard the same news report. She said it was just an unconfirmed report, and the submarine wasn't named. You know how the news media screw things up. I wouldn't put a lot of stock in it."

"The news anchor said it's landed right on *Loihi*, the undersea volcano off the Big Island. He didn't say it was unconfirmed."

Marisa held her hand over the phone, while she asked, "What station were you guys watching?

"Channel four," they both answered.

Taking her hand off the phone, she asked, "Becky, what channel were you watching?"

"Channel five."

"My kids were watching channel four. Can you tell me exactly what they said on channel five?"

"They–John McLenny, the anchor, actually–said that a volcanologist on the Big Island had confirmed that a US Navy submarine had sunk and was lying on the bottom of the ocean on top of *Loihi*, the volcano that's about twenty miles from Hawaii. He said the volcano's getting ready to erupt and the Navy is planning an emergency rescue attempt. The boat's more than a half-mile below the surface.

"McLenny didn't say nothing about whether anyone's still alive on the sub or which boat it was or how they're going to get the crew off the sub. He said they talked to Admiral Green and got the brushoff. Green just told him that the Navy won't give out the position or mission of any Navy submarine after it leaves port."

"So, Green didn't deny it?" Marisa asked.

"No. That's one reason I'm so upset," Becky answered. "I figure if he knew it wasn't true, he'd deny it. Doing that wouldn't give away the position of our sub, but it would reassure the families of the crew. Right? What's he got to lose by denying it? So, I figure it's true."

"I see your point. It's been on at least two channels, too, so there must be something to it. But we don't know if it's the JPC, right? It could be one of the other subs."

"Maybe," Becky said. "But all the rest have been out to sea for a couple of weeks. They shouldn't still be hanging around in Hawaiian waters. The JPC, on the other hand...."

"I see your point. The others are probably in the South China Sea by now, or wherever they're going." Marisa paused to think. "I don't think we can get any info tonight. I'll let you know what I find out tomorrow."

"Thanks. I'll keep my ears open, too. 'Bye."

"What did she say?" Missy asked.

"She heard the same report on another channel. Let's check all the news channels at ten. By then, they might have more information."

"Do you think Dad's in trouble?" Rudy asked.

"He's been in a lot more danger before, I'm sure," Marisa answered. She was speculating, of course. Mike Polanski never talked about his missions. "Don't ask, don't tell" had been his mantra long before it was applied to sexual preferences in the military.

Marisa always worried about him when he left, but her gnawing uncertainty about his return had just become part of her life over the years. *You've got a good man. You can't drive yourself nuts worrying about whether you'll keep him,* she told herself. This time, though, was different, and despite her best efforts to control her thoughts, she felt real fear, along with an obligation to hide it from her children.

After the kids went to bed, she picked up the phone and called Ellen Farriott.

Chapter 8

30 January 2020

3:20 a.m., Loihi Seamount

Daniel Farriott lay on his bunk in his underwear and stared at the ceiling less than five feet above his bed. He recognized his stateroom was a luxury. It was his private place, after all, and his crew had no such place. Even the beds were shared, each sailor taking one shift per day, and the bottom of the bunk above was less than a foot above their heads. Times like these, he was glad he was the skipper. Rank had its privileges.

Nevertheless, the walls and the ceiling were beginning to close in on him. It was different when they were speeding through the sea. Every day had something new to experience, even if they were underwater. They were always busy. A busy submarine, he knew, was a happy submarine.

But here, just lying on the bottom, was a nightmare that wouldn't stop. He had a sense of helplessness that he couldn't get rid of. It was getting to him. He couldn't imagine how his crew was holding together. He knew they faced much more privation than he did. So far, though, there'd only been two incidents since Dennis Lozano's injury.

The first one hadn't been serious. One seaman took exception to the music another had on his iPod. The seaman was using earphones, as required, but then the man began singing along with the music. The lyrics, unfortunately, were graphic and offensive to the man who overheard them. He objected, and a brawl resulted. His LCPO had intervened, calmed things down, and disciplined both men. There might have been residual irritation, but that was it.

The second incident was more problematic. One sailor, a white man from the deep south, had balked at an order given by a petty officer, who happened to be black. This had led to another brawl, accompanied by several nasty racial slurs. This time, the LCPO didn't get there until after the seaman struck the petty officer across the face with a wrench. It was a wonder he hadn't fractured the man's skull. It was bad enough as it was, though. He'd broken the man's nose. When they got back to shore, he'd face charges for assault on a superior, with certain time in the stockade. For the present, though, nothing much could be done except to confine him to his bunk room when off duty. The JPC had no brig.

Incidents like that were doubly intolerable on a submarine, as they affected the morale of the entire crew and tended to result in divisions. As in other confined spaces, like prisons, cliques could form, often based on racial or religious lines. Cliques were anathema to submarine commanders. The crew of a submarine had to be one band of brothers. And sisters, these days.

Daniel knew that the two incidents had been handled, but they hadn't been forgotten. One incident tended to lead to another, and it was only a matter of time before there would be major disruption of their ability to act as a team and fulfill their mission.

He sighed. He wasn't going to get any sleep this shift. He decided to make the rounds of the submarine, interact with his men and try to cheer people up. At least the end of the ordeal was within sight. They'd picked up sonar echoes from the surface. A ship was up there, and he had no doubt it was a rescue vehicle. Some of them might be out of the sub within the next twenty-four hours. Of course, he couldn't tell the crew that. Not before he had actually heard it from COMPACFLT. But he could tell his crew that rescue would be "soon."

He sat on the edge of his bunk and stretched his arms upward, something he couldn't do while standing because of the low ceiling. Then he stood and slipped on his uniform. He was about to leave when there was a knock on his door. "Communication from

COMPACFLT, Sir. It's encoded and for your eyes only," the radioman said.

"Thank you," he said, and accepted the envelope in the radioman's hand.

He decoded the message and was pleased by the first few sentences. Now, he had a definite time and specifics for a rescue attempt. The last sentence of the message, however, made him groan audibly. They were, indeed, going to be rescued soon. That was good. Or at least most of them would be. Others were going to have to stay on the JPC for quite a while longer, until the JPC itself could be salvaged. They needed a skeleton crew on board during the salvage. He was one of those who would have to stay, and he had the unenviable task of choosing who his fellow coffin-mates would be.

His COB would have to stay. They would also need their Weapons Officer and Engineer. Should he keep the XO? He still had his doubts about her, but since the initial sinking, they'd worked well together. And what if something happened to him? He needed a backup. He deferred that decision. He decided to keep the Damage Control Assistant on board. He was particularly competent, an outstanding officer. The Communications Officer would have to stay. So would his Reactor Control Assistant. As for the enlisted personnel, he'd talk to the other officers and the COB before choosing.

He could see the logic in COMPACFLT's position. The JPC was worth a billion dollars. If they could salvage it, they should. And to do it properly, sufficient crew had to be aboard to handle any problems that might come up. But Daniel also knew that salvage of an intact submarine with personnel aboard from this depth was unprecedented. In fact, the last time the US Navy had tried to salvage an entire submarine, the sub had broken in half a thousand feet below the surface. Granted, that submarine had a big hole in its side from an explosion. The JPC was intact. *That should make it easier to salvage*, he thought.

Despite that, he guessed that any man or woman he selected to stay on board would have at least a fifty percent chance of dying. *Who do I want to die with?* he asked himself. It was irrelevant, of course. He'd choose the people whose competence was needed. The best. Military service was like that. The most competent were often chosen to be the first to die.

7:20 a.m., Hickam Air Force Base, Oahu

The *Groton III* Submarine Rescue Diving Recompression System (SRDRS) rescue vehicle arrived at Hickam Air Force Base in an Air Force C-4M transport aircraft. From there, it was taken to Sub Base Pearl Harbor in a special transport land vehicle also flown from its home port in San Diego. Divers then piggy-backed it to a Virginia class attack submarine for transport to Loihi. The attack submarine was to act as its mother ship until a surface vessel relieved it. Thereafter, the submarine would circle the site and provide security for the rescue operation.

1:08 p.m., COMSUBPAC, Bldg. 619, Pearl Harbor

"Doctor Wilkes, I can't tell you how much harm has been done by this news getting out," said Admiral Green, on a secure line to Wilkes. "The news media have been all over the story. It's attracting very unwelcome national and international attention. Family members of submarine crews are panicked and demanding information. All of this interferes with my ability to solve the problem at hand."

"What can I say?" Russell Wilkes asked. "A secretary overheard my telephone call with Susan Cho. She was standing behind me and I didn't see her until I hung up. I told her to keep it quiet, but she obviously didn't. I'm really very sorry. It was not my intention to spill the beans."

"Apology accepted. But it's time to clam up now. If someone asks you a question, simply respond with a 'no comment'."

"I've tried my best to do just that, but it's difficult. I've only been setting the media straight when they're clearly off the path about Loihi. I don't want them to publish false material."

"Doctor Wilkes, I don't believe I have any alternative but to cut you off from any further information regarding the JPC. Your services will no longer be required."

"Admiral, I beg you to reconsider. I take the daily pulse of Loihi via seismography. The information I can supply to you may be critical to your success in rescuing your crew and salvaging the boat. Please accept my offer of further assistance."

"Assistance? I'm afraid the information you've given us has come at too high a price. I will certainly welcome any information you wish to share. I respect your knowledge in your chosen field. But the information exchange will have to be one-way from now on. This operation is too important to be jeopardized by loose lips. Good day, sir." He hung up.

The problem was worse than he had told Wilkes. Although Loihi was within the territorial waters of the United States and they could declare a no-navigation zone around it, they had no practical way of keeping the Russians away. What were they going to do? Blow them out of the water? No. They'd be busy enough working with the JPC. The last thing they needed was an international diplomatic crisis on top of an already difficult operation.

The only alternative was to complete the rescue and salvage before the Russians and Chinese could get there. Achieving that would cut even further into their planning time. What had already been a tight deadline was now even tighter.

They would have to act before they had all the information they needed. It was like betting the farm on seven card stud before you had your fifth card. That made Admiral Green very uneasy.

He checked his watch and sighed. He had a half-hour to think over what he would tell Ellen Farriott and Marisa Polanski. Ellen had called early in the morning, and he'd reluctantly agreed to meet her and Marisa. He had to tell them something. Of course, he already knew what he would say, but he was still looking for a way to avoid telling them too much. He refilled his coffee cup from the machine and carried it to his desk. He closed the door and thought while he sipped the black brew.

Twenty minutes later, his intercom buzzed. "They're here," Trudy said.

"Send them in," he said. He stood behind his desk when they entered and motioned to two chairs in front of the desk. "Please sit down," he said.

When they were seated, he began. "You'll need to keep what I'm about to say absolutely confidential," he said. "Do I have your word on that?"

"Can I tell the partners of other crew members?" Marisa asked, thinking of Becky Morton.

"No, but they'll know soon enough. Don't tell your children, either."

"That's going to be hard," Ellen said. "Our kids need to know."

"Not yet, they don't. I need your promise to keep this secret."

"Okay. I'll agree," Ellen said. She looked at Marisa, who also nodded.

"Good. We're going to do a rescue, hopefully before the end of the week. We don't want the Russians or Chinese interfering with it. They read all our papers. We know they'll be on their way here, but we don't expect them to arrive for several days. The less they know about this, the better. That's why we have to keep this secret.

"I can confirm that the JPC is the ship involved. It's disabled, but the crew is okay, except for one man who has some burns. A rescue craft is on its way, and we plan to bring most of the crew up as soon as we can. Don't hold me to the timing, though. It depends on a lot of factors I can't control, like weather, wave activity, etc."

"You said 'Most of them.' Why not bring all of the crew up?" Marisa asked.

"We need a skeleton crew aboard during the salvage of the JPC. We can't leave it unattended until salvage vessels are ready to pick the sub up."

Marisa went cold. "How many?" she asked.

"My guess is less than twenty, maybe a dozen."

"And that will include the skipper and the COB?" Ellen asked.

"Your husband will have to stay. Who he selects to be with him is his decision, but yes, I would think he would select his COB. He would want his best people with him."

Ellen took a deep breath. "How long before the salvage attempt?" she asked.

"Salvage ships are on their way. They'll be here in three or four days. The timing will depend on the weather. We don't want to try it in high seas. It might be another week before we feel comfortable in proceeding."

"What do you think the chance of success are?" Marisa asked.

"Very good," Green lied.

"Can you give us more details?"

"No, I can't. We have a lot of planning to do, and the rest of the operation is classified. I've told you everything I can tell you. I only ask that you keep this quiet until after the crew is rescued. After that, the secret will be impossible to contain anyway. But keeping this secret for the next few days will be critical for us, critical for your husbands, too. We don't need interference from unfriendly vessels nearby."

Ellen stood up. She reached out her hand. "Thank you," she said, as he shook it.

Marisa stood also, looked directly in Admiral Green's eyes, and said, "I know you haven't told us the whole truth, but my husband and I have been in the

Navy a long time. He's a wonderful man. You bring him back to me." She turned, without offering her hand.

Admiral Green understood that he'd been issued an order. He'd try his best to obey it. But right now, he had work to do and a flight to catch.

3:40 p.m., Pacific Ocean, above Loihi Seamount

When Susan and the *Iwi* reached Loihi, the *Groton III* was floating on the surface. A destroyer or cruiser–she couldn't tell which–was a half mile away, apparently circling the site, providing security, but the submarine that had brought the *Groton III* was nowhere to be seen. She wondered if it was underwater, a potential obstacle for her.

Admiral Green's aide, Lieutenant Moran, found her on the deck and briefed her on the next day's activities. "The submarine won't be in your way," Moran said. " We won't need it for the rescue. A surface ship will be here to provide support in a few hours. Tomorrow, at 0500, we'll start bringing the crew to the surface. We'll transfer them from the SRDRS directly to the surface vessel. We want the first batch of crew members coming up just after dawn. What happens on the bottom doesn't need light–as you know, it's always dark down there–but the transfer from the *Groton III* to the surface vessel will be safer in daylight. That ship has a helipad, so after the submariners are assessed for injuries, we can fly them directly to Pearl Harbor."

"So, they get to go straight home?"

"They'll be taken to a secure facility at Pearl Harbor for debriefing. We'll get them home to their families as soon as we can."

"I understand. When the mission's over."

He was silent.

"With the early start, I'll eat soon and hit the sack."

"We'll hold a final briefing at 1930. Plan to be finished eating by then."

"Will do. Thanks."

She checked her watch. 5:00 pm, or 1700 military time. Three bells, navy time. She had two and a half hours before the briefing. She went to the *Iwi*s galley and filled a plate from the steam table. This wasn't the navy. Eating was much less disciplined. On the *Iwi*, personnel ate dinner when they wanted, anytime between five and seven-thirty. She chose mahimahi, rice, mixed veggies, a nice helping of salad. She poured herself a cup of coffee, added a little powdered cream and sugar, and sat down to a leisurely dinner.

She had an hour and a half to kill before the briefing, so she went to the deck and watched the sun descend over the waves. Sunset was at 5:57 p.m. according to her smart watch. The sky was already gold and purple around the edges, and the seas were at evening calm, with rollers rocking the *Iwi* gently. It was a beautiful evening, tranquil and encouraging, until her cellular rang and Russel Wilkes ruined all that.

"I'm looking at the current seismometers, and there's something unusual going on at Loihi," he said. "The mini-earthquake frequency is increasing. It's all pre-eruptive activity, but more irregular than usual. Anyway, I'm concerned. I can't say just what's going to happen or when. But something's up, for sure. You might want to be extra careful if you're anywhere near Loihi. Be ready for surprises."

"Thank you, Russell. I'll be extra careful."

"Then you are near? I thought the rescue would come sometime soon, but you know, your Admiral Green isn't telling me much these days. I'm not in the loop, it seems."

"Well, you were fired," she said, with a joking tone. "You can't really blame him, can you? After all, the leak came from your office."

"It did. And I do regret that. Where are you right now?"

"I wish I could tell you. Sorry."

There was silence on the other end.

"Listen. I'm concerned about you, that's all. Volcanoes are dangerous. Even ones that are under the ocean. Particularly ones that are below the ocean. When I saw that red glow when we were down there, and I thought of what it represented–and I know we weren't actually there. It was just virtual reality, of course–but still, I had this image of real evil, and you being caught up in it, and I guess I'm just telling you to be very, very careful, that's all."

"Thanks," she said. She felt compelled to add, "I'm touched by your concern. I'm a big girl, though. I can take care of myself. I appreciate your warning, and I'll heed it."

"I know. My fear is irrational. You'll just be on the surface, running the *Hululua* by Gertrude. Just promise me you'll be careful."

She couldn't contradict him. "I promise. And I'll call you when it's all done."

"Please do. I'm very concerned about this whole operation. So many things could go wrong...."

"We can't let them go wrong, can we? The consequences would be unthinkable."

"Aye. That's the problem, right there. When people feel a strong obligation, they do whatever they must do to meet that obligation, don't they? And that's what I'm afraid of. Because I know you'll take risks if you must. And the ones I can think of are major risks, not just theoretical ones, so it scares the hell out of me."

"I have to leave now. I have to attend a.... a meeting." She didn't want to say a "briefing." "I'll call you when I get a chance. Keep me informed of any new developments on Loihi. Bye." She hung up. The whole conversation had unsettled her. It wasn't just his pointing out dangers to her. It was the level of his concern for her that was surprising.

She walked to the briefing and shifted her mind toward the immediate problem at hand. She'd deal with her feelings regarding Russell Wilkes later, when she had the time.

9:05 p.m., Pacific Ocean, above Loihi Seamount

Admiral Green had decided to monitor the rescue from the deck of the *Iwi* rather than from the *Groton III*s mother ship. Watching the rescue from the perspective of the *Hululua o Maui* would give him an even better view than those aboard the *Groton III* had.. Besides, by watching the rescue, he felt he might see something that might be of value during the subsequent salvage of the JPC, planned for the week after the rescue of most of the crew.

The night before the rescue, he couldn't sleep. Instead, he paced the deck of the *Iwi* and tried to find holes in their plans. Everything looked good on paper. But a rescue had never been attempted before at this depth.? No one knew what could go wrong, but everyone involved doubted that the operation would go off exactly as planned. From experience, Green knew that in operations as complex as this one, something always went wrong. He could imagine all sorts of scenarios that might end up in disaster. Hatches could get stuck. Pumps could malfunction. Human beings could make stupid errors. An earthquake could hit just as the bolts were being tightened between the JPC and the rescue vehicle. He shuddered at the thought. Even after all bolts were tightened, a strong enough earthquake could still rip the two vessels apart. Currents could prevent the SRDRS locking. The list of potential problems seemed endless.

Unfortunately, he had no way to prevent any of the scenarios he imagined. If they happened, they happened. When he finally went to bed, he prayed that they'd be lucky the next day. They needed luck, a lot of it.

Chapter 9

31 January 2020

2;24 a.m., Loihi Seamount

The temperature in the JPC had risen another degree. Daniel Farriott didn't know what else they could do to decrease it. If they couldn't vent heat to the ambient water around them, because the ambient water was already warm, they were stuck with it. They'd already done everything they could, but it wasn't enough.

The problem wasn't life-threatening, but it was uncomfortable. Sweat rolled down people's bodies as they worked, even if they stripped to shorts and removed their shirts. Desalination required energy from the reactor, meaning more heat. As a result, water was rationed and full showers could not be taken, so everyone stank. They needed whatever water they had to replenish the water they lost in sweat. When each shift took their turns on their hot beds, the mattresses were still damp from the previous occupant's sweat. The resulting sleeplessness caused friction and an overall loss of morale.

Daniel was counting the hours until rescue. He only hoped it would come before the tensions among the crew erupted. They had their own social volcano brewing inside the sub, aggravated by the impending eruption outside. So far, he'd been able to keep tempers down, but he knew full well that any spark could set off a disastrous rebellion.

Adding to the tension was the worsening condition of Dennis Lozano. He was running a fever and was often delirious. Clearly, he needed to be in a hospital. The man was dying from an injury that everyone on board thought would have been serious but not life-threatening under normal circumstances.

He was a popular man but a pain in the ass, often giving voice to feelings that all the crew shared. He could make them laugh at their plight at the same time as he made his superiors cringe. Daniel knew that Doc was doing everything he could for him. He also knew that the crew didn't feel it was enough.

"Skipper, we've got a whisper campaign going," Mike Polanski said. "When I make rounds, guys are talking, and as soon as they see me, they clam up and won't meet my eyes. It's all over the boat. I don't know what's coming or when, or who's the ringleader, but a storm is brewing. We got rough waters ahead."

"Have any ideas of what to do about it?" Daniel asked.

"Get us the hell out of here. Nothing else is going to work."

"Let the crew know we'll have most of them up top within twenty-four hours."

"You sure you want to tell them that? If it doesn't happen, there'll be a riot."

"That's why I've been keeping it quiet. I've had estimates, but you know how things get screwed up. Nothing ever happens as soon as it's supposed to. But the word just came in from above. An SRDRS is already topside. They're planning to start down to pick some of us up at 0700. They'll send two guys down to help us load. That leaves room for eighteen crew members to ride up. I want Lozano to be one of the first to go. You can pick the rest."

"I'll send some of the guys I think may be ready to raise hell. Let's get them out of here."

"Be careful. Everybody wants to be the first out of here. You don't want to be seen as rewarding bad behavior," Daniel said.

"Good point. I'll mix in some of the best people, too."

"Don't forget. Some of us have to stay behind. Have you told them yet?"

"Skipper, I got that handled. Every person I selected to stay behind is a volunteer. I didn't order anybody to stay. I just talked to each one individually, told them what the need was, and asked them if they'd be willing to stay. If they said no, my plan was to scratch them off the list, then swear them to secrecy, no matter whether they said no or yes."

"So how many said no?" Farriott asked.

"Not a damned one. I asked good people. Good people do what's right when the going gets tough."

"So how many are staying?"

"Eleven. I'd settled on ten. Then Celia Hutchinson comes up to me. She's pissed because she overheard me talking to one of the guys and I hadn't asked her to stay. She thinks I passed her over because she's female," Mike said.

"Did you?"

"Maybe, unconsciously. But she's a sonar tech, and I thought, 'What do we need with sonar during the salvage?' "

"We don't want anything near us during the lift, and we'll be blind without sonar," Daniel said.

"That's just what she said. Made sense to me, so she's staying behind with us."

6:30 a.m., Pacific Ocean, above Loihi Seamount

The *Groton III* was a remotely-controlled, battery-powered cylinder fifty-two feet long and nine feet in diameter. Its hull was built of carbon-reinforced fiberglass, twice as strong as steel and half the weight. Nevertheless, it weighed a little over eighty tons. Its operational depth limit was four thousand feet, less than the Mystic and Avalon class Deep Submarine Rescue Vehicles (DSRV's) of the past, but sufficient for this job. It could rescue up to twenty sailors at a time and could perform safe decompression of them if they were exposed to high pressures, up to ten atmospheres. In this, it was different from its predecessors. Decompression would not be required for the crew of the JPC, as the sailors inside the submarine were at an internal pressure of only one atmosphere, the same as at the surface. No divers would be able to work at the one hundred atmosphere pressure outside the JPC's hull. Thus, supplemental attachment of the vehicle to the JPC by divers, which might otherwise be done for safety, was not possible due to the depth.

Instead, the vehicle would find the JPC and attach to it directly over its rescue escape hatch. Water would be pumped from between the JPC and the *Groton III*, creating a suction lock of the two vessels. Crew members of the *Groton III* would then enter the transfer chamber and bolt the two vessels together with eyebolts. The hatch to the JPC could then be opened, and up to eighteen sailors would enter the *Groton III* for transport to the surface.

The process was very similar to the one used in attaching the Space Shuttle to the International Space Station, except that the pressure differential was a hundred times greater than what was encountered in space, and the two ocean vessels were subject to water currents that could pull the vessels apart, whereas the International Space Station floated in a vacuum.

Once the sailors had exited the transfer chamber and entered the main transport chamber of the *Groton III*, the *Groton III*s crew would secure the transfer chamber, close the hatch to the JPC, and remove the eyebolts. They would then exit the locking chamber, secure its entrance and flood the chamber to remove the suction lock to the JPC. The *Groton III* would move to the surface to discharge the rescued crew members. The process would need to be repeated six times until all personnel were rescued.

The *Groton III* was remotely controlled from the surface by cable, which allowed more precision and less time delay than the Gertrude that Susan used to control the *Hululua.* However, for this mission, two rescue personnel would be sent down to ensure locking of the eyebolts. They could also render whatever medical assistance might be needed to the crew of the JPC on the way up. If necessary, they could over-ride the surface controls and operate the *Groton III* manually.

The SRDRS could lock to a bottomed submarine in a three-mile-per-hour current, but until the eyebolts were secured, stronger currents could change the orientation of the *Groton III* to the JPC, breaking the hydraulic seal, flooding the locking chamber, and killing anyone inside it at the time. For this reason, the hatch to the JPC could not be opened until the eyebolts were in place. Otherwise, the entire submarine could flood. If this were to happen, death of the entire crew would occur within seconds due to the immense pressure. The two rescue personnel were at most risk, because they would be in the locking chamber before the eyebolts were placed. They were volunteers who considered this risk to be just part of their jobs.

The cables holding the JPC to the floating dock presented two threats to the operators of the SRDRS. First, the cables could entangle the *Groton III*s drive train during the rescue. Second, they could prevent a solid lock of the *Groton III* to the JPC.

To prevent these potential problems, Admiral Green, Susan, and the *Groton III* pilot agreed that Susan would pilot the *Hululua* as it descended with the *Groton III* and hold the cables out of the way until the *Groton III* had safely locked to the JPC. Once loaded with men, the *Groton III* would make itself buoyant by filling its ballast tanks with air, break the water seal with the JPC, and refrain from using its engines until it had floated well above the cables. From there, it could proceed to the surface safely. The *Hululua* would then return to the *Iwi* and recharge its batteries, hopefully in time for the next dive.

For these maneuvers, Susan had insisted on piloting the *Hululua* from depth herself, relieving Admiral Green from the necessity of requesting it. She needed the increased precision available only with direct control of the submersible, as opposed to robotic control, for this delicate and critical operation.

Susan had configured the *Hululua o Maui* differently for the rescue attempt. Because the secrecy of the mission was already compromised, the communication cable which had linked her to the *Iwi* was gone. That removed one potential danger–that her communication cable would entangle the SRDRS's drive train–but it meant that any communications she had would be broadcast further in the surrounding ocean. She still had a Gertrude, but since the water itself conveyed the audio message, not a cable line from the surface, the audio emissions of the Gertrude could be heard by any vessel within three miles of the JPC. Anyone with the appropriate codes could transcribe the transmissions. The encryption would prevent any nearby Russian or Chinese subs from understanding what was said immediately, but if they had knowledge of the subject of the transmissions–the rescue of a downed submarine–their code-breakers would have a leg up on breaking the code.

Admiral Green expected unfriendly vessels to converge on the site eventually. Submarines were a bigger problem than surface ships. They were harder to detect and could sneak in closer. They weren't there already only because they either were thousands of miles away when the media broadcast the news or because their home countries had not been able to communicate with them while they remained submerged. Eventually, they'd show up. By that time, though, Admiral Green hoped the mission would be successfully completed.

If Susan needed to talk to the surface support ships from the *Iwi*, she could use a secure satellite phone she'd been given, although she was told to keep talk to a minimum and be as non-specific as possible. She could not, for example, mention the name of the vessel on the bottom or any unnecessary details of its configuration. If she wanted to talk to people on the SRDRS, however, she had to use the Gertrude.

Her job was simple, at least on paper. She was to direct the *Hululua* to the depths, then grasp and deflect the cables out of the way of the Navy SRDRS rescue vehicle. Once the SRDRS rose above the cables, she could return to the *Iwi*, exchange batteries, and return to the JPC to repeat the process, until all the sailors, except for the skeleton crew, were on the surface.

She doubted it would be that easy.

Chapter 10

1 February 2020

4:30 a.m., Loihi Seamount

Daniel Farriott was beginning to feel that he was losing control. His helplessness was so clear to him that it was almost palpable, a solid, disgusting thing that had to be obvious to every man in the crew. Daniel had no idea how to deal with his own rising dread, much less that of his crew.

The shaking of the JPC was nearly constant, unnerving them and creating a growing sense of impending disaster. Every time it stopped, the crew gave a collective sigh of relief, but then a minute, ten minutes, or an hour later, the shaking would start again, tumbling them from exhausted sleep, disrupting work they were doing, and threatening the steam pipes that had already roasted one of their mates.

Every crew member was shaken, physically and emotionally, as the ground beneath them moved left and right, forward and backward, up and down, in an unpredictable pattern, a *danse macabre* over which they had no control. The JPC crew wallowed in their own helplessness. Few had full confidence in their officers any longer. Daniel still maintained command, but he knew that his control was tenuous and might be lost at any time.

In his stateroom, he said a prayer, on his knees like when he was a kid. "Get us out of here before it's too late," he prayed, not knowing who he was asking. *Someone with a lot more power than I have*, he thought. It made no difference. He was used to solving his own problems. What he got from his prayers was not a burst of self-confidence so much as it was a slowing in the deterioration of his own sense of worth.

One of the problems, he knew, was sleeplessness. Too often, after falling into a dreamless sleep, they were shaken awake, coming conscious with a sense of dread that made falling asleep again impossible. His crew that slept in upper bunks were particularly affected. It was one thing to be shaken out of a bunk a foot from the floor and another to awaken in the act of falling five feet to a floor made of hard steel.

One more hour he knew he could take. One more day, he could push himself to stand. One more week, and he knew that no one on the crew would be able to function any longer, himself included. There was a limit and an end, and they were near to it. In his dreams, he felt they were on a moving train heading toward a chasm with no bridge. They were speeding toward the end of the rails with no way to stop the train.

And he was the man in charge, a fake superman weakened by kryptonite, just as helpless as the most ineffective man on his crew. A man with a fancier uniform than the lowest seaman, but just as helpless.

He pulled himself upright. He wasn't going to sleep, he knew. He made his way to the bridge. He wanted to be there when things started happening.

The rescue, if it came as promised, would be just in the nick of time. Another hour or two and the SRDRS would be alongside them. What a relief it would be to have some of the crew on their way up. He checked his watch. 0630. Another half hour before they expected to hear anything. Sonar would pick up activity first. Then there would be a Gertrude message, probably just as the SRDRS started down.

He waited.

His anxiety grew as he paced the bridge, waiting for a sign of their rescue. They hadn't heard a thing yet, not by Gertrude nor by sonar, and they should have. It was 0700 and then 0730 with no signs of any rescue activity. He knew something was not right but he couldn't show his anxiety. "These guys are on Navy time," he commented, then laughed at his own joke. No one else laughed.

4:45 a.m., Pacific Ocean, above Loihi Seamount

Susan Cho was just instructing Admiral Green on the use of the virtual reality goggles when his satellite phone rang. He hung the goggles back on the rack and answered the phone.

Ted Rosen, COMPACFLT, was on the line. "I have three pieces of bad news for you," he said. "The first is that the crew of the SRDRS found a malfunction when they did their checklist. The engineers think they can fix it, but we have to fly parts to them from Pearl Harbor. They called me first to expedite flying the parts, and I told them I'd call you, since I needed to talk to you anyway. So, you can stand down on the *Iwi.* With good luck, they'll be ready to go tomorrow morning.

"The second bad news is that we can't get the pontoons you wanted in the time frame necessary. So, we've changed your plan. We're going to loop four cables around the JPC, on the stern, the bow, and just in front of and behind the sail. The cables are plenty strong enough. They'll do the trick. We'll lift her up with two winch ships locked together. It's maybe not as fool-proof as the pontoon idea you had, because there will be more motion due to wave action than there would be using the pontoons. We'll also have to be very careful to keep the cables under equal tension, so the lift itself will be more technically demanding, but it's a hell of a lot faster to set up. We have the cables and ships ready to go. They're on their way to you as we speak.

"The rescue will be run by Rear Admiral Ralph Kennedy. He's in R & S, Rescue & Salvage. You'll be an advisor. I want you there, but this is primarily a surface mission, not a submarine operation. It's more in the R & S area of expertise than in yours.

"When will they get here?" Green asked.

"Figure a week. In the meantime, you can get most of the crew off. The CO and a few critical personnel will have to stay behind and do whatever needs to be done on the way up."

"They're not happy about being left down there. It's not a pleasant environment. The volcano's heating up, and they're getting shaken by some pretty significant earthquakes. The sooner we can get them out of there, the better."

"We're doing our best. Help is on its way."

"Understood. I'm just concerned...."

"I'm told you have a top-notch CO down there. I'm sure he'll handle whatever comes up. You need to have faith in him."

"He is, and I do. But he's sitting on an active volcano a half-mile below the surface. His crew must be near the breaking point by now. This delay is going to be hard for them to accept."

"Nothing you or I can do about it. Shit happens."

"Right. I'd better let the folks on the *Iwi* know what's going on. Thanks for calling."

"Don't you want to hear the third piece of bad news?"

Green frowned. "There's more? You've already given me enough to worry about."

"Right. You have my sympathy. Anyway, our sonar array detected a submarine headed in your direction. From its sonar signature, it's probably Chinese. Their subs aren't as fast as ours, and it's still a long way from you, so we figure it'll take another four days before it gets in your backyard. You should have the rescue done by then, but I you'll have to watch out for that sub during the salvage attempt."

"Just when I thought life was complicated enough. Okay, we're ready for it. We'll keep communications to a minimum and have one of our subs intercept it and warn the Chinese off if it gets too close. It'll be a nuisance, but I doubt the Chinese will interfere & if we can keep them far enough away, they won't get much of an intelligence coup from being here."

Admiral Green let the bridge know the day's mission was scrubbed, then walked back to where Susan Cho was waiting, her goggles on her lap. "We're stalled. Waiting for parts for the SRDRS. Should be arriving later today, and we'll give it a go when they're ready, hopefully tomorrow morning."

"Great. Another beautiful day of rest at sea," she said. "You tell the folks down below yet?"

"Not yet. They're not going to be happy."

"I'm not happy, either. I'm all psyched up for a busy couple of days. We don't have to waste this time, though. We can send the *Hululua* down and check the JPC up close. Make a practice run, so to speak. I'll give you a guided tour. It might be interesting for you. I can even have them hook up the Gertrude cable again, too, so you can talk to the crew. We'll be talking at low volume right next to them, so the sound won't carry more than a thousand feet or so."

"Why not?" he answered. He put the goggles back on and took a seat beside her.

Two hours later, the *Hululua* was on the bottom, exploring the terrain around the JPC.

Susan aimed the cameras at a red glow a hundred feet up-slope from the JPC. "That's red-hot lava being cooled by the ocean. It wasn't there the last time I was here," she said. They watched it, and the area slowly bulged outward. A foot-wide ball broke off, with the lava from where it fractured momentarily glowing yellow until the ocean cooled it down to a dull red again. In the meantime, the ball rolled downhill, eventually striking a pinnacle, where it fragmented into hundreds of smaller fragments. The lights of the *Hululua* then reflected on a shimmering in the water that rose from the area, looking almost like a bubble rising. "Russell Wilkes calls that a lava bomb," Susan said. "I'm told that the energy from the lava is transmitted to the water all at once when it explodes. All the heat goes to the water, and it rises, a bubble of hot water in the midst of cold water. That water might be five hundred or six hundred degrees. We don't want to be above any lava bombs that explode."

They circled the submarine. Green saw a shimmering very near the aft half of the boat. "That shimmering, right near the submarine? Is that hot water rising?" he asked.

"Right. A hot water vent must have opened almost underneath them. That's why they're having so much trouble maintaining temperature."

Green imagined what they must be going through, stuck a half mile below the surface in this hostile, unstable environment. "They must be going through hell in there," he said.

"Want to talk to them with the Gertrude?" Susan asked.

"Sure." She turned it on and gave him thumbs-up to indicate he should start talking. "This is Admiral Green," he said. "Do you copy?"

"We copy. Fine to talk to you, sir," he heard in response. The speech was distorted by the Gertrude, and he couldn't identify the voice.

"Please let me speak to Commander Farriott," Green said.

"Speaking. How's the rescue going, sir? It's obvious it's been delayed, but we haven't heard anything from above."

"Right. The delay's going to be short-term. The rescue vehicle needs a part that's being flown in from Pearl. Rescue won't happen today, but it will happen within the next couple days, hopefully tomorrow morning. I'm talking to you from the *Iwi* through the Gertrude on the *Hululua."*

"My crew's near the breaking point, sir. It's very stressful being down here, and the heat is getting to be a critical problem. We had a ... command situation after the rescue I'd announced didn't happen this morning. One of my crew members went wild and had to be restrained. He'll face time in the brig after we come up."

"Understood. We're doing everything we can to get you out of there ASAP."

"I'll relay the news to my crew. We'll deal with it."

"Good. I'll buy you a beer at the officer's club when we get you back to Pearl."

"I'll take you up on that offer, sir."

"Okay. We're heading up to the surface," Green said. "Reassure your crew. We're here, and it won't be long. Your ordeal is almost over."

"Thanks. Say hi to Ellen for me. Tell her I love her."

"I'll be hanging around here until you're all up safely. Then you can say hi to her yourself."

"Right, sir. Out."

"Heading topside," Susan said. Green just nodded. A half hour later, the *Hululua* was being hoisted onto the *Iwi* and Green took his goggles off. He rubbed his nose while Susan took off her own.

"While we were doing that, I almost forgot I was still on the surface," he said. "When we went up again, I felt guilty for leaving them behind. Then I realized I was still on top. That made it worse." He sighed. "Anyway, thanks for the tour. You can imagine what it's like, but when you see it first-hand.... well, it makes a hell of an impact."

"I wish Russell could have seen this. The topography's changed a lot from a couple days ago."

Admiral Green's face hardened. "I'm afraid we can't risk a leak."

"Too bad. His input could have been very helpful. I see what happens down there, but he sees the implications of it."

6:20 p.m., Foster Village Subdivision, Honolulu

Ellen Farriott prepared dinner in a daze broken finally by conflict in the next room. Steven and Penny were happy kids, and tonight, their happiness grated upon her. Steven, in particular, was behaving like the eleven-year old towhead he was, taking advantage of his natural athletic ability while playing tag with Penny, his eight-year-old, less-endowed sister. Something crashed in the living room, followed by a yell of pain and shouting.

Ellen rushed into the living room. A lamp lay on its side, its bulb shattered. Glass was all over the floor and some shards were lodged in Penny's bare foot. She was howling, bleeding, and holding her foot, while pushing away Steven, who was sheepishly trying to help her. Bloody footprints on the wooden floor made Ellen happy they'd decided against carpeting the floor.

Ellen's first reaction was to yell at them, but she held herself back. It wasn't the right time. These kids might not have a father tomorrow. She forced herself to be calm. "Stevie, get a dustpan and a broom and clean up that mess," she said. "I'll take care of your sister." She picked up Penny and carried her to the bathroom, where she sat her on the toilet seat while she found a washcloth under the sink. She examined the foot, pulled a half-inch glass sliver from Penny's sole, then rinsed her foot and put antibiotic cream and a bandage on it.

"What were you doing?" she asked, now calm again.

"Just playing tag. I was it, and I had Stevie cornered on the couch. He tried to escape by jumping over the lamp, but his foot caught the thingy on the top of it. The bulb busted when it hit the floor, and I stepped on some glass."

Ellen was about to scold her when she remembered the lasagna in the oven. "Oh, damn. The lasagna," she said, and ran out to rescue it. When she got to the kitchen, the timer was dinging, but she didn't know how long it had been signaling. She pulled on her oven gloves, grabbed the lasagna, and set it on the top of the stove, burning her forearm in the process. She ran some cold water over her burned forearm until the pain eased, then checked the lasagna. It was a little overcooked, but not too badly, she thought. They could eat everything except some of the corners that were dried out and black.

She returned to the living room, which looked a lot better. All the large pieces of glass had been picked up and were in the waste basket, and Steven had taken the shade off the lamp. He looked like he was about to try to remove the remainder of the bulb from the socket.

"Steven, unplug that lamp before you try to get the bulb out," she said. "Better yet, leave it to me. I don't want you cutting your fingers. Go get a new bulb from the garage."

She put on a rubber kitchen glove and used that to protect her hand while she unscrewed the broken bulb. By that time, Steven had a new bulb in his hand. She screwed the bulb in, plugged the lamp back in, and was rewarded with a bright glow. "See, honey, you could have electrocuted yourself if you hadn't unplugged it first," she said. "Never work on something electrical while it's still plugged in."

Her thoughts drifted to Daniel, and a sudden dread took her breath away. Now dizzy, she sat down, closed her eyes, and leaned back on the couch. What would she do if he didn't return? Ever. How would she cope with the kids as a single parent? She was already about to blow her mind and he'd only been gone for a little more than a week. She realized how much she missed him, how precious he was both to her and the kids, and how ashamed she was of her own infidelity. Sure, it was hard to have him gone so much, but others had been tested in the same way and had behaved with honor. She had not, and she felt her face redden as she realized how mortified she would be if anyone ever found out.

She only noticed that tears were flowing down her face when she opened her eyes and saw her two children standing in front of her and staring at her. Her vision was blurred by the tears, and she brushed them away with her forearm. She held Steven and Penny to her in a group hug and said, "I love you guys so much. Even though you're a couple of rascals."

"I'm sorry we made you sad, mommy," Penny said, tears rolling down her cheeks in response to her mother's.

"It's not you," Ellen said. "It's just been a hard day for me. I miss your dad, but I'm fine now. Except that I need to get your lasagna served. Can you help me with that?"

Penny nodded.

"Steven, put the shade back on, please. Then come to dinner."

He held the lamp shade in his hand. "It's a little crooked," he said.

"We'll straighten it after dinner. Just put it back on right now. Be careful where you walk, too. I doubt you got all the glass. We'll clean it all over again together after dinner, but right now, let's eat."

That night, she lay alone in her king-size bed and resolved to end her affair with Victor, once and for all. She had sworn to herself to end it several times before, of course, but then she'd been weak and had given way to him. This time, though, it would be different.

She planned the breakup in her mind. She'd go to his apartment and tell him. Flat out, no uncertainty.

Chapter 11

2 February 2020

4:00 a.m., Pacific Ocean, above Loihi Seamount

Susan awoke and dressed, keeping one eye closed and using minimal light to preserve her night vision. She went on deck and enjoyed a spectacular view of the Milky Way. *This is one of the real perks of this job*, she thought. *Not everyone gets to see the stars like this.* She studied the sky until lights began to pop on all over the ship and the Iwi crew began work, preparing the *Hululua o Maui* for launch.

She grabbed a cup of coffee from the galley and walked to the *Hululua.* By the time of launching at five, she was ready to go, sitting in the *Hululua*, earphones on.

To avoid collisions and since she knew the topography, the plan was for the *Hululua* to descend fifteen minutes before the *Groton III* rescue module. The *Groton III* would be remotely operated by tether from the surface, not by Gertrude like the *Hululua* when it was in robotic mode, and would follow her down, tracking her directly to the JPC.

To be sure the *Groton III* operators could see her, she flashed her lights intermittently. Battery power was at a premium, so she minimized the lights until she was at depth, then turned them on to get her orientation. She scanned with the cameras three hundred and sixty degrees before picking up the microphone and saying, "At depth. Proceeding to target. Over."

"Roger. We read you loud and clear. We're ten fathoms above you. Over," the *Groton III* operators replied. Sixty feet.

She used her on-board computer to track to the JPC but had to take many side-steps to avoid steam vents. They were much more prominent than she remembered from her previous visit the day before. Also, when she approached the JPC, she could see a red glow in the water, where sediment reflected the light of molten lava below it. The scenery was surreal, more hostile than before. She took a brief video to show Admiral Green later, then skirted the glowing zone, circling the caldera toward the JPC on its outer edge.

Just before she saw the JPC, she felt the tremors of an earthquake. The *Hululua* pitched like an airplane in turbulence, and she had to fight a change in current to continue on her desired course. The water distortion from the steam vents wavered in the light from the *Hululua* and several coral branches broke off and rolled down the slope into the caldera.

When she saw the JPC, she could tell that it had settled further with the earthquakes. Broken coral branches lay about it, particularly on the uphill side of the outer rim of the caldera. The submarine was at a slightly greater tilt than it had been, and the cables tangling it to the dock waved in a slight current.

"Target sighted," Susan said. "Current appears to be about two knots. It seems to have slid downhill a bit from its prior position but appears intact. Positioning to hold cables out of your way. Will let you know when it's safe to come down. Over."

"Will maintain position until your signal, over."

"Roger. Out."

She maneuvered until she was downstream of the JPC, then proceeded to the starboard cable. She grasped this with the port grasper on her third try, thinking all the time of the toy machines in the arcades, where kids waste money trying to grasp a toy with a mechanical crane.

Holding the cable in her port grasper, she maneuvered to the JPC's port side and grasped the cable there in her starboard grasper. She then reversed and very slowly backed away from the JPC. The port cable broke loose from her grasper when it tightened while the starboard cable was still loose, but she re-grasped it and held it while she pulled it down and away.

"Clear to proceed," she said. "I'm holding debris away from target. Over."

"Roger. Coming down. Over."

She watched as the rescue module slowly descended, then positioned itself directly over the JPC's escape hatch. It slowly lowered itself onto the JPC. She saw a shimmering flow of water downward as the rescue module pumped colder surface water from the space between the module's rescue chamber and the escape hatch. The rescue module settled on the JPC like a mosquito on a forearm, wavering at first and then solidly bonding as a hundred atmospheres of pressure compressed the O-rings between the two vessels.

She hovered and waited, holding the cables away, cognizant of the steam vents close to her and monitoring the water temperature with care. It seemed like a long time, accentuated by several tremors, before she heard anything further from the *Groton III.*

5:10 a.m., *Groton III*, above Loihi Seamount

Two men sat in the *Groton III*'s main chamber and wondered if they would be alive at the end of the day. Their job was simple but dangerous. They were the ones who had to enter the evacuation chamber before the SRDRS was bolted to the submarine. If the chamber leaked because the seal was broken between the Groton and the JPC, say from a strong current or earthquake movement of the submarine, they would be dead in an instant, crushed from the pressure like cockroaches under the heel of a boot.

The senior man was Bartlett "Buck" Gebhart, an E-7 Navy Seal. He'd been part of so many dangerous operations, most of them covert, that this one had appeared to be a walk in the park to him, at least until their final briefing the night before. He hadn't realized that the JPC was sitting on top of a f–ing volcano, that the currents were unpredictable, that earthquakes were a constant threat, and that rescue from that depth had never been successfully accomplished by anyone, though the Soviets were rumored to have made a disastrous attempt at one.

The junior man was Clarence "Cool" Chittenden. A slow-talking southern man, he was as tough as they came. Also a Seal, he was one stripe behind Gebhart, an E-6, with a reputation of being quiet and functional when everyone around him was in full panic. He'd seen a lot of action and wasn't proud of the number of enemy he'd hurt or killed. He prayed before and after every mission and was pleased that, so far at least, God had answered his prayers and blessed his exploits.

They sat on benches in the main chamber, leaning back against the wall, facing each other. They'd practiced enough times that they didn't need to talk about what was coming. If the mission got screwed up, it wouldn't be because they screwed up. It wasn't as if they had control over anything, anyway. Right now, they were basically in an elevator going down. Other people were guiding the *Groton III* from the surface by cable. So, all they had to do was relax.

Cool had his eyes closed and his lips were moving. *Son of a bitch is praying,* Buck thought. *Each to his own.* Buck didn't pray. He just did his job.

The *Groton III* rocked a bit with the current as it descended. Otherwise, it was hard to tell they were even going down. When they heard the motors whirring and they started moving sideways, they'd know they were close to the bottom. There would be some jostling side-to-side and maybe a barely noticeable feeling of descending again. Then a stop and a hiss, followed by a loud whirring of the pumps as water was pumped out of the gap between the submarine and the locking chamber, bringing the pressure within the gap to one atmosphere. With the outside pressure being a hundred atmospheres, that would tentatively lock the JPC to the *Groton III.* Once that was done, they could open their hatch, pump out any remaining water in the gap, and bolt the two vehicles together.

"Nearing the bottom," they heard over the intercom.

Buck stood up, stretched, and said. "Show time, dude. Let's get our tools."

He lifted a power wrench from its hanger on the wall and set it on the floor. It was the same size as a jackhammer and weighed almost fifty pounds. He put three one-inch-wide by six-inch-long bolts, with their associated brackets, in sleeves on his work vest, and slipped on the vest. Cool did the same. They both sat down again, facing each other.

"I hope your ugly mug isn't the last human face I see before I ride with the angels," Cool said.

"Maybe a ride with the fishes, but not with the angels," Buck replied. "You think you'll go to heaven after you're squashed into fish food?"

"Yep. All my sins been forgiven. I just saw to it."

They were jostled sideways as the motors started.

"They're moving us into place," Cool said.

"I do believe you're right," Buck replied. He felt the *Groton III* drop and the two of them swayed a bit from side to side. Then, they felt their descent stop. A moment later, the pumps began their task.

Buck spun the wheel that opened the door between the exchange chamber and the main chamber. He bowed and waved his hand, saying, After you, my friend."

Cool smiled and stepped through and Buck followed and locked the door behind him. "We ain't in danger yet," he said. "Not until we open up that next little door.

Cool noticed the swaying back and forth before Buck did. "What the hell is that?" he asked.

"From what they told us at the briefing, I'd say it's a seaquake," Buck said.

"I'm not opening that door until the shaking stops," Cool said.

"Me neither."

They waited while the pumps whirred. Toward the end of the pumping, the motors labored against the one hundred atmospheres. Finally, the whirring stopped. The shaking stopped shortly afterward. An "All Clear" sign activated from the surface flashed green. Buck listened and, hearing nothing from the pump and no hissing noises that might indicate a leak, opened the outer hatch, his tools ready. Below him, he saw the hull of the JPC, with two inches of residual water. He pushed a button and the residual water was pumped away. The two of them jumped in, grabbed a bolt apiece, and had them in place thirty seconds later. Two more bolts were placed before they felt secure. The last two bolts completed the job.

"One down and we're still alive," Buck said.

"Don't jinx us. We got eleven more chances to kill ourselves today," Cool replied.

They banged on the escape hatch of the JPC, and a moment later, it raised. A pale face popped above. Its expression was not so much a grin as a face of awe. The man raised his right arm. Buck grabbed it. Cool then grabbed his left hand and they hauled him aboard.

"We got an injured man next," the man said. "His arm's burnt. Be careful with him. He can't climb up a ladder, so we'll have to haul him up with a rope. I'm supposed to help you guys with him."

A moment later, a screaming Dennis Lozano lay on the floor of the exchange chamber.

When the exchange chamber was full, they unlocked the door to the main chamber and the first batch of rescued sailors walked through. Lozano was carried, still whimpering, but his screaming had stopped. They locked the door, filled up the exchange chamber with sailors once again, unlocked the main chamber door to allow the second group through and locked the main chamber door once again.

"That's it for this round. Eighteen's our maximum," Buck shouted to the sailors left in the JPC. "Close your hatch and let us know it's secure. Then we'll detach and go up topside."

A banging from below came a minute later.

"Ready to unscrew?" Buck said. Cool nodded. They unscrewed the bolts, throwing each one into the evacuation chamber. Then they climbed out of the gap, slammed their own hatch shut, locked it, and gave each other a high five. They gathered and organized the bolts for the next run before they entered the main chamber, locking the door behind them.

Buck went to the microphone on the wall. "All secure & ready to come up," he said. "You can release us from the JPC."

Soon, a gurgle of water signaled the breaking of the pressure lock, and with a jerk, the *Groton III* began to ascend.

Buck smiled at Cool. "Only got to be in this chamber with the bolts off eight more times," he said. "I figure we only used up two of our nine lives on this one. Still got seven left, and only eight chances to lose them."

Chapter 12

3 February 2020

1:10 p.m., Pacific Ocean, above Loihi Seamount

When Susan entered the *Hululua* for the fifth rescue run, she was exhausted. The three runs the prior day had been taxing but successful, and the first run this morning had been no different, though the JPC had shifted its position a bit overnight. Each time she dived, however, she became a little more concerned. What she was doing was dangerous and required her full attention. Providing that attention for hours on end was tiring. She was glad this was the last run. It wasn't exciting anymore. It was just dangerous.

She knew halfway down that something had changed. Suddenly, she felt the *Hululua* quiver and her instruments wavered, showing some instability in the *Hululua*'s position. It wasn't a big change, just a foot or two, but it was unusual. She wondered whether she'd encountered a rip current, something akin to a jet stream, but in water. Then, a transmission from the JPC told her what it really was. "There's been a tremor. Bigger than usual. We've settled with another three degrees of roll to starboard. We've detected an increase in current as well."

Neither change was welcome. The roll to starboard might make it hard for the *Groton III* to attach to the JPC's escape hatch, and maneuvering was always more difficult with a current running.

She responded by dropping the nose of the *Hululua.* The faster she got down there, the better. She'd need as much bottom time as she could get.

When she reached her depth and turned on her lights a moment later, she was struck by how different the bottom looked. Some of the tube worms were upset, lying on their sides. A shimmering fountain of hot water squirted from a large vent that had opened since she'd last been there. When she saw the JPC, she could immediately tell the difference. It had slid another ten feet downhill and was lying at more of a tilt. To the port side of its midpoint, shimmering in the water indicated another vent, not more than thirty feet away from the JPC's escape hatch.

"*Groton III,* this is *Hululua,*" she broadcast on the Gertrude. "You have a thermal vent off the port side. You'll have to approach from starboard this time. You don't want to go over that vent. Over."

"Roger. It'll be tricky. We have a little current running. Over."

"I'll tell you how to avoid the vent when you come into view. I'm going to grab the cables now. Please stay off until I have them secured. Over."

If they're coming from starboard and I want to stay out of the way, I'll have to park on the port side, she thought. That would put her on the side of the vent. Not where she wanted to be, but that's what she'd try to do. She circled around and slowly approached the JPC from the port stern side, angling toward it, running very slowly and monitoring the temperature gauges the whole time.

The cables in front of her were undulating in the current, looking like black encrusted sea serpents. She waited for one to wave in her direction. She tried to grab it but barely missed as it waved back. A moment later, it swung back toward her, and this time, she was able to grab it.

She reversed her screws, easing slowly backward, until the cable was nearly taut, then angled across the JPC's bow to where the starboard cable was. She grasped this cable on the first try, then reversed, keeping as close as she could toward the JPC's stern, but away from the steam vent. She tried to park on the JPC's port side, but the temperature was too high there. She settled down on the starboard side, letting the cables slide through her claws, so that she was as far away from the JPC as possible.

The *Groton III*, she knew, had to settle on the JPC's escape hatch at almost a right angle. Otherwise, it would impact on the submarine's sail. When it did that, it would be almost on top of the *Hululua.* Tough, she thought. Not a damn thing she could do about it except try to keep as much out of the way as possible.

"Cables secure," she broadcast. "Watch for me. I'm very close to you. Over."

"We're settling down. Temperature rising. We out of that vent? Over."

"You need to reverse about fifteen feet. Then, angle downward a bit. Your stern is very close to a tubeworm colony. Over."

"We have direct vision of the escape hatch. Settling down on it now."

She watched as the *Groton III* descended, barely moving. The bow of the *Groton III* was only a few feet from the vent, and its stern was threatening the tubeworm colony. It's port side was not more than two feet from the *Hululua*, completely blocking her view.

"You're about two feet away from me, right in front of my cameras. Can't see a thing. Over."

"Trying to latch on but we're not getting a good seal. We'll have to maneuver a bit. Sorry if we jostle you. Over."

Great, she thought. If she moved backward, though, she'd pull the cable from the grasper. She settled the *Hululua* on the bottom. Sediment flew up, blocking any view she still had. She felt like she'd just flown into a cloud.

"Trying again. We seem to be getting a good seal this time. You okay? Over."

"Blind but otherwise fine. You just grazed me. A little too cozy. Over," she replied.

"Just snuggling up. Enjoy! The Navy does it deeper. Over."

"Your weight's pushing me into the muck. Not my idea of a good time. Over," Susan said, hearing the concern in her own voice.

"We're latched on now. Going to put a few bolts in, then open the can. Be patient. Over."

"Roger. Over." She waited while the *Groton III* scraped against her hull, making a sound that caused a shiver down her spine, like a chalk on a blackboard. She waited, her heart pounding with each scrape against her hull, for what seemed an hour before she heard their next transmission.

"All loaded. Latch secured. Removing bolts. Over."

"Roger. Let me know when you disengage. Over," Susan said.

"Disengage in five, four, three, two, one. Over."

The *Hululua* lurched as the Groton popped loose and drifted toward it, pushing the *Hululua* further into the mud. One cable came loose from her grasper.

"Loose cable," she said. "Ascend slowly. I'll try to keep it out of your way. Over."

She maneuvered forward but heard a chattering sound as she did so. She knew the sound–a bent propeller. That was going to slow her down. As she watched the *Groton III* ascend, she saw the loose cable tighten and the Groton's ascent stopped. *Damn*, she thought. The cable was caught on the *Groton III.*

"The loose cable is caught on something. Stop ascending, and I'll try to get you untethered. Over."

She ascended slowly, the *Hululua* vibrating fiercely because of the bent propeller. She followed the cable. It was hung up on a cleat on the Groton's hull. "You're going to have to descend a foot or two for me to get you unhooked," she said. "It's hung up on a cleat. At least your drive train is free for now. But descend very slowly. I'm right below you. Over."

"Roger. Will do. Dumping buoyancy now. Over."

She saw bubbles rising from the Groton's venting tube. When the cable became slack, she grabbed it with her port grasper and reversed her engines. As she backed away, the cable came loose. "Okay to ascend now. You're clear. Over."

"Roger. Ascending."

She waited until the *Groton III* was a hundred feet above her, then dropped both cables and headed upward herself. She checked her batteries and was dismayed when she saw how little charge remained. The

Hululua wasn't going to make it to the surface. Not with a bent propeller.

"Guys, I'm going to need some help getting to the surface. I have a bent propeller and too little battery charge remaining. Can I hitch a ride with you? Over."

"Happy to help if we can. What do you want us to do? Over."

"If you can hang where you are for a minute, I can come from below and grab you with my graspers. If you can lift me up to within a couple hundred feet of the surface, I think I can make it from there on my own. Over," Susan said.

"Come on up. We'll wait for you. Over."

She circled as she ascended. When she got to the level of the *Groton III,* she saw a guard rail on its upper deck. She eased forward, grasped it with her starboard grasper and turned off her engine.

"I'm hooked onto your deck rail. Okay to proceed with ascent. Take it slow. No jerking around. Over," she said.

"Going up. Let us know if you have any problems. Over."

"Thanks. No problems now. Over."

The *Groton III* rose slowly out of the black zone with the *Hululua* attached. To be safe, she held on until her depth gauge showed two hundred feet. She opened the grasper, waited until the *Groton III* was well above her, then started her own engines and made her way to the *Iwi.*

When they pulled the *Hululua* on the deck for inspection, she saw not just a bent propeller but a bent driveshaft. "We can't repair this here," the mechanic said. "She's got to go back to Honolulu. We'll need to order a new drive shaft. This baby's out of commission for six weeks, at least.'

Susan was okay with that. She'd faced more danger and excitement than she'd bargained for, and was exhausted, ready for a break. She hit her bunk on the *Iwi* and fell into a deep sleep.

5:20 p.m., *Groton III*, above Loihi Seamount

Buck Gebhart and Cool Chittenden watched the last crew members disembark. Chittenden turned to Buck and said, "I think we used up ten of our nine lives on that one. Got minus one left."

"You must be dead then, right?"

"I think I could be rejuvenated with a couple cold ones. Think we can talk 'em into flying us back to Pearl for a little R & R?"

"Dude, I think they've got other plans for us. They're talking about a salvage now. Still some crew on that sub, too. I think we're stuck here till it's all done.

"Damn."

5:40 p.m., COMSUBPAC, Bldg. 619, Pearl Harbor

Admiral Green pored over the photographs and videos Susan had brought back from her exploratory descent with Russell Wilkes, recordings from the tour she had given him two days before, and the brief films she'd taken during the rescue dives. What he saw didn't make him happy. "Do you think we can do it?" he asked Jerry Wentzel.

"Not with just the *Groton III*," Wentzel replied. "The *Hululua*'s out of commission, and her sister ship back on Oahu is too small to do the job. You'll need to send for help."

Green stared at him, trying to assess how sure Wentzel was. Wentzel stared right back at him, never blinking. Green broke his gaze first. He knew Wentzel was right. Jerry Wentzel was the top submarine engineer for the Navy. Green had only met him the day before, but Wentzel's sterling reputation preceded him. He was a legend in the submarine service, the man everyone went to when they had a problem of enormous complexity. If he said the *Hululua* couldn't push a cable under the JPC, that's just the way it was. They'd have to find another way.

"The stern cable's no problem," Wentzel continued. "According to the most recent photos, you've got a couple feet of leeway under the hull there. Should be easy to push a cable under it. But you need a cable under the front, too. The only way you're going to be able to do it is to ram a cable driver under the sub, right through the rock or coral or whatever's in the way. To do that, you'll need a bigger submersible, one with more powerful graspers and more maneuverability than the one you have."

"You have any ideas?"

"I do. We've been working on a bigger, better submersible. CINCPAC's already put it on alert, in fact. I can't tell you anything more about it without getting clearance, but if you'll put me on a secure line, I'll make sure you get it ASAP."

"This thing is so classified that you can't tell a Rear Admiral about it without getting permission?"

Wentzel smiled. "Need to know," he said.

Green frowned. "All right," he said. "We'll get you a secure line. Where to?"

"Pentagon. I have the number."

Green got up, walked out, and came back a moment later. He walked Wentzel across the office to a sound-proofed room. "It's in there." He handed him a sheet of paper with a number written on it. "Dial this access code first, then the number you're calling. I'll leave you alone. Come back when you're ready."

He walked back to his office, frustrated. Sometimes the Navy just made things too damn complicated. It didn't have to be this difficult.

It was a full half-hour before Wentzel returned. He locked the door after him, then said, "It's all set up. They'll put the thing on a C-4M. We should have it here in forty-eight hours."

"Did you get clearance to tell me about it?"

Wentzel nodded. "It's an experimental manned submersible. It can go to six thousand feet without problems, probably to eight thousand actually, but it's not cleared for that yet. It can take a four-man crew but can be run with only two. It's four times the weight of the *Hululua* and its graspers are much more powerful. Its engines are far more powerful, too. Amazing, actually."

"What's it supposed to be good for?"

"Espionage. Tapping undersea cables. Stuff like that. Plus some other activities you don't want to know about."

"Are they sending a crew with it?"

"Two guys. They've been test-piloting it and know it well. I talked them into giving the other two seats to your *Hululua* driver and that British volcano expert. We need him to tell us about the rock we'll have to ram through."

"Good. Those two are familiar with the bottom there. It's kind of a weird environment." He took a deep breath. "They're civilians, you know. I can't make them go down there. Could be dangerous. They'll need clearance, too. Particularly the Brit. I've barred him from any further information, since he was responsible for the leak to the press.

"I'm sure you'll find a way to persuade them. And the Pentagon has already cleared them both. The leak was a big-time mistake, but we expect he's learned from it."

"Can we get the submersible on site in four or five days then?"

"If things go well. You can attempt the salvage the next day, so figure six days total. Will you have surface ships ready?

"Should be on site late tomorrow. It'll take another day before they're configured properly. That gives us a day or two's leeway before your submersible arrives.

"Should be interesting." Wentzel paused and shrugged. "It should work. Of course, we've never done it before. Not at that depth, anyway. It's all theoretical at this point."

"It's not just salvaging the JPC," Green said. "It's removing a danger to Honolulu, too."

"Not my field. Sounds far-fetched to me, but your volcano guy's the expert. I'd have to defer to his judgment."

"I believe him," Green said. "None of us can tell how big the danger is, but there's a lot of fire-power aboard the JPC. If it all went... Well, let's just say we don't want to take the chance."

"Let's go over the plan again," Wentzel said. "You've got two ships above, and they're hooked together with steel I-beams, leaving a seventy-foot gap between them. Right?"

"Right," Green confirmed.

"Each ship has four heavy-duty winches on them, and they have four eight-thousand-foot cables, two on ship A and two on ship B. One cable goes under the stern of the JPC from Ship A and is run back up to the surface to ship B. Once we get a cable under the bow, we run that one from Ship B to ship A. Am I on track so far?"

"Right on."

"Then we run the bow and stern winches on both ships to lift the JPC off the bottom. We lift it up maybe fifty feet and then run two more cables, one just ahead of the sail, and the other just behind the sail. We need to do that before we start lifting that floating dock off the bottom, because our cables will break if we don't. To me, the JPC is at maximum danger point when it's suspended by only two cables, so we want to place those additional cables as quickly as possible."

"Yes," Green said. "Particularly the cable before the mast. Once that one's taut, the dock weight isn't so important anymore, because the tether is to the bow intake ports, and we'll have one cable on either side of those."

"Okay. Then, we run all the winches at the same rate so that they're all taking in the same length of line and the cables aren't dragging against the side of the JPC any more than necessary. We lift the JPC to two hundred feet depth, the maximum depth where we can safely send divers down to cut the JPC loose from the dock cables. That's another danger point, because when those cables pop loose, there'll be a sudden shift of weight, and the JPC will bounce around on its supports. Your crew will need to be ready to abandon ship, just as a precaution."

"I agree," said Green.

"Then we bring the divers who cut the dock loose back into the *Groton III* and decompress them there while we bring the JPC to the surface and inflate its ballast tanks with air, making it buoyant. The danger's over as soon as that's done. We can tow it home to the shipyard and have it ready for action within a couple of months. And everybody's happy, right?"

"Yes. Very happy," said Green, smiling.

"Okay. But when you're doing something this complex, you know damn well it won't go the way you planned it. So, let's spend the next hour listing all the things that could possibly go wrong.

"It might take a lot longer than an hour," Green said. "It'll be a long list."

Chapter 13
4 February 2020

12:55 p.m., Pacific Submarine Base, Pearl Harbor

A yeoman sat outside the submarine base amphitheater and checked the ID's of each spouse before the person was admitted to the briefing. Ellen and Marisa were in the middle of the pack, and by the time they entered, the auditorium already had about sixty women and a few men seated within it.

They waited for another thirty minutes before Lieutenant Moran arrived and asked them to stand for Admiral Green's entrance. Both Ellen and Marisa had brought books to read–they knew how the Navy worked.

"Please sit down," Admiral Green said, and he paused while they all did this.

"If you watch the news, you've heard that an American submarine had a mishap a few days ago resulting in its sinking off the coast of the Big Island," he began. We are going to brief you on events regarding that, but we must warn you that any information you hear is classified. We will ask you to sign a form indicating that nothing you hear at this briefing will be disclosed to anyone. Not the news media, not your kids. Not your parents or friends. No one. You may only speak of this to your spouses, when you see them again.

"Lieutenant Moran, would you please distribute the forms," he continued. "Please read them, then sign them at the X. We will pick them up in fifteen minutes. If you have any questions regarding the forms, Lieutenant Moran will be happy to answer them. If you don't wish to sign, you may leave now."

When Lieutenant Moran had all the signed forms in his hands again, Admiral Green began the actual briefing.

"Most of you have already seen news media accounts of a submarine that has sunk and is lying on the bottom off the Big Island. I can confirm that the submarine they are referring to is the JPC.

"During a routine exercise, the JPC encountered debris, probably from the Japanese tsunami. This debris fouled the JPC's propulsion system and resulting in its settling to the bottom.

"We have been in contact with the officers and crew of the JPC from day one and can assure you that your loved ones are doing well. A rescue mission was undertaken a couple days ago. Most of the officers and men serving on the JPC have been rescued and brought here to Pearl Harbor for debriefing. One man sustained burns and is being treated for that at Tripler Hospital. He is expected to recover. A few other individuals have minor injuries, not requiring hospitalization. Most, however, are completely healthy and anxious to see you.

"We are keeping them isolated from the press until they can be fully debriefed and until the submarine itself can be brought up from the depths. We hope that will be done within the next few days. Until then, we do want to keep the specifics of the mishap to ourselves. Other countries might derive a major intelligence coup by access to classified information about the capabilities of our submarine fleet. We have ordered the crew not to answer questions regarding the mishap, including the depth or location of the submarine, its operational mission, the systems used to rescue its personnel, or any difficulties that arose during this ordeal. Please do not ask them such questions and do not expect them to answer if you do. I must warn you that disclosing classified material is a felony, and any leaking of information will be tracked to its source and perpetrators will be prosecuted.

"Busses are waiting to transport you to your loved ones. You will have two hours to converse with them. Lieutenant Moran will call your names. When you hear your name, please line up behind the driver, who will escort you to his or her bus, and from there to the debriefing center." He closed his briefing folder. "Thank you for your attention and for your service to your country."

Lieutenant Moran began to call out names. After each group of twenty or so was gathered, the bus driver would leave with the spouses or significant others. After three buses had left, only eight spouses were left in the hall.

Admiral Green returned to the lectern.

"Those of you who are still remaining will have to wait a bit longer. Your loved ones have volunteered to assist in the process of salvaging the JPC. Unfortunately, to do this properly, we need to have a skeleton crew aboard the JPC. This salvage will take a few more days to accomplish.

"I'm sorry to disappoint you, but I felt you deserved a personal explanation for why your loved ones aren't on base with the rest of the crew. Please bear with us. We plan to bring all them back to you as soon as possible. They are all in good condition, but they have one more task to do before they can return to you. They are the best of the best, and I salute them, and you should also.

"So, I would ask that you return now to your own vehicles and go home. You may tell your children their parent is fine, but please don't tell them anything more. I can't stress the importance of this enough. We don't want any foreign powers interfering with the salvage we plan. The welfare of your loved ones depends upon your keeping this secret."

He looked around the room and asked, "Are there any questions? If not, you are free to go."

One by one, the spouses left the room in silence. A few glared at Admiral Green before they left, but no one asked any questions. Finally, Ellen and Marisa were the only two left in the room with him. Ellen shook his hand and thanked him for the briefing. Then she said, "I only have one question. The salvage, how dangerous is it?"

Admiral Green's hesitation gave her the answer she anticipated–and dreaded–before he told her, "It should go off without a hitch."

Marisa and Ellen walked toward Ellen's car. Ellen wavered and stopped halfway to the car, tears running down her cheeks. Her head spun in a hateful whirlwind of guilt. She could not think, could not assess, could not walk, could not talk. Through the fog and storm in her head, she barely heard Marisa's voice talking to her, nor hugging her, then speaking to her with words that initially made no sense. Finally, she came to her senses enough that she understood.

"I'm driving. You're in no shape to do it," Marisa said. "Give me the keys." Ellen reached in her purse, found the keys to her car, and give them to Marisa. Marisa held her around the waist, leading her. When they neared the car, Ellen headed toward the driver's seat, but Marisa steered her to the passenger seat. She helped Ellen fasten her seat belt, then went to the driver's seat.

"We're going to your house, where we're both going to have a shot of Uncle Jack, if you have some." She put the car into gear and drove to Ellen's home, leaving the car in the driveway. Ellen sat there like a zombie until Marisa guided her out, helped her unlock the front door, and sat her down on the living room couch.

"Where's the booze?" she asked.

"Cabinet. Under the stove."

Marisa found a bottle and two glasses, put two ice cubes in each glass, and poured generous shots in both glasses. She brought one back for Ellen and kept the other for herself. She sat down opposite Ellen and sipped a small amount from her glass. "My man's too tough to die," she said. "And your man's too smart. They're going to be just fine. Let's drink to that." She made eye contact with Ellen while she downed the shot.

Ellen stared back at her, then set the glass down on the coffee table before her. "I'm not fit to make that toast," she said. "I let him down, and I don't know if he's going to live long enough for me to make it up to him."

"You're a Navy wife, not a fucking goddess," Marisa said. "It's tough. We all screw up. But there are times when we have to just be there for our guys. Times like this. So, get it together. You've got to. Just like I've got to. Make the damn toast, drink it up, and carry on."

Ellen made the toast, but she couldn't shake the thought that her life and the lives of her kids and husband were going to change, and it wasn't going to be a change for the better. And it was all her fault.

Marisa waited while Ellen sipped her drink. Then she rose. "I've got to pick up my kids," she said. "Can you drive me home now?" She handed the keys back to Ellen. At the door, she turned and said, "I don't want to know what your problem is, but my guess is it's not unique. We all live a hard life. I think you're a good person. Otherwise, I wouldn't be here. You need help, you call on me. I don't give a damn if you're an officer's wife. We hang together. You remember that."

After she dropped Marisa off and returned home, Ellen made some coffee and sipped it, deep in thought. Then she headed to the school and picked up Penny and Steven. By that time, she was under control, and she also knew that she now had something critical for her, something she hadn't had since childhood. Ellen had a female friend she completely trusted.

Chapter 14

7 February 2020

7:15 p.m., Hilo, Island of Hawaii

"This really isn't a safe place for us," Russell said, smiling.

"And why not? It's lovely," Susan asked. The restaurant overlooked an estuary on the Big Island. Their table was set on a platform that extended over the water. Underwater lights illuminated an abundance of fish feeding below them. The dim light, candles, and palm trees completed the picture. They were enjoying a wonderful meal in a beautiful, romantic tropical paradise. She didn't know how it could get better than this. Except, of course, for the daunting fact that this evening might be the very last either one of them experienced. Talk about an elephant in the room! This one was a mammoth.

"We're in a tsunami zone," Russell answered. "If Loihi blows while we're here, we could be underwater in minutes."

"Good gracious, Russell," she said. "What a thing to say. You just ruined a very romantic mood. I hope you're proud of yourself."

"Sorry. It's the real world I must live in. But it was a bad joke, I guess. I don't think it's going to happen now. Not really. Of course, tomorrow might be a different story. That will be an adventure, indeed."

"We're going to get through it, right?" she said, smiling. "We'll make all the right decisions and save the world, and then we'll bask in our glory and live happily ever after."

He lifted his wine glass. "I'll propose a toast to that. May our team win. Damn the volcano," he said.

"We shouldn't take the chance of offending the volcano goddess, Madame Pele. I'd propose an alteration to the toast. Bless the volcano, but keep us safe from it."

"Agreed. Madame Pele, if you heard, please pardon my poor phrasing." They clicked their glasses together and laughed.

After dinner, they drove to his small bungalow in Mountain View. It wasn't the first time she had been to his pad. Later, as she lay in bed after making love, she wondered if it was the last time she would ever be in his bed or anyone else's. *So be it,* she thought. *Whatever will be will be.* She slept beside him, happy in this moment and not letting the worries of tomorrow disrupt the pleasures of love today.

The next morning, it was all business. They got up before dawn, packed his car with equipment, and drove to Hilo harbor where they loaded everything onto the *Iwi.* By dawn, they were out of the harbor and headed toward Loihi.

Three hours later, they joined a flotilla of ships parked over Loihi. The *Groton III* was there, along with its support ship. Two other winch ships were coupled together like the twin hulls of a catamaran, except that the struts joining them were a hundred feet long. A destroyer circled the perimeter. Susan had no doubt that at least one submarine circled below, providing security from unwelcome undersea vessels.

The vessel that caught her attention immediately, though, was a mini-submarine tethered to the *Groton III*'s support ship. It seemed larger than the *Hulului*, probably twice as long, but most of it was underwater, so she could only see the twenty percent of the hull that protruded above the surface. She couldn't see its lighting configuration or its graspers or its drive train, and she had no idea what its communications capabilities were. No matter. It was this boat and its crew that Russell and she would bet their lives on. As a scientist, she seldom took chances based upon faith alone. This was an exception, and it made her uncomfortable.

She turned to Russell. "I need data," she said. "Let's get the dinghy to take us over there and see if that boat and its crew are any good."

"Righto," he answered.

Chapter 15

8 February 2020

11:17 a.m., Pacific Ocean, above Loihi Seamount

Susan and Russell sat in a briefing room with the two pilots of the submersible they would take below, Lieutenant Commander Herb Chaplin and Lieutenant Dick Tanner. Chaplin did most of the talking and was clearly in charge. He'd already given them a tour of the submersible and a safety briefing.

"We just call it the *XMS*," Lieutenant Commander Chaplin said. "It stands for X-mini-submarine. Someday we'll give it a real name, but this one's still a prototype."

"What can it do?" Susan asked.

"Most of it's classified, but it can go as deep as we need and we can stay down for at least twenty-four hours.

It has two sets of graspers, fore and aft, and they're powerful buggers.

"Dick and I've been putting it through its paces for about four months now. We've had to make some modifications as a result–we find glitches and then fix them–but overall, it's a great boat. Really maneuverable. Good video inside. Comfortable seating. Tremendous capabilities."

"Have you taken four people down in it yet?" Susan asked.

"Can't say as we have. Nah. It's been Dick–Lieutenant Tanner–and I most of the time. Sometimes, we take a suit down, somebody from the company that built the thing, or sometimes one of the Navy officers who oversee the project. This will be the first time we have both passenger seats filled."

"How do we see what's going on outside?"

"Virtual reality goggles, same as you have on the *Hululua*, except better. They're state of the art. You'll be able to see everything I see, hear everything I hear. All in beautiful 3-D and stereo."

"So, what's the plan?" Susan asked.

"We'll go down ahead of the first cable, pick it up when it dangles in front of us, noose that around the stern and bring it back up to the surface. Cable 2 will be trickier, I'm told. That one needs to go in front of the sail. Trouble is, that part of the JPC's lying on the bottom right now. So, the winches on the support ships above will have to lift the stern with the number 1 cable just a foot or two and we'll drive a threader under the bow, sliding it between the bow and the bottom. If coral or rocks are in the way, we'll hammer right through them. The threader will be hooked to the number 2 cable, so we'll pull that cable through and bring it to the surface. The winches on both cables will then lift the JPC off the bottom.

" With those two cables holding the boat up, it should be easy to place two more cables, one at the bow, and the other behind the sail. Once those are in place, we lift the JPC up. No sweat."

"The last time we went down, the JPC had moved," Susan said. "It slipped downhill about ten feet. I think the stern's still off the bottom, but you might have even more problems with the second cable,"

Chaplin frowned. "Okay. We'll have to deal with that. We'll see what needs to be done and do it."

"How about the dock that's stuck to it?" Russell asked.

"We lift that up, too. Once we get her to the depth where divers can work, they cut the attachments to the JPC, and the junk falls to the bottom again. Good riddance."

"What do you want us to do?" Susan asked.

"Sit back and relax until we get near the bottom. I already showed you the alternate camera. You can control that. Floodlights, too. Once we get down, we'll be focused on setting the cables. We'd like you two to check out what's going on around us, keep us advised of any problems you see. We'll be looking forward. We need you guys to cover our back and sides."

"How about communications? Can we talk to the JPC?"

"We'll have to. They'll have to help while we're coming up. The dock will make the bow heavier than the stern, for example. They can help us level out the weight by blowing whatever ballast air they have into their forward tanks. Then, they even it out again after the dock's cut loose. There are a lot of little details that need to be worked out on the spot. That's why there's still crew aboard."

"I have no seismograph here, and I'm feeling a bit out of touch. Any word on what Loihi's doing?" Russell asked.

"I spoke to the JPC's commander earlier today by Gertrude," Chaplin said. "Lot of shaking going on down there, I'm told, and it's getting hot. They're going to be glad to get out of there. If you want more info, you'll probably have to call the Volcano Observatory. They can set up a line from the *Iwi*, I suspect. Be careful what you say, though. It won't be a secure line."

"No, it won't, and I certainly understand the problems with leaks," Russell said, glancing at Susan. "I expect I'll just have to remain ignorant. Of course, I'll see exactly what's going on tomorrow, won't I?"

"Yup. You will. We all will." Chaplin paused. "I guess we're done here, then. Any more questions?"

Susan stood. "I'm satisfied. See you in the morning."

"We'll send a dinghy for you at 0400. Eat a good breakfast before then. We won't be back to the surface until after noon, I expect," Chaplin said.

Susan nodded. It'll be a long day, she thought.

As they were walking back to the dinghy, Russell said, "Good plan. Sounds like a piece of cake."

"Let's hope it's not devil's food," Susan said. She knew it wasn't going to be that simple.

4:20 a.m., Loihi Seamount

Daniel lay on his bunk in his skivvies and stared at the ceiling. He was sweating profusely despite being almost naked. Only emergency lights were shining, as they'd nearly shut down the reactor to decrease heat production, so the ceiling was lit only by a dull glow from the hallway outside his quarters. The door was open for ventilation. There was little need for privacy anymore, with only twelve crew and officers remaining on board.

Thank God, the rest of the crew were gone. He envied the ones who had left and were probably either at home or sitting in an air-conditioned debriefing center at Pearl Harbor by now. With them gone, though, the remaining crew had been busy. He'd personally had only an hour or two of fitful sleep in the last two days.

It was too hot to get a sound sleep. They'd done everything they could to control the heat, and it wasn't enough. With another hundred crew on board, they would have been roasting. As it was, no one was wearing shirts anymore. Most of the crew were down to skivvies. Wendy Peyton and Celia Hutchinson wore sports bras and exercise shorts.

He checked his watch. 0423. Time to get up and get to work. He slipped on shorts, walked to the mess hall and poured himself a cup of cold coffee. He put an ice cube in it from the dispenser, swirled it around, and drank it down in one gulp, ice and all. Then he refilled the cup and repeated the process.

They'd stopped eating heated food or drinking heated beverages a couple days before. Cold cereal was now the favorite breakfast, and he ate it with some chilled canned milk. It tasted heavenly. So did cold coffee.

Wendy Peyton joined him, putting a bit of canned milk in her own cold coffee. "One more day," she said. "Then we're out of here."

"Hope so. I've had enough of this tour."

A tremor shook them, spilling Wendy's coffee. She scowled as she went to get a napkin. She returned just before the spilled coffee got to the edge of the table and wiped it up before it could hit the floor. "I like dancing, but I'm tired as hell of being 'all shook up,' " she said.

Scotty McLean, their Weapons Officer, and Tim Patrick, their Engineer, came in and sat at the next table. Both chugged glasses of cold, freshly-desalinated water before attacking their cheerios.

Patrick leaned over and said, "I got a patch on that latest steam leak. We should be okay unless the fitting gets shaken loose again."

"Good. Let's hope it stays this time," Daniel said.

"Should. We used a lot of duct tape on it. McGyver would approve."

Buzz Henderson, Nuclear Assistant Officer, came in next. He was the antithesis of anyone's image of a nuclear engineer, with an irreverent sense of humor, an athletic grace, and a constant smile on his face, even in the worst circumstances.

He sauntered over and sat next to Patrick. "I love eatin' in the dark," he said, glancing at the emergency light above. "Romantic, I guess, as long as you don't mind that everybody around you smells like stale sweat, the food is cold and tasteless, and there ain't no booze or wine. 'Course it makes it lots easier for my boys, too, 'cause the reactor's a lot safer with all them control rods stuffed in. Keep it up and we'll all stop glowin' in the dark pretty soon."

"Don't get too used to the leisure life," Daniel said. "Soon as we get off this volcano, it's going to get cold. About twelve hours from now, we're all going to be back in uniform and the reactor's going to be running full blast."

"Won't that be a kick?" Scotty McLean said. "You think it'll ever really happen?"

"We should be hearing something more about an hour from now," Daniel said.

"I'm going to be monitoring the sonar pretty carefully," Wendy said. "Chances are we'll hear them working at it a long time before they get out the Gertrude. When Celia hears the screws of a mini-sub, it'll be a really good sign."

Daniel was about to answer when a nasty shock hit them. Their communications officer, who was just coming in, fell to the floor, and his coffee cup flew across the hall and smashed on the bulkhead. They held onto the tables, unsteady for what seemed to be a full minute before the shaking stopped.

"What the hell was that?" Buzz asked. "Somebody dropping depth charges on us?"

"Don't know, but it seemed like more than just an earthquake," Farriott answered. " We need to assess for damages. Everybody check your own sections. Let me know what you find." He turned to Wendy Peyton. "XO, see if sonar heard anything unusual. Then report back to me. I'll be in the command center. If anybody sees our COB, send him in my direction."

He chugged the rest of his cereal and helped the communications officer to his feet. "You okay?" he asked.

"I guess. My wrist hurts. May have busted it."

"If so, we'll have you seen at Tripler pretty soon. See Doc and ask him if he thinks you need a splint."

"Aye, sir."

Daniel headed toward the sail and command center. When he got there, he checked all the gauges. A few red lights were blinking, and he sent crewmen or officers to investigate, whoever was knowledgeable and available. Rank didn't mean much on a submarine with only twelve crew. Everybody had to pitch in and do manual labor, stuck as they were in a hell-hole on the bottom of the ocean.

He was sure this tremor wasn't just a bigger version of what had been going on for days. Something new was happening, and he suspected it wasn't good news. A half hour later, he had confirmation.

Wendy Peyton called from sonar. "Sonar is tracking something moving above us on the mountain. There's a lot of noise, a rushing sort of sound, and active sonar shows changes in the landscape. Bottom line is we've got an eruption going on. There's lava flowing above us."

"Is it coming in our direction?" Daniel asked.

"Can't tell. It's moving too slowly for us to get a fix on where it's going. But it's uphill of us. Seems to me that sooner or later, it's going to close in on us."

Chapter 16

9 February 2020

5:00 a.m., XMS submersible, above Loihi Seamount

The XMS began its descent. It had four seats, two in front and two behind. Susan and Russell sat in the back seats, and Chaplin and Tanner took the pilot seats.

As soon as they sat down, Chaplin began a second safety briefing, outlining escape procedures and emergency equipment. "Of course, if we get in trouble at that depth, we're dead meat, so most of this is irrelevant," he said. "What we should be talking about is how to stay out of trouble.

"The first thing to know is that we go up and down steep. Fasten your seat belts and get ready for a wild ride. The second thing you need to know is how to work the cameras. If you're blind and deaf, you're worthless.

"Dr. Cho, you've got two toggle switches and a video-game-like controller in front of you," said Chaplin. "That runs the alternate camera. It's self-explanatory. Play with it and you'll figure it out. Flip the right toggle away from you and the alternate camera turns on. If you flip it toward you, you're looking at the camera I'm controlling. You control the other one. The control stick points both the lights and the camera. Focus it by turning it clockwise or counterclockwise. The zoom is a little dial on top of the stick. The dial below it controls the sound volume. Any questions?"

"Got it," said Susan.

Russell fitted the Virtual Reality goggles over his glasses and said, "I'm ready."

"Hang onto your seats," Chaplin said. He switched on the power and the XMS shot forward and began spiraling downward.

Susan was amazed. She guessed they were descending at a sixty-degree angle. It was like descending on a roller-coaster. She hung from her shoulder straps and watched the depth indicator in the periphery of her goggles. It seemed like no time before they were at a thousand feet, then two thousand, and finally they were leveling off at three thousand feet.

At that point, she turned on the lights and did a visual sweep of the terrain with her alternate camera.

After a moment, Russell grabbed her arm. "Go back to the right again," he said.

She complied, slowly retracing what the camera had already shown her.

"Stop there," he said. "Do you see it? That red glow there? It's a rift eruption. That's lava flowing downhill. It's not the same as above water. It's slower, because the water cools it, and it flickers from red to black for the same reason. But it's definitely a lava flow.

"I see it," she said. She spoke to Chaplin. "We've got lava flowing below us. Don't go directly above it or we'll get cooked, but come at it from the side. We need to look at it more closely."

"Right. I see it," Chaplin said. I'll go down to that level and come at it from the side, like you say. How close can we get to it?"

"Stay ten meters away and monitor our temperature. Watch out for areas where the water shimmers. That water can get to be six hundred degrees. Maybe higher. You don't want to pass through those areas."

"Roger. Thanks for the tip. Our temperature gauges max out at 250 degrees Fahrenheit, by the way. Guess nobody figured we'd have to worry about water hotter than boiling temperature."

"Then you'll have to be doubly cautious about approaching water that appears to glimmer," Russell said. You can't see it without light, of course, and the only light down here comes from molten lava, phosphorescent creatures, and our own lights. So, you have to have your lights facing straight forward."

They descended another hundred feet and circled slowly until they were facing directly at the red glow from about a hundred feet away. Chaplin eased the submersible closer to the glow, stopping about twenty feet away. From there, hovering, they could see lava billowing out over a three-foot round area. The area bulged outward until a ball of lava broke off from the flow and rolled down the slope, blackening as its edges were cooled by the sea water. Each time a globe broke off, the red-hot lava glowed bright yellow for a minute, gradually turning to red and then dark red just before breaking off and falling.

Russell timed the event, then did some calculations. "It's a lava tube emptying on the side of the mountain," he said. "Each one of those globs contains about a half a cubic yard of lava, so this flow is running at about thirty cubic yards of lava per hour. Not much as volcanoes go--Kilauea regularly puts out 20,000 cubic yards of lava per hour--but it still can cause trouble if it's in the wrong place, and there are probably dozens of others. Where's the JPC in relation to this one?"

Susan switched to the alternate camera and searched. In a moment, she answered. "My best guess, based on the terrain, is that it's about fifty feet below us and two hundred feet to starboard, but the lights aren't strong enough to carry that far. We'll have to go looking for it."

"Roger," Chaplin said. "We'll mosey in that direction." The submersible backed away from the active lava flow, then turned to starboard, running at slow velocity. He flipped a switch and a pinging noise began. "I just turned on active sonar. The JPC should stand out on that like a sore thumb," he said.

"Got it," he said, a moment later. "You weren't far off." He turned off the sonar.

"Stop dead," Russell said. "You're headed straight over a vent. Back up and circle around it."

"Where?" Chaplin asked. "Okay. I see it now. Subtle." He reversed and went slowly forward, angling significantly to the right of the glimmer. He whistled. "Two hundred degrees outside," he said. "You caught us just in time."

"They're easy to see once you know what you're looking for. You have to be constantly searching for them, though. That one was hot enough to cook our instruments. The cameras are particularly sensitive to heat."

"Glad you saw it then, Doc. We would have been in a world of hurt without our cameras."

Soon, the stern of the JPC came into view. "See that bare flat area above it?" Susan said. "The JPC's slid another ten feet downhill from where it was last time we were here."

They circled the submarine, keeping fifty feet away from it. "No problem getting the first cable around it," Chaplin said. "Stern's a good three feet off the ground. It's going to be tough to get the second cable under, though."

"Can you focus up the hill a bit, just forward of the sail?" Russell asked. "A little higher. Okay, there. Cone in just a bit closer, please."

Chaplin complied. They were hovering close to the JPC now, perhaps thirty feet away. Above the JPC, about thirty feet up-slope from it, was a three-foot-round rock caught in a patch of tube worms.

"Just as I thought. It's a lava bomb, like the one we saw being produced a little while ago," Russell said. "There must be a lava tube emptying above the JPC. These tubes come and go. They can close if the flow slows, then open in another location when the flow picks up again. I don't see any glow up-slope right now. Let's hope it stays that way. If these things get rolling, they can pack a wallop when they hit something downslope. They're deceptive, you know. They're black on the outside, but for a long time, the lava on the inside stays molten. If they roll and hit something hard enough, they can break up and release all their energy at once. Like a bomb. Very destructive."

"Great," said Chaplin. "This place gives me the willies. Let's find our cable and put it where it needs to be." He made tight circles as he directed the XMS upward. Susan heard pinging from the active sonar again.

"I've got the cable on sonar," Tanner said. "Bearing twelve degrees starboard and seventy feet ahead." The XMS turned slightly to the right and eventually the cable came into view. Chaplin hovered the XMS ten feet away and adjusted buoyancy so that they descended until the bottom of the cable was five or six feet below them. "Grab that bugger," he said.

Tanner manipulated the graspers, while Chaplin focused the main camera to give a perfect picture of the cable. One grasper locked onto the cable. "Got it," Tanner said.

"Okay. Time to get out the Gertrude. We need to talk to the surface and to the guys inside. He lowered a microphone from the ceiling until it was in front of his mouth. "Surface, this is the XMS. We've got the cable. Give us a hundred feet of slack, please. Over."

"Roger. Beginning now. Over."

Chaplin allowed the XMS to descend. Because it was negatively buoyant, it was, in essence, hanging from the cable.

"That's a hundred. Want more? Over."

"Not yet. We'll find the sub again, then tell you how much we need. Over." Chaplin turned on the active sonar. A moment later, Tanner said, "Thirty feet below us and a hundred forty behind us. Bearing 175 degrees."

"Roger." He flipped on the Gertrude. "Give us another fifty feet. Over."

"Roger. Beginning now. Over."

"Susan, you can help us here. We're going to try to loop this thing over the stern. I'll be looking through the main camera. I need you to look through the alternate camera and guide me. We'll come in from the stern. I figure the cable will hang on the starboard side of the submarine, and we'll be on the port side. The cable will loop down below us. We want to get it just forward of the drive train bulges. If we do that, it won't slip off. Got it?"

"Right. I'm looking through the alternate camera right now. Trying to find the loop of cable.... Okay. I have it. Let me know when you see the stern of the JPC."

Chaplin waited until he was aligned with the JPC before turning the Gertrude on again. "JPC, this is Lieutenant Commander Chaplin on the Submersible XMS. We're going to help you get out of here. Do you read? Over."

"This is Lieutenant Commander Peyton, the XO on the JPC. We read. Great to hear from you. Over."

"We're slipping a lasso over your tail. You'll hear it dragging on you as we bring the far end back up to the surface. Don't sweat it. What I need you to do is get ready to pump as much air as you have into your buoyancy chambers and then pump it to the stern. We want your stern as buoyant as possible. Don't do it yet, though. Wait until I tell you. Understand? Over."

"Roger. Understood. We're prepping & will stand by. We don't have enough extra air to be buoyant, but we do have some. Over."

"After we get the first cable laid, we'll lift up your stern a bit. We need to get another cable forward of your sail, and that will give us some room to maneuver. It'll be a lot harder. We'll have to drive that one in. We'll let you know when we're ready to start. Over."

It was then that the ground began shaking. The submersible swayed as the water around it flowed back and forth. Lava bombs rolled downhill, one settling less than ten feet from the JPC's prow. Fortunately, it didn't explode. The tremor lasted almost a minute before the sea became calm again.

Chaplin wiped his brow. "I figured this was going too easy," he said. "Let's get that cable around the stern and head toward the surface before the next one hits. We don't want to get slammed against the JPC while we're setting it. We're going to have to sneak in close to pull this off. If she's a moving target, we could be shit out of luck."

5:28 a.m., Loihi Seamount

Inside the JPC, Wendy Peyton leaned forward in her seat. She was dripping sweat and had already soaked a towel she used to keep sweat from running down her forehead and into her eyes.

The temperature was still rising, well beyond the point of comfort. The only saving grace was that the air conditioners removed most moisture from the air, so sweating was effective at cooling the body. If she leaned backward, though, air couldn't circulate behind her trunk. Her damp back stuck to the plastic chair until her body temperature rose to the point where she couldn't tolerate it.

CDR Farriott, Polanski, and she listened to the Gertrude chatter, intent on keeping track of what was going on outside the JPC's hull. Sometimes the XMS talked to the ships on the surface and sometimes to the JPC itself. It made no difference. They could hear all conversations transmitted into the water, no matter who the talk was directed at. There were no telephone lines in the deep ocean.

She was handling the communications, freeing CDR Farriott to command the submarine. He sat a short distance away from her, next to the intercom microphone, ready to bark orders into it when necessary.

They had already blown as much air as possible into their stern buoyancy tanks. It wasn't much, but it did tend to lift the stern a foot or two further off the bottom. Inside the sub, they noticed a slight decrease in the angle of fore to aft tilt. It wasn't much. If they walked toward the bow, they still walked uphill. They also had a ten-degree list to port, and that was more awkward for them. It felt like one leg was longer than the other when you moved fore or aft, and you had to watch your head to keep it from bumping into the equipment on the uphill side.

She stood up and stretched, taking a risk, she knew. An earthquake could come at any time and knock her off her feet. She had the bruises to prove it. But she just couldn't sit any longer. She lowered her hands and grasped the seat back, holding on. She'd been lucky she hadn't broken a hip the first time. She didn't want to have to depend on luck a second time.

"JPC, this is Lieutenant Tanner on the XMS. We're coming in. You'll hear some scraping on your hull. Over," she heard.

She flipped the Gertrude microphone on. "Roger," she answered. "We're ready for you. Over."

A slight earth tremor made her sit down again.

"You've got a bit of movement. We're holding. Don't want a collision. Over."

"Come when you're ready. We're okay. Over."

Two or three minutes later, she heard a scraping on the hull. She couldn't tell where it was coming from. It just seemed to emanate from all around her. "I hope that's you on our hull. Otherwise, we've got a hell of a rat problem. Over."

"Just us sea rats. We're under your stern. Just doing a bit of adjustment, then we'll tighten up and run for the surface. You'll hear a long squeal as the cable gets pulled around you and taken up above. We'll deliver the free end to the surface winch, then be back down to do a visual inspection of the cable after it's hooked at both ends to the winches above. We'll make sure it's still in good position before we let them start lifting your stern. Over."

"Roger. When you get to the surface, say hello to Mister Sun for us. We haven't seen him for a while. Over."

"Will do. Out."

After a minute, the intermittent scratching sound on the hull gave way to a whine that began at a low pitch and then rose in pitch as the velocity of the cable looping around the hull increased. The whine lasted for half an hour and then lost pitch and ceased, replaced by rattling and scraping once again.

"They must be up on the surface and feeding it to the winch on the other ship," Farriott said.

"I guess. Not much to do now except wait, I guess," she answered.

They waited another hour, punctuated only by intermittent scraping against the hull. Then the intercom signaled. Farriott picked it up. He listened, then said, "Roger. Thank you." He turned to Wendy. "Sonar's picked up the XMS coming down again."

Soon, the scratching started. After a moment, Tanner's voice came on. "We're inspecting your stern. We'll need to drag the cable three or four feet forward, then we'll ask them to take out the slack. When that's done, we'll confirm that the cable's position on your stern is okay, then ask them to lift your stern. We'll have to ascend and recharge before coming down again and driving a second cable just forward of your sail, but we want to be sure you're all set before we go up. We won't have that much time to drive that second cable. Over."

"Roger. Standing by. Over."

Five minutes passed. "Surface, cable's in ideal position," Tanner's voice said. "Take in ten feet of slack. Over."

Wendy heard a scraping sound, then felt a jerk.

"Surface, you're tight now. Take out six more feet of slack."

Wendy felt the deck tilt changing as the stern rose off the bottom.

"JPC, we're going up again to pick up a second cable in a minute," Tanner said. "Just inspecting where we're going to have to put it first. It's going to be tight. No picnic. This is going to be the hardest part of this whole mission. Over."

"Roger," Wendy answered. "We can feel ourselves floating. Must be some rollers up top. Over."

"Not too bad. Four-footers. Pretty smooth. Heading up now. We'll recharge, then be back down in three hours. Don't go anywhere. Over."

"Wish we could. Out." She hung the Gertrude on the rack, then stood up again, holding on.

Farriott also arose. "Interesting sensation, isn't it?" he asked. "Our bow's grinding into the bottom, while our stern rises and falls with the surface waves. Not what you usually feel on a submarine. More like what you feel on the surface."

"It's a prescription for seasickness," she said. "Any of our guys susceptible?"

"Hope not. I guess we'll find out. In the meantime, let's have some chow."

By intercom, he notified the rest of the crew of the break in activity. They walked together to the mess hall, holding to the side rails for safety. They were almost there when a large tremor hit them, followed a moment later by an explosive impact against their hull.

8:18 a.m., Pacific Ocean, above Loihi Seamount

The XMS broke the surface between the two winch ships, which formed a seventy-foot wide pool between them. The struts linking them had some give, but not much, and the two ships functioned almost like a single ship, a catamaran-shaped stable platform that looked and functioned like a floating dock. The XMS approached the starboard ship and soon was tethered to a grating, from which the crew could disembark and climb a ladder to the main deck.

While they lunched, crew members from the support ship changed their batteries. When they returned, Susan noticed a thirty-foot-long curved piece of metal hanging on a cable from amidships. It hung about ten feet off the water. "What's that?" she asked.

"That's our needle," Chaplin answered. "We have to drive that thing under the JPC. We push it from one side, then pull it from the other. Any coral that gets in the way gets smashed. The cable's hooked to it, so once it's free of the coral and the JPC, we carry it back up to the surface, and the surface crew on the other ship removes the needle from the cable and hooks the cable to the winch on the other ship. Then we winch it up and lift the JPC off the bottom."

"You make it sound easy."

"I figure we have a 50-50 chance of doing it right the first time. Securing that cable is the toughest thing we're going to have to do. Anyway, it's show time. Let's get to it."

They entered the XMS and started the electric motors. The ship crew released their lines, and they were on their way down. A half-hour later, they were a hundred feet above the bottom, their lights on, searching for the JPC.

"Looks different. Something's happened," Russell said. "Must have been another earthquake while we were gone. A strong one. See that shimmering right above the JPC? Susan, can you redirect the light away from it?" She complied.

"See that glow? It's subtle, but when we take the light away, you can see it. That's a lava flow waiting to break loose. The surface is still intact, but it's getting hot, and pretty soon, it'll break through."

"I've got the JPC a hundred feet ahead of us by sonar," Tanner said. "The needle's hanging right above it. We should be seeing it in a minute."

"Can we take a moment to check out this lava flow?" Russell asked.

"Sorry. No time for sightseeing right now. This is going to take all the time we've got," Chaplin said, shaking his head. He piloted the XMS forward slowly until the needle was directly in front of them. He hovered four feet from it. "Grab that bugger," he said to Tanner.

Susan aimed the alternate camera forward, so she could see what was going on. She saw the hook-like needle and then the metal arm of the starboard grasper advancing. The hand of the grasper closed over it, grabbing it. "Locked on. Now for the tricky part," Tanner said. He advanced the port grasper, manipulated it so that it was three feet below the starboard one, and wobbled it forward until it was ready to grasp the needle. It wasn't easy getting it in perfect position, and it took about fifteen minutes to accomplish. After it was held by both graspers, he loosened one grasper after the other, turning the needle so that it pointed directly forward.

Tanner got the Gertrude working. "Surface, we have the needle. Give us fifty feet of slack. Over," he said.

Once the cable became slack, Chaplin let the XMS descend. They moved just above the JPC, forward of her sail and hovered there. "Give me the Gertrude," he said to Tanner. Tanner handed it over. "JPC, we're going to drive another cable under the hull. Shift your buoyancy forward if you can. Over."

"Roger. We're doing it now," Wendy said. "Check our hull when you get a chance. We had an explosion outside. Pretty powerful. Don't know what it was. Over."

"Lava bomb," Russell said. "Has to be."

"We'll check it out," Chaplin said. "You look okay from this side, but we'll have to wait to check out your port side. You'll feel impacts when we drive this thing home. Be ready for them. Over."

"Understood. We'll fasten our seat belts. Over."

Chaplin adjusted the tilt of the XMS so that their bow was thirty degrees downward, and they descended until the needle hit bottom.

"I can't see the needle tip with my camera light," Chaplin said to Susan. "Get the alternate camera aimed below us. I want to know where the tip of the needle is."

Susan adjusted the alternate camera until the needle tip was in view. She noticed that its tip was flattened, with flukes like the bottom of an anchor. *Clever*, she thought. "It's on the bottom aiming a little bit upward, maybe five feet from the JPC," she said. "Tip is a foot off the ground right now."

"Tell me when the tip's flat to the bottom and aiming below the JPC, about four feet forward of the sail." He started to increase their tilt, forty degrees, then forty-five. Susan hung from her shoulder straps and seat belt.

"Stop. You're perfect right now," Susan said.

"Hold a second," Russell said. "Susan, show me that rock just beyond those tubeworms."

She adjusted the camera and focused in.

"See those ridges? That's pahoehoe. It's very solid rock. You're never going to drive through that. I'd suggest moving a couple of feet forward. You won't have as much room to maneuver, but there's looser material there, and you'll have a better chance of driving through it.

"Okay," Chaplin said. He backed up and came back three feet in front of where they had been. "You approve?" he asked.

"Righto."

"Then, we'll try to drive it under now. Hang onto your seats." He drove the XMS forward, the needle tip making a six-inch-wide groove in the bottom. The tip slid under the hull. Then they stopped. He pressed on the accelerator. Nothing happened. They did not move.

"We'll have to re-grab it. We're pushing it down into the rock now. Have to grab it a little lower. You ready?" he asked Tanner.

"Top grasper's loose," Tanner said. A moment later. "Bottom grasper's loose."

Susan watched the maneuver. With the graspers partially loosened but still keeping hold, the XMS slid downward on the curve of the needle and re-grasped it four feet lower. Tanner revved the motor, engaging the clutch, and the XMS jumped forward another three feet before stopping once again.

"Good. We made some progress. Now, I think we need to grasp up above again," Chaplin said. They repeated the maneuver, this time moving upward. They moved forward only another foot.

"Let's try a little higher," Chaplin said. They shifted upward another four feet and this time were rewarded by six feet of progress. After four more such maneuvers, Chaplin was satisfied. "Let's see if we can grab the needle from the other side of the sub," he said.

Tanner loosened the graspers and they maneuvered the XMS to the port side of the JPC. Susan focused the alternate camera on the JPC's hull, looking where they expected the needle to be. It was there, but it was something else that attracted her attention. "Wow. Look at that," she said.

"That's what a lava bomb can do," Russell said.

The JPC's hull was discolored over a six-foot area and pock marks testified to the impact of molten lava. The needle protruded just below the discolored area.

"At least we didn't drive the needle right into that discolored area," Chaplin said. "I doubt we'd be able to drive it through an intact hull, but you can't say how strong this one is." He lowered the XMS until Tanner could grasp the needle with the rear graspers. When Tanner gave him thumbs-up, he gunned the propulsors, heading forward and upward. The XMS shot forward.

"You're still holding the needle. It's loose from the sub," Susan said. The cable's under and seems to be about three meters forward of the sail.

"Great," said Tanner. "That's just where we want it." He turned on the Gertrude. "Topside, we're coming up. Give us fifty feet of slack, please."

He pushed air into their buoyancy tanks so that the XMS was positively buoyant. They passively rose until their upward progress stopped, their bow tilted downward by the cable.

"Give us another fifty feet of slack," he said. A minute later, they leveled out and began to rise again. They rose only about twenty feet before the cable caught once more.

"The cable must be hanging up somewhere down below. Our natural buoyancy isn't enough to keep it moving," Tanner said. "We'll have to use power to shake it loose." He started the engines and eased the control stick forward until the cable loosened and the XMS shot upward again.

He had to repeat that process several times more before the XMS broke surface next to the winch ship.

9:37 a.m., Pacific Ocean, above Loihi Seamount

By the time the winch ship had removed the needle from the cable and attached the cable to the winch, the XMS was ready to head down again. They planned to first witness the JPC's lift off the bottom, after which they'd loop a third cable just behind the bow of the JPC, then return to the surface to deliver the third cable to the winch ship. Then, they'd head down to pick up a fourth cable, and position it just behind the sail.

The trip down was smooth and uncomplicated, and they found the JPC easily. They hovered fifty feet above it and thirty feet to starboard. "Now for the tricky part," Chaplin said. He got on the Gertrude. "JPC, we're ready to begin lifting. You'll need to adjust your buoyancy way forward, if it isn't there already, since the one cable we have on your bow is near amidships. Copy? Over."

"We still have buoyancy forward," Wendy answered. "That last cable screeched like a banshee as you pulled it up, and it seemed to catch several times. Over."

"Not surprising. The cable was stuck between the ground and your hull," Chaplin answered. "Surface, we have the sub in view. The number 2 cable is in place and it looks like it has about twenty feet of slack in it. Let's take out ten feet on either side. Will give you further instructions after that."

"Roger. Give us ten minutes to set up. Over."

Chaplin hung up the Gertrude. "They don't want to drag the cables against the side any more than they have to," he explained. "That means both winches, one on each winch ship, have to start and stop at the same side. They want it balanced, too, with the weight evenly distributed. Unfortunately, they can't do that right now, because the fore cable is closer to the midline than the aft one is. So, we compensate by blowing air into the fore compartments. Then we level the boat out. Once that's done, we'll have to have all four winches, two on each cable, work simultaneously."

"XMS, we're ready to take out slack. You ready? Over," the surface coordinator asked.

"We're ready," Chaplin said. "Over."

"JPC, you ready? Over."

"Roger," Wendy answered. "We're anxious to begin ascent. Over."

"Will begin in thirty seconds. Over."

Susan turned on the alternate camera's lights and focused on the cables. She soon saw them all move, then the bow of the JPC gave a slight jerk. The number 2 cables now were off the ground and taut.

"Surface, this is JPC," Peyton said. "Our stern is up two degrees. If you want us level during the lift, I'd suggest lifting on the fore cables about three feet. Over."

"Roger. Will do. Let us know if we need to do more. Over."

A moment later, Susan saw the bow lift off the bottom. "Hot damn," she said. They're off the bottom."

"Surface, this is JPC. We're level and suspended. We can feel the difference in our motion. Please lift us up. Over."

"Surface, XMS confirms," Chaplin said. "Ready to lift fifty feet. We will then inspect. Over."

"Roger. Beginning lift in five, four, three, two, one. Over."

The JPC's rise was imperceptible at first, but slowly it rose, swinging slightly on its tethers. Its rise stopped when it was fifty feet above the bottom. The hawsers from the floating dock below now stretched toward its intake manifolds, with another twenty feet or so of cables still on the bottom.

"Look at the bottom, where the submarine was," Russell said.

It took Susan a few moments to see what he saw, and she only saw it clearly when she turned off the lights. Just forward of the place where the sail had rested and where their bow cable had been, the bottom glowed red.

"No wonder they were so hot in there," Russell said. "They had a lava tube ready to open up right beneath them."

Chaplin shrugged. "Nothing we need to do about it now. Good thing we got them off that thing. Let's go grab our other two cables. We can't lift up both the sub and that damned dock without all four of them." He engaged the motor and they headed upward.

10:42 a.m., JPC, above Loihi Seamount

The most immediate change Daniel Farriott noted was in the temperature around them. Within ten minutes of getting off the bottom, the temperature dropped to tolerable levels. Their soaked shorts and skivvies began to dry, and sweat no longer rolled down their chests and backs.

"XO, we're going to be hanging here for a while. Why don't you put a shirt on? You're going to be freezing in a while." he said.

Wendy flashed him a smile. "It feels great, doesn't it? I'll be back in a minute."

"Grab your escape suit while you're at it. We'll want those right next to us on the way up. They won't be useful until we're within a couple hundred feet of the surface, but by then we might be too busy to get them when we need them."

"Roger. Will do." She climbed down the ladder, leaving him in the command center.

"You, too," he ordered Mike Polanski. "Then check on the crew & report back here. I want escape suits next to every man on this boat."

"Right, skipper. I'll get it done."

He called the reactor room on the intercom and ordered Buzz Henderson to bring the reactor up to standard power. Now that they were in colder water, they could dissipate the heat of the reactor enough to provide optimal electrical power so their dimmed lights could be brightened. When full power came to the lights, the glare hurt his eyes. It had been a week since he'd seen full illumination.

He waited until the XO came back before changing his own clothes. None of their clothes were clean, of course. They couldn't wash them at depth, particularly with their energy usage minimized. He put on the best of his shirts, then carried his own SEIE-8 escape suit up to the bridge. He hung it out of the way, in a place where it would be easy to grab in an emergency, right next to Wendy's suit.

The SEIE (Submarine Escape Immersion Equipment) suits were red, insulated, full-body protective suits that provided enough air supply for an escape from as deep as six hundred feet. Because of the possibility of decompression problems–the bends and/or air embolism–when used at that depth, however, their use was safer if the escapees were within one or two hundred feet of the surface. All his crew were trained in escape procedures from two hundred feet.

He hoped they wouldn't need them, but you never could tell. He wanted them nearby. He would have preferred that they be worn, but that would have hampered their movements.

He stood in the middle of the room, closing his eyes and feeling the rocking of the boat as the surface waves pulled them up and down, forward and backward. It was an unusual feeling in a submarine. Surface disturbances didn't normally penetrate to the depths they ran in. As it was, the motion was muted by the elasticity of three thousand feet of steel cables linking them to the surface. As they rose and the cables shortened, the rocking would increase, of course. At the same time, the air in their buoyancy tanks would expand due to the decreased pressure and make them more buoyant. Then, they'd get rid of that damned dock or whatever it was that they'd hit. They might even be positively buoyant once that was gone. He imagined the exultation they would all feel once they were floating on the surface.

His naval career was probably over, he thought. There would be an inquiry, lots of finger-pointing. Even if they ruled that the incident was not the result of dereliction of duty, it would be a blot on his record. He might be better off leaving the Navy when the inquiries were over. He'd have to talk it over with Ellen when he got home.

He smiled when he thought of her. He'd banished thoughts of her and the kids while they'd been under. He always did. But then, on the way home, he'd get out their pictures, knowing he'd have to prepare for that other life, the one on shore, where he slept in a real bed and partied and made love and enjoyed sunshine.

He was heading home after a prolonged stay in a surreal, stressful environment as alien to his surface way of life as another planet. But somehow, he knew when they were under the sheets, together again, he would remember what to do.

His reverie was broken when the Gertrude intervened. "JPC, this is Chaplin aboard the XMS. We're down with your third cable. This will go around your bow. You'll hear it scraping on you as we loop it around you. Over."

"This is LTC Peyton," Wendy answered. "Roger. We'll be ready. How's our hull? Any damage you can see? We took quite an impact down there. Over."

"We see some discoloration and pitting over a fairly wide area right under that second cable. I don't think it's all from that impact you felt. It's worse on the port side but extends all the way to the starboard side. The bottom was hot where you were sitting. We saw that after we lifted you up. Maybe the heat caused the discoloration. Anyway, we need to get these cables laid. Divers will take a closer look at it when you get near the surface. Over."

"Any recommendations for us? Over."

"Nothing special. Just be ready for the unexpected. You're probably doing that anyway. Over."

"We are. We're better off already. We can control our temperature again. Over."

"Glad to hear it. I'm signing off. Need to concentrate on laying this cable. Out."

Hull discoloration? Important, but probably not dangerous, Daniel thought. They'd check it out at the shipyard at Pearl. He was glad they'd told him about it. He could think about the implications while they were being elevated. It was better to be over-prepared than under-prepared.

"XO, make sure everyone knows to keep their SEIE escape suits right next to them. Anything you can imagine can go wrong as they're dredging us up. Also, warn the weapons people about possible hull damage right next to them. If they hear or see anything unusual, I want to know about it right away."

"I'll let them know," Wendy said. She left the bridge, heading forward.

Chapter 17

10 February 2020

6:33 a.m., Pacific Ocean, above Loihi Seamount

Admiral Green's chopper pilot had to be extra careful during the landing on the support vessel. The wind was a factor, and so was the rolling of the deck caused by Carlotta, the tropical depression now passing due south of them. Carlotta hadn't hit the islands, but it had made its presence known by causing larger surf than usual and a doubling of the normal trade winds. Adding to the problem was Tropical Storm Dante, still to the east of them, but affecting the surface conditions as well. It wasn't a perfect day to bring the JPC up, but you couldn't always have everything the way you wanted, could you? You had to play the cards you were dealt.

They were ready. The fourth cable had been placed into position. The XMS was tethered off the port bow. All eight winches were loaded with cable and ready to run.

Admiral Green watched the sun rise from the bridge of the starboard winch ship. It was a beautiful morning, though a rising sea made standing without holding on to something perilous. The sun rose into a sky with few clouds, and the absence of a band of redness on the horizon gave testimony to the lack of moisture in the air.

The sky was peaceful, but the ocean was not. An irregular cross swell hit them, arising from the two separate tropical storms to the south and southeast of them. These created rollers that peaked at six to thirteen feet, depending upon where they crossed each other. The ocean, as he watched, had a checkerboard appearance, with whitecaps showing where the kings and knights were. On board, he was tossed to the right and left, but also to the back and front, in a pattern that was impossible to predict. Sailors subject to seasickness were going to have a rough day.

Green was there to observe and consult. He was not the Admiral-in-charge of this operation. That honor belonged to another Admiral, one well-versed in surface operations in support of the fleet. Admiral Green knew submarines, but he did not know surface procedures. Thus, he had to take a back seat and watch while Rear Admiral Ralph Kennedy barked commands at his staff.

"Winch crews, are you clear for beginning the ascent?" Kennedy asked. He then listened as the leaders of each of the eight winch teams–four on his own vessel and four on the port vessel tethered a hundred feet away–reported they were ready to begin.

"JPC. Are you ready to come up?" he asked on the Gertrude.

"This is CDR Farriott. We're more than ready to proceed," he heard.

"On my count, winch her up twenty feet," he said.

He began a countdown from ten. When he got to "One," he didn't hesitate. He simply said, a second later, "Begin. Stop and report when you've taken in twenty feet." It seemed only a moment later when all the winch crews reported back with the words, “Holding at twenty feet."

"Cable tensions, please." Kennedy ordered. He waited for the measurements to come back. They were almost identical. Almost. Cable two on the port side showed slightly less tension than the others. "Number two port winch, take in one more foot. Then report tension." he ordered.

"Cable tension increased by 1823 pounds," he heard a moment later. The tension on the #2 port cable was now a little more than on the other cables. "Close enough," he said to Green. "Raise another twenty feet," he ordered.

The crews followed the standard procedure, and this time, the cables had nearly the same tension after the winching was finished.

"Give me another twenty feet," he ordered. He adjusted for a lack of tension in the port #2 cable once again. "What goes with that crew?" he commented. "Can't they count to twenty? My guess is they have an incompetent crew chief, and they haven't calibrated their counters properly."

"Ascend another twenty feet," he ordered. He checked his watch. It had taken them more than an hour to lift the JPC only sixty feet. He made a calculation, then commented, "We need to speed this up. At this rate, we're going to be lifting for fifty hours,"

"Report when you're ready to ascend fifty feet," he ordered. When all eight winch crews confirmed they were ready, he ordered. "Ascend fifty feet."

Once again, the #2 port winch reported less tension than the others. Kennedy sighed. "This incompetent crew is costing us time," he said. "I've got more than a thousand sailors involved with this operation, all of them being tossed around in difficult seas, and they're screwing up." He picked up the intercom. "Number two port winch, raise two feet and report tension," he ordered. Once again, the cable tension was a bit more than the others afterward. "All winch crews ascend fifty feet," he ordered. After the tension check, once again, Port #2 winch had less tension than the others.

"Admiral, something's going on here," Green said. "We need to figure out what's happening. One crew shouldn't be repeatedly behind the others."

"I know what's going on," Admiral Kennedy said. "This crew has a problem with their calibration. They must not have checked it before we started. I'll hash it out with the crew chief personally after it's over. In the meantime, I've got a submarine to salvage." He glared, then turned away. "Ascend another fifty feet," he said.

"Admiral, there are other alternatives," Green insisted. "We need to send a submersible down to check the JPC. If we can't do that, at least, we need to contact the JPC and get their input."

"What are they going to tell us? That the heads aren't working?" Kennedy answered. "They can't see anything outside their submarine. How are they going to give us useful information about the tensions in the cables lifting them?" He turned his attention back to the matter at hand. "Port crew #2, give me two more feet of ascension," he ordered.

Admiral Green gave up. Kennedy was in charge. He had no right to question his commands. But he couldn't shake a nagging feeling that something was wrong, and it wasn't just an incompetent winch crew.

8:22 a.m., JPC, above Loihi Seamount

"What the hell? We're going up, anyway," Mike Polanski said.

"I can't stand that noise, though. It's like bad chalk on a chalkboard," Celia Hutchinson said. "Loud as hell, too. Rips my eardrums apart."

Celia could hear noises and interpret them better than anyone else on board, but even she was stumped.

"It repeats every time we get rocked side to side by the surface waves. It's a scratching sound, particularly when we rock to port. But when we go up, it's a lot louder and more constant, more of a squeal than a scratching. Then we stop, and a minute later, it's super loud for a second. Each time our elevator goes up, I hear the squeal. Then, a few seconds later, it's the same sound but super loud, just for a few seconds"

"You hear anything like that ever before?" he asked.

"Yeah. A few times. Once when we got tossed around by an earthquake while we were sitting on the bottom. Same sort of squeal. I figured the hull was scraping against coral or something. But it was a little more high-pitched, more of a squeak, like a mouse. This is more like a soprano in a death scene."

The saying, "It isn't over until the fat lady sings," came to Mike's mind. It unsettled him. "I'll tell the skipper. He'll want to hear it himself," he said.

He headed for the bridge. While he walked, he thought about Celia. She was an amazing woman, he knew. There was no privacy on a submarine. She'd handled it by ignoring it. If some sailor stared at her when she was changing uniforms, she'd just stand before him and say something like, "What, you never seen tits before?" That would be enough.

His own Marisa, he thought, would do fine on a submarine. She had a lot of the same spunk Celia had. *Soon*, he thought. He always enjoyed their first screw after sea duty. When he thought about it, though, he enjoyed all their screws. The last one, right before he left for sea duty again, that one was always fantastic. Something to sustain them both for a couple of months. Something special every time.

He climbed the ladder to the bridge. The skipper was seated there, his eyes on all the LED's in front of him. "Hutchinson's hearing some sort of squeal every time we go up. She says it sounds like a dying soprano in an opera. You want to hear it?" Mike asked.

"Dying soprano? Sure," CDR Farriott said. "You're in charge," he said to Wendy Peyton. He followed Polanski down the ladder.

When they got to the sonar area, Hutchinson handed them both earphones. "You can hear it every time we ascend, but it's not really loud until after the ascent. Then, just for a few seconds, it gets loud as hell. I have to off my earphones to save my ears."

Polanski and Farriott put on their earphones. At first, Mike heard nothing but a dull scraping sound, not very loud, but regular, and Hutchinson was right. It got louder when they rocked to port. Then, he felt a sensation of ascension, very similar to the sensation he always expected after elevator doors closed. A second later, he heard it, a steady high-pitched squeal. It was indeed like a soprano voice, except that there was no vibrato. It was steady, changing neither timbre nor amplitude, and continued until he felt the ascension stop. He heard nothing for a minute or two, and then heard an intense loud squeal. It was the same sound, but a hundred times louder. All three of them had to take their earphones off.

"Impressive," Farriott said. "I figured it must be some sort of resonance effect at first, maybe vibration in the cables, but that wouldn't explain that loud scream at the end." He smiled. "It does sound like a soprano who just got stabbed, doesn't it? You have any ideas, COB?"

Polanski shook his head. "Not a clue, sir. Got to have something to do with the ascent, though. Maybe we should ask the surface folks, see if they have any ideas."

"I agree. Any idea where it's coming from?" he asked Hutchinson.

"I'd say right next to us," she answered. "Probably from the JPC itself. Could be noise transmitted down the cables, though. Those things could be acting like piano wires."

"Right. Good point. I'll ask the surface to get their sonar people on it. If it's us, they should be able to tell. Good work, bringing that to our attention. It could be important."

"Just doin' my job, sir."

Farriott and Polanski returned to the command center. "Anything interesting?" Wendy Peyton asked.

"You should listen to it yourself. See if you have any thoughts about it," Farriott said. "Why don't you drop down there while we're contacting the surface? I'll relieve you here."

He got out the Gertrude and called to the surface, asking for Admiral Green. Polanski listened in on the speaker phone, while Farriott told the Admiral what they'd heard and asked him if he had any ideas.

"It has to be related to the port #2 winch," Green said. "That one's been lagging a foot or two with every fifty-foot ascent sequence. The winch crew has been adjusting the cable tension by lifting the port side cable a foot or two until the tension matches what they're measuring on the other cables. My guess is when you hear the squeal amplified, it's when they're adjusting the tension."

"That sounds like the cable's scraping against the hull Why just one cable, though?" Farriott asked. "Why not all of them?"

"It might have something to do with the discoloration and pitting the XMS saw," Green answered."

"Could the cable be cutting into our hull? Hope it doesn't cut us in half," Farriott said.

"Unlikely. The damage to your hull wasn't that bad when the XMS looked at it, and that was after three thousand feet of cable had been dragged around the hull. I don't think that dragging the cable just a few feet more would do much damage. You have maybe sixty sequences of lift, with only about two feet of adjustment each time. That's only a hundred and twenty feet of cable scraping against you."

"True. But there's a heck of a lot more tension on the cables now than there was when that cable was being passed. The tension might exacerbate the damage already done."

"Possible." Admiral Green paused. "I'll need to check with the engineers and get back to you. I'll also let Admiral Kennedy know what you're hearing. We'll get our topside sonar to listen for the noise, see if we can tell you for sure where it's coming from. In the meantime, we need to bring you guys up to the top, so my recommendation is to continue the lift. You're already a third of the way there."

"Glad to hear that, Sir. We're all anxious to see topside again." Farriott said.

"I bet you are," Admiral Green replied.

9:33 a.m., Pacific Ocean, above Loihi Seamount

It took Green longer than he wanted to get a secure connection to Jerry Wentzel. He told him what he knew about the squealing during the lift, the discoloration of the hull, and the recurrent necessity to adjust the port #2 winch.

"Weird," Wentzel said. "That hull is made of a carbon-fiber-reinforced polymer. It's stronger than the strongest steel. There's no way that a simple cable should be able to cut through it."

"I know," Admiral Green replied. "Let me ask you this, though. If the polymer were to be exposed to great heat, could the heat alter the strength of the material?"

"Sure, but it's irrelevant. The sub's in water. It would never get hot enough for heat to be a factor."

"Not even if it were exposed to molten lava?"

Wentzel was silent. Green waited. Finally, Wentzel said, "Manufacture of that polymer depends upon carefully controlling the temperature and speed at which it cools. If the material were reheated almost to its melting point in an unstructured environment, it could lose most of its strength. It could become brittle, very susceptible to abrasion. It would discolor, too, darken noticeably."

"Our minisub did notice that. And when the JPC was lifted off the surface, the bottom where it had settled was glowing red."

"Then you may have a real problem," Wentzel said. "The cable could be cutting right through the outer hull."

"What should we do about it?"

"Stop making those tension corrections. Believe the winch crew when they say they've collected fifty feet of cable. My bet is that with each fifty-foot ascent sequence, the cable cuts through a little more of the hull. The cable is lax afterward because the cable's taking a short cut into the hull rather than curving around it. The only way to stop that is to minimize dragging against the hull when the cable's fully loaded. So far, the inner hull is intact. If it weren't, your guys wouldn't still be alive. Besides, the inner hull was probably insulated from the heat. It's probably still very strong. But if the cable keeps cutting.... well, all bets are off."

"I'll relay that to Admiral Kennedy," Green said. "Thanks for the help. Any other words of wisdom?"

"Just this. The inner hull will withstand pressure, but if the outer hull's not intact, the inner hull may not be strong enough to sustain a bending force. You need to get that floating dock loose as soon as you can. It's straining the whole system, particularly the two cables in front, and your shifting of air to make the front more buoyant may not be effective if the outer hull is compromised. The air you pumped in front might have leaked away."

"We're planning to cut the cables or hawsers linking the dock to the sub, but we can't do that until the JPC gets above two-hundred-foot depth," Green said. "Once we do, divers can use underwater cutting torches to cut the dock loose."

"That'll be a relief for you, I'm sure."

"It will. Once that's done, we can shut the JPC down, take the skeleton crew off, and haul the JPC back to Pearl Harbor for repairs. It'll be a real relief for the crew. They've been through an ordeal." He paused.

"I've got to sign off and convey this to Admiral Kennedy," Green added. "Thanks for the help."

"Always happy to be of service."

Green hung up and returned to the bridge. He went directly to Kennedy and told him what Wentzel had recommended. Kennedy listened, weighed what he heard, and replied, "This whole system relies upon distributing the weight over all four cables evenly. We've got to keep the tension on that second cable the same as what the others are. Otherwise, the first cable will snap. What I'll do, though, is try to adjust the tension of the second cable by pulling on both ends of the cable at the same time. That will stop the cable from dragging over the surface. And we'll adjust the tension every hundred feet, not every fifty feet."

"You're the salvage expert, but it makes sense to me," Green said, though he still had some reservations. "How far do we have to go?"

"We're just above fifteen hundred feet from the surface. Another thirteen hundred and we can stop and cut that damned dock loose."

4:50 p.m., Pacific Ocean, above Loihi Seamount

The remnants of Tropical Depression Carlotta were 569 miles south southwest of the Big Island, and Tropical Storm Dante was 270 miles due south. Carlotta was breaking up, but the waves the cyclonic winds created reflected her past glory, heavy rollers averaging eight feet in height. Dante's waves were enlarging as the storm moved closer to them and over the last twenty-four hours had reached six-foot height. The result was a cross-chop that lifted the two support ships whose winches were raising the JPC asymmetrically. The bow of the port ship would be ten feet higher than the starboard ship, and then a moment later, the starboard ship's bow would be higher. As a result, the JPC rolled along its long axis, tilting ten to fifteen degrees to port, and then up to fifteen degrees to starboard.

The second result was that the cables–all four of them–dragged back and forth along the JPC's hull, causing an ungodly squealing that the crew within the submarine could not escape. If the pitching from side to side wasn't bad enough, the squealing that accompanied it made the circumstances unbearable. The squealing was uncomfortably loud in the area just forward of the sail, where the second cable lay. The crew avoided this area, to the extent possible, but the enlisted quarters were there. Since sleep was impossible, and several officer's billets were available, Farriott moved the enlisted crew to these for rest periods.

Now that the JPC was near the surface, though, their work was almost done, and Daniel felt it was time to evacuate unnecessary crew from the JPC. They were two hundred feet below the surface, within safe emergency escape depth. The ascension was stopped, so that divers could cut the dock loose. Once the dock's attachments to the JPC were severed, the submarine could be brought to the surface, the reactor shut down, and the JPC floated back to Pearl Harbor suspended between the two salvage ships that currently supported it.

"COB, Buzz Henderson will set the reactor to minimal power," Farriott said. "After that, I want our crew gathered near the escape port, in their SEIE escape suits. I'm not waiting for us to be bobbing at the surface. I want as many as possible out of here before they cut the cables loose to that damned dock. That's going to be tricky and dangerous, and I don't see the need for exposing our personnel to that risk. We're evacuating everyone but Henderson, Peyton, you, and me. Once we get rid of that dock, Henderson can shut down the reactor, and we four will rise to the surface and turn the JPC over to the salvage people."

"Sounds like a plan," Polanski said. He went down the ladder to assemble the crew. After he left, Farriott notified Green of his plan. The sailors above would need to have a boat launched to pick up his crew when they hit the surface. It was still night time, but each of the SEIE' s had a strobe light. Moreover, the boat could drop a line to guide his sailors up. Farriott thought the risk was acceptable, and he knew that the divers would start down at the crack of dawn. He wanted his crew on the surface before the cables were cut to the dock. They couldn't wait for sunlight.

Within an hour, the crew members designated for escape were assembled next to the airlock that served the emergency escape hatch. They all wore SEIE's and Polanski reviewed their use with them. Then, they began to leave. It was a slow process, as only two crew could be evacuated at a time. They entered the escape chamber, the chamber was flooded, those inside released the outer door and escaped, the chamber was pumped dry, and the next two entered. The result was that, even under ideal circumstances, only eight crew members could be evacuated per hour. As it was, within two hours, the crew of the JPC had been reduced to only four.

Daniel felt a great sense of relief when Green told him that all evacuees had been picked up and were in good condition.

"Divers coming down. You'll hear them banging on your hull," the Gertrude barked.

"Roger. We're ready," Farriott said. He turned to Wendy Peyton. "Tell Henderson and Polanski to get their SEIE's on. We should, too. They'll be hot and hard to work in, but we can't be too safe. If anything goes wrong, it will happen fast. We need to be prepared for the worst."

Chapter 18

11 February 2020

6:40 a.m., Groton III, 200 feet below Pacific Ocean surface, above Loihi Seamount

Navy Seal Pete Martino never considered any dive to be routine. Routine killed people, because it led to complacency, sloppiness, and errors. So, for him, every dive had to be carefully planned. Flawless execution depended upon anticipation of everything that could go wrong.

That said, he judged this dive was likely to be going to be easier than most. Except for some surface chop, which would be irrelevant at their depth, the conditions were ideal. They faced no significant currents, the water was clear, the water temperature was warm, and their decompression could be leisurely, while relaxing aboard the *Groton III*, their support ship. At two hundred feet, a fair amount of daylight still filtered down, so their need for artificial illumination was minimal. The *Groton III* would drop them off and pick them up at depth, so they would never have to face the surface chop. The acetylene and oxygen tanks that supported their oxyacetylene torches would be on the *Groton III* and would not need to be carried with them.

He and Navy Seal Tasi Sampaga, his friend and co-diver, went over their checklist prior to the dive, checking both themselves and each other for any problems. For this dive, they would use a 10/40 trimix, a gas mixture of ten percent oxygen, forty percent helium, and fifty percent nitrogen, to avoid both the problem of oxygen toxicity and nitrogen narcosis at the seven-atmosphere (200 foot) depth in which they would work. Martino and Sampaga both checked the mix of gases themselves, to be sure it was accurate. Oxygen toxicity could damage lungs and eyes over time, and nitrogen narcosis could produce a dangerous euphoria at depth that could interfere with judgment. Both problems could be reduced by trimix, but the gas mix had to be accurate. Just as sky divers inspect their own parachutes, deep ocean divers personally measure their own gas mixtures.

Their breathing mixture was piped to their head gear through flexible tubing. A second tubing that spiraled around the air hose carried warm water that circulated inside their suits, keeping them from becoming hypothermic. In the tropics, this was less of a problem than it might have been in colder waters or at greater depths, but at seven atmospheres of pressure, neoprene suits, as worn by sport scuba divers, would provide minimal insulation. Air bubbles within the neoprene would be compressed to a seventh of their normal volume at depth, eliminating their insulation effect. Instead, heated water circulating within their suits kept their bodies warm enough that hypothermia, which could lead to the bends, was averted.

Two more tubes carried oxygen and acetylene for their cutting torch. The gases ran into an ignition chamber, where they were spark-ignited. The resultant flame was forced out a tiny portal into the ocean, where it could melt steel before its heat was dissipated by the boiling of ocean water.

"I'll take the port cable, and you take the starboard one," Pete said. "I'll cut mine first, since it's on the downhill side. The submarine will probably roll to starboard after I cut it, since all the debris will then be hanging from the starboard intake. Be ready for that. Make sure you're well above the cable when I cut the thing. It's going to whip loose when it goes. Those buggers can cut your arm off," Pete said.

"Watch yourself, dude. I don't want to have to dive for your pecker after it's cut off," Sampaga answered.

Pete laughed. "Time to go," he said. He put his helmet on and took a deep breath. He adjusted the seal between his body and his head, zipped his suit closed, plugged the warm water hose into his suit, and turned it on. He could feel the heat flowing to his chest, and then to his legs and arms. The seal held and air flowed as he took another deep breath. His helmet covered his entire head, so he could talk with it on. A microphone picked up his speech, and a Gertrude transmitted it to the *Groton III* and to his buddy, Sampaga. "Gas is flowing fine," he said, smiling at the sound of his own voice, squeaky from the helium.

Sampaga put his own suit on, went through the same procedure, then put his helmet on. "Check. We're both good." He sounded like Mickey Mouse, strange for a man weighing near two hundred and twenty pounds.

They flooded the escape lock and opened the hatch in the bottom. "Ladies first," Pete said, "I'll hand you the torch when you're outside."

Sampaga gave him a well-gloved middle finger, stepped through the hatch and disappeared. He rapped on the side of the *Groton III* to signal, and Pete pushed the cutting torch into the hatch and into Sampaga's hand, then entered the water himself.

When he met Sampaga on the port side of the submarine, he saw the cable exiting the intake of the JPC and disappearing into the blackness below, but he couldn't see the dock hanging from it until he took out his flashlight and aimed it downward. Seventy feet below him his light caught a ragged formless mass. Barnacles glinted in the light. "Nasty looking son of a bitch," he said. He pulled on the cable leading to it. It didn't budge. He tapped the cable with his torch tip and listened for the tone it made. The higher the pitch, the more tension it was under. "Heavy, too. This cable's really taut. We're going to have to be really careful with it. You check out the starboard one?"

"Yeah. Same deal. Just as tight."

"We want to stay on this side, with the sub between us and the starboard cable. That one might snap from the new weight when we cut this one."

"Roger. I'll buy that."

"*Groton III*, you read us? Over," Pete asked.

"This is Admiral Green. We read you loud and clear. Over," he heard.

"We're going to cut this dock loose now. The cable's about an inch thick. Tell the JPC crew that everything's going to jump when we let it loose. Have them hang on. Over."

"Roger. Will do. Over."

Sampaga swam behind Pete and lifted all their tubing above the JPC. He took a position near the sail and clipped himself onto an eyebolt there. By doing this, he stabilized his partner so Pete could concentrate on cutting the cable without thrashing around to maintain his position. "I'm ready," he said when he was clipped.

Pete reached for the acetylene torch and turned it on. He positioned himself aft and above the cable, extending his arms to make sure he was as far away as possible from the torch, where the water would be scalding hot and rising. His gloves were insulated, but his arms were not. He knew from experience to keep them away from the water above the area he was cutting.

It didn't take long. The cable turned red hot and he could see a groove forming, and then it parted with a noise like a shotgun being fired. The JPC jumped upward as the dock was momentarily in free fall, and then as the starboard dock cable caught the mass of the dock, the JPC began to rotate. Pete heard an ear-shattering squeal coming from the second support cable just aft of his position. As the JPC stopped rotating, the starboard intake port now on its downside, he saw air escaping from a long groove cut in the hull by the support cable. His blood ran cold at the implications. The JPC had a hull breach.

"We got to cut that last cable. That damned dock needs to go," he said to Sampaga, then realized that his buddy was tethered on the other side of the cable that was cutting the JPC in half. "Come forward with me, he ordered. I don't want that support cable between us."

7:22 a.m., Aboard the JPC, 200 feet below Pacific Ocean surface, above Loihi Seamount

Inside the JPC, things suddenly went topsy-turvy. Farriott was thrown to the deck and slid down to the starboard bulkhead as the JPC rolled fifty degrees to starboard. He was able to stand there, with one foot on the bulkhead and the other on the deck.

Wendy Peyton caught the photonic mast as she slid past it. She pulled herself up the sloping deck until she could drape her trunk around the mast. From there, she could clamber upward until she could stand with her feet on the mast and her buttock on the deck.

Farriott oriented himself and was about to make a grab for the helmsman's chair when he noticed that his ears were popping. The implications left him cold. He forced his voice to be calm. "Hull breach. We're taking in water somewhere," he said. "Can you reach the microphone?"

"I've got it," Wendy said.

"Get hold of Buzz and the COB. Tell them to prepare to abandon ship, then meet us at the escape hatch."

Wendy broadcast these orders, then helped Farriott scramble up to where she was standing. They stood belly to belly for a moment, both balancing on a sloping platform less than a foot wide, and their eyes met. Farriott recovered quickly. "Get to the escape hatch. Use it if you need to. I have to stay near communications to keep track of Polanski and Buzz. When they're safe, I'll join you." He boosted her up until she could reach the ladder leading aft.

She clambered aft and returned a moment later, holding a fire hose. She lowered this to where he could easily grasp it, then tied it to a pipe at shoulder height. "Hang onto this and you can walk right up the deck," she said.

"Thanks. Now get to the escape hatch. That's an order. Wait inside it. As soon as you have two people in there, use it. Escape solo if you must. Don't wait for the rest of us."

"Aye, aye, sir." She disappeared, heading aft.

She'd been gone only a few seconds before Polanski's voice came onto the speaker. "Henderson's ready to shut down the reactor. Request permission."

"Permission granted. You have flashlights?"

"Affirmative. We've already got water around our ankles. Flowing from forward of us. The current's not too stromg. We can walk aft through it."

"Keep your eyes open coming back. Watch your balance, too. It'll be hard to walk on the slope."

"No problem. I've done it before. Not with a current, though."

"Help Lieutenant Henderson if he needs it." Buzz Henderson wasn't nearly as experienced. He'd be sure to stumble, Farriott thought.

The lights went out a moment later, and Farriott was in pitch black. He turned on the flashlight built into his escape suit and climbed up to the ladder leading aft. He walked backward toward the escape hatch, which was aft of him. Water ran from forward over his feet halfway up his calves. Soon, he was outside the hatch door It was open, and he ducked his head in, making sure Peyton was inside. The escape chamber was at forty-five degrees from vertical, and she was lying on its downhill side.

"Henderson and Polanski are on their way back here. When they get here, you and Buzz take the first exit. Polanski and I will take the next."

"Aye, aye, sir," she answered.

"I'm going to close the door. If there's a sudden flood, it might be hard to do, and you can't escape without the door being closed."

"Sir, please don't. I'll take my chances. If you close it, it will delay Henderson getting in. The rest of you, too. Seconds may make a difference."

He thought a moment. "You're right. I'll leave it open. If I see water rushing, though, I'll slam it and lock it. If you see that happening, flood the chamber and save yourself."

He climbed out of the chamber and shone his flashlight aft. Any extra light he could give them would help, he knew. He couldn't communicate with them as they made their way forward from the reactor, but he could at least give them some extra light.

A short time later, he saw their lights. Their progress was slow but steady. When they reached him, he directed Henderson inside the chamber.

"You and Peyton get out of here," he said. "We'll join you on the surface in a minute." He locked the door behind Henderson and waited outside, listening while the escape chamber filled with water. He smiled with relief when he heard the outer hatch door open and close. The hatch door indicator confirmed its closure, and he pushed the button to pump the chamber dry again. When the pressure indicator showed the chamber to be at two atmospheres pressure, he could pull the chamber door open without a significant whoosh of air or water outward. *The air in here must already be at nearly two atmospheres,* he realized. *We must already be half-flooded.*

Polanski was still entering the chamber when Daniel's ears popped again, the boat seemed to jump upward, a flood of water hit Farriott in the chest, and the heavy steel door to the escape chamber slammed nearly shut, catching Polanski's foot before he could pull it away.

7:48 a.m., 200 feet below Pacific Ocean surface, above Loihi Seamount

To cut the second cable, now rotated forty-five degrees under the sub, Sampaga draped himself over the bow and deflated his buoyancy compensator, in order to make himself as negatively buoyant as possible. Pete, still tethered to him, hung on the other side of the JPC, providing a counterweight to keep Sampaga from sliding downhill. Sampaga lay on the bow of the JPC, spread-eagled to give as much stability as possible. He was careful to keep above and to the side of the cable as he cut it. It didn't take long. With the entire weight of the dock hanging from a single cable, he only needed to cut half of it before it gave way. When it did, the dock shot downward and the JPC jumped upward as the stretched support cables holding it jerked it toward the surface. The sub then slammed down again, with a screech and a thunderous crack. Pete was tossed up and down as the submarine slammed against its restraints. When he regained his balance, he saw that the second cable, the one that had cut into the hull, had broken and no longer supported the middle of the submarine. As he watched in horror, the groove it had cut in the hull began to spread. "Let's get the hell out of here," he yelled to Sampaga. He had just enough time to inflate his buoyancy compensator before the split hull, its lower side already separated by almost six inches, fractured with a crack like a cannon. He and Sampaga were caught in a rush of escaping air. They fell through an air bubble twenty feet in diameter, and then were sucked downward by the current produced as the front third of the JPC rolled off the first cable and disappeared into the depths,

Pete fought the current, turning himself right side up and driving toward the surface. When he looked upward, though, he saw the back two thirds of the JPC sliding forward on the two cables still holding it. As he watched, the third cable, now overstressed by the dead weight of a submarine filled with water instead of air, gave way. He and Sampaga swam for their lives sideways, and the remainder of the JPC missed them by ten feet, but they were still caught by the downward rush of water accompanying the remainder of the JPC as it dropped into the depths.

He jerked as he came to the end of his air hose and jerked again as Sampaga reached the end of the tether linking him to Pete. He looked down at Sampaga and realized that the heavier man's air hose had parted. It was shooting around, undulating like a long snake as it free-flowed masses of air into the ocean. Sampaga had no air.

He inhaled and found his own air supply compromised. The leak of compressed air from Sampaga's hose dropped the pressure in the compressor feeding both of them, reducing his own air supply as well. He could breathe but only by forcibly inhaling.

"Mayday," he said. "Sampaga's hose ruptured. Clamp off his air supply. I'm coming up, but I'll need all the air I can get. Be prepared for resuscitation. Sampaga's got no air at all right now. We're about a hundred feet below you. It's going to be close." He began climbing up his own air supply tube. He calculated how fast he could go. If he went too fast, he'd risk getting the bends. If he went too slow, Sampaga would drown. "Sampaga, just hang there. I'll pull you in," he said. "Don't exert yourself. Let me do the work." He didn't expect a verbal reply, but Sampaga gave him an "Okay" sign.

He was breathing hard for a minute before Sampaga's air tube went still and the bubbles stopped coming from it. After that, he could inhale with ease. He pulled himself upward steadily until he followed the tube to the access port into the *Groton III.* He stopped outside and pushed Sampaga while Gebhart and Chittenden pulled his limp body out of the water, then he climbed into the transfer chamber himself. When they were both in, Chittenden locked the chamber.

"We'll stay at three atmospheres pressure," Gebhart barked. "That should prevent the bends. We can decompress at our leisure. We'll bring the oxygen tension up to 20%, too. That'll help us get rid of our nitrogen. Might help Sampaga, too."

In the meantime, Gebhart and Pete worked on Sampaga. He'd gone limp, unconscious. They pulled off his helmet and Gebhart started CPR, while Pete worked on getting his buddy's dive suit off.

7:52 a.m., Pacific Ocean surface, above Loihi Seamount

On the surface, Admiral Green was tossed to the deck as the winch ship suddenly rolled to port. He jumped up, embarrassed to be caught off balance at sea, to hear a torrent of profanity from Admiral Kennedy.

He turned to the ship's Executive Officer, standing next to him. "What just happened?" he asked.

"We lost the JPC. She broke loose. It looks like she's headed to the bottom."

Green went cold. "What about the crew left aboard?"

"Don't know, sir. Four were still aboard. We're looking for people in escape suits, but we haven't seen any yet."

"Two people in rescue gear just came up," a sailor yelled. "Look off the port bow."

The XO grabbed some binoculars, focused them, and perused the ocean until he confirmed the sighting. "There they are. They look fine. Send a boat to pick them up," he ordered.

"Let me borrow your glasses," Green said. He looked through the binoculars and saw two figures in the ocean. One was black. "That's got to be Henderson," he said. The other was Caucasian, small-framed. "The other doesn't look like Farriott or Polanski. It's probably their XO, Peyton."

His heart skipped a beat. Daniel Farriott, in his mind, was an immensely talented Navy man, one with a great future, and a friend. Mike Polanski, too, was a tremendous asset, one who had proven himself time and again. The loss of either one of them would be a personal loss to him, as well as a major loss to the Navy.

The captain of the winch ship was on the communications line. He hung up and then said, "The *Groton III* reports two divers aboard. Both are in the decompression chamber. One had a near drowning and is being resuscitated. He's still unconscious but breathing with some help. He'll need medical attention and may have some brain injury from lack of oxygen. Martino, the uninjured Seal, says the JPC broke apart. The bow broke loose at the second cable. Then, when the sub flooded, the third cable snapped. The JPC just missed the divers as it headed to the bottom. The air tube of the injured diver tore loose from his helmet. Fortunately, he was tethered to the other diver, who pulled him back to the *Groton III*."

"One more person bobbing off amidships," the sailor with the binoculars yelled.

"Give me those," Green ordered. He focused but couldn't tell who it was. Was it Farriott or Polanski? Whoever it was flailed around without any apparent purpose. Green was sure the man was in trouble when he saw swirls of red in the water around him. The man was bleeding. A lot.

7:50 a.m., JPC, 200 feet below Pacific Ocean surface, above Loihi Seamount

Daniel knew he was in trouble when the pressure in his ears suddenly rose. A second later, the pressure wave slammed the hatch door on Mike Polanski's foot. Daniel pulled at the door, hoping to relieve the pressure on Polanski's foot, and was relieved when Polanski's boot slid inside. A torrent of sea water slammed Daniel against the hatch door. He hung onto the hatch for dear life, knowing that if he were washed further into the submarine, there would be no chance of escape for him. He could breathe the air in his SEIE while he waited for the current to diminish.

After the flood slowed, he started swimming toward the bow, grabbing protruding machinery to pull himself along. He was halfway there when the JPC turned upside down, throwing him against a protruding pipe. He felt something snap in his left thigh and a searing pain shot down his leg. The sub then turned turtle once again and he lost all sense of position in the blackness. A wall of air hit him next, apparently rising air trapped in the sail or the aft of the JPC and now released as the JPC headed downward, aft down. He was rolled, slammed into bulkheads, and pitched about, completely out of control. He could see light in front of him, though, and tried to swim for it, only to evoke a searing pain in his injured leg. He changed his tactics, pulling with his hands while pumping with his one good leg, still aiming for the round window of light above him

When he broke into the open ocean, he was tumbled in the wake of the sinking boat and rolled in the water head over heels. When he regained control of himself, he looked again for the light, which now seemed dimmer than it had been. No matter. Life was light. Light was survival. He gritted his teeth and swam for it.

He could only use one leg. Any attempt to use the other was rewarded with agonizing pain. He looked down at his leg and saw what looked like black ink flowing out of a tear in his rescue suit. Blood, black in color because no red light penetrated that deep in the ocean. And the tear meant that he'd lost a lot of his air supply and buoyancy. Instead of floating to the surface, he'd have to kick for it. He realized he'd be lucky to make it. He had no idea how deep he was, but he also knew that his only chance for survival was to reach the surface.

He forced himself to stay calm. He concentrated, ensuring that every kick upward was a productive one. He took off the shoe of the foot of his good leg so that his foot could catch the water better and propel him, even though bending his leg upward to do this caused a searing pain in his injured leg. Forcing himself to ignore the pain, he pumped upward, his hands and arms flailing, his good leg kicking. A picture in his mind of Ellen and the kids gave him the determination he needed to make this supreme and painful effort. *They will not grow up fatherless,* he told himself. *And Ellen will not have to cry at my funeral.*

He looked upward again. Was he closer? He couldn't tell. He decided not to look up again. It was too discouraging. He avoided looking up for the next few minutes, or maybe it was hours. He couldn't tell, but it seemed like hours to him since he'd pulled himself out of the dying JPC.

Finally, he couldn't stand not knowing any longer and he looked up to get his bearings. The light was brighter. He was making progress, but he still couldn't see much surface detail. Maybe another hundred feet to go, he thought.

He pumped, desperate now to make it. His leg muscles began to cramp from the effort. Still he pumped, his jaw set in determination, his good leg acting almost automatically now. He was too disoriented to recognize the effects of excess nitrogen and carbon dioxide and diminished oxygen upon his mental capacity.

When he broke through the surface, he didn't know he'd done it, and he flailed in the ocean, still trying to climb upward, until a boat picked him up. His thigh bent at ninety degrees and his broken bone stabbed through his muscle and skin as they pulled him aboard, but he didn't have the strength or will to scream. When his rescuers took the hood off his SEIE, allowing him to breathe fresh air again, he didn't know they'd done it, because he'd fallen into unconsciousness.

7:50 a.m., JPC, 200 feet below Pacific Ocean surface, above Loihi Seamount

The door slammed shut on Mike's foot with such force that it crushed his big toe despite the steel toecap in his shoe. He screamed, trying to pull his foot out, and the door slid over the toe cap and caught on his sole. He yanked again and the door slammed the rest of the way closed. He tried to push it open again but couldn't budge it. He was locked in, by pressure if not by the door lock. The only way to get out was to flood the chamber. Then he could open the outer door.

The lights were out, along with the electricity. He was trapped in the rescue chamber in utter blackness, being tossed from side to side as the chamber changed orientation. He pushed at the escape hatch, but it, too, could not be budged. He had to increase the pressure in the chamber if he wanted to get out. But he couldn't see his hand in front of his face and couldn't find the controls. He also knew he'd have to do it manually. With no electricity, just pushing a button wouldn't hack it.

He activated the strobe light on his rescue suit. This gave him a flash of light every second, and using this, he found the flip valve that allowed water to flow into the chamber. He put on his helmet and waited for the chamber to fill. It seemed to take forever, and while it filled, the whole chamber seemed to flip upside down. The escape hatch now seemed to be at his side, not above him.

He understood the implications. It meant that the JPC was going down, and every second he waited took him deeper. He put it out of his mind. He had to wait until the pressure equalized. That wouldn't happen until the chamber was full of water.

His ears popped repeatedly, and he held his head at a tilt, a scuba divers trick that kept his Eustachian tubes maximally open. Otherwise, his eardrums or the membranes leading to the inner ear canals that controlled his sense of balance would rupture, giving him vertigo that could be fatal in this situation. He kept breathing so that his lungs wouldn't be compressed, using the limited air available in his SEIE. When the rescue chamber was nearly full, he attached an air hose and re-inflated his suit. He wanted as much air and buoyancy as possible.

Finally, he opened the hatch, oriented himself, and headed upward. He had no idea how far it was to the surface, and he could barely see the glow above, but he headed for it, paddling with the efficient hand and foot movements he'd learned years before as a Navy Seal.

The suit was rated for escape from six hundred feet, but he had no idea how deep he was when he exited the hatch. *Cool it,* he told himself. *It's not going to help you to get excited.* He slowed his breathing and monitored his heart rate, willing it to slow down. He watched the bubbles escaping from his two pressure relief valves and made sure his progress upward was slightly slower than these rising bubbles. If the manual was right, he had twenty-five minutes before he'd go unconscious. If he was lucky, he'd be on the surface by then. If not.... well, he'd had a good run.

8:02 a. m., Pacific Ocean surface, above Loihi Seamount

"All that god-damned work, and we got nothing for it," Kennedy said, throwing his hands up in the air. "I was just about ready to relax. I thought we'd pulled it off." He ended with a string of profanity, then sat down. "Okay. Now we've got to think. What can we do to salvage this ungodly mess?"

"We need to know where the JPC's settled," Green said. "How deep is it? Particularly the bow portion. That's where the munitions are. We need to get those away from that volcano. The rest of the JPC's not a vital issue. I'm not sure it's worth salvaging, now that the hull has fractured."

"Right," Kennedy answered. "Sonar can give us an idea where it is. Then we can send the XMS down to check it out. Maybe we can even use the mini-sub to roll it downslope to the bottom, so it's off that damned volcano." He gave an order to charge up the XMS for another mission. As an afterthought, he said, "See if that lady oceanographer and her volcanologist friend will go along with them."

"The *Iwi*'s on its way back to Hilo. Their job was done once the cables were laid. Should I ask the *Iwi* to bring them back?" Green asked.

"Nah. I don't want to wait for them, and Chaplin and Tanner have been down there. They can tell us what's going on. The XMS needs a full charge, though, and they're probably tired from today's activities. We'll let them get a good night's sleep and send them down in the morning.

"In the meantime," Kennedy said, "we've got a hell of a lot of cable to wind up. By next morning, I want cables one and three wound on the starboard winch ship and cable four wound up on the port ship. Cable two is busted, so one half can go starboard, and the other half port. Right now, though, the cables are tethering our two winch ships together. We'll need to separate them before we can move back to Pearl. We'll leave the struts in place holding them together until we see what the XMS can tell us, but we can start on the cables now." He gave the order to proceed.

A seaman with binoculars yelled out, "One more rescue suit on the surface off the port bow."

Green grabbed the binoculars. Someone was bobbing on the surface, but he wasn't moving. He turned to the XO, who seemed the least busy of the officers around him. "Get someone over there with oxygen ASAP," he ordered. "Get that hood off him and let him breathe some clean air. If he's still breathing at all, that is." He knew the body floating there was Mike Polanski's, but he didn't know if the man was still alive.

He watched as a boat rushed out to Polanski. Crew members loaded Polanski into the boat and brought him to the ship. Green couldn't see what happened afterward, because he had no line of sight. He turned again to the XO. "Please have your men call me when they know how that man is doing."

A half hour later, the XO handed him a phone. "Here's the report on your sailor," he said.

"Admiral, this is HM1 Perkins," he heard. "I understand you want to know the condition of Master Chief Petty Officer Polanski."

"I do. I know the man well."

"He's alive, breathing okay, and he's stable. It looks like he's got a bad case of the bends, though. He's not moving his arms or legs. We're going to transfer him to the *Groton III* for treatment in their decompression chamber."

Shit, Green thought, but what he said was, "You do that. Thank you for the information."

Chapter 19

12 February 2020

5:10 a.m., Pacific Ocean surface, above Loihi Seamount

"According to the sonar, the bow's five hundred feet deeper than the JPC was before. It's still on the slope of Loihi, but it's far enough down that our cables aren't long enough to loop around it and still reach the surface," Kennedy said. "We want you to check if there's something sturdy we can grab onto. You should have access to the inside of the sub. Look for something that you can tie a cable around. If you can, we'll either tow the bow over deep ocean and sink it or bring it to the surface. We'll need two cables on it to do the latter. One cable won't be strong enough."

"Do we drag a cable down with us?" Chaplin asked.

"No. We'll lower one to you if and when you need it. The problem is, there's not much to grab hold of on the bow. You'll have to look inside, but we realize the XMS is too large to go inside. The other problem is that the cables will need to be fitted with some kind of hook. That can't be done until we see inside and have some idea what we'll be hooking onto," Kennedy said.

"So, it's a fishing expedition. You want us to find the fish and then tell you how to catch it. Right?"

"Right."

"We can do that." Chaplin turned to Tanner. "Let's get to it."

An hour later, they were on the bottom, searching for the bow of the JPC. Where they searched, the slope was steeper and the tube worms that thrived around volcanic vents were absent. Still, there was life, plenty of it. Chaplin's only regret was that they didn't have time to video it.

"There it is," Tanner said, pointing with the alternate light beam and camera. The bow was lying on its starboard side in a depression on the side of the mountain. They circled it, taking videos of it for the benefit of those topside, before coming in closer.

The walls of the depression were steep and reasonably high, so they had only a limited look inside. The hull was cleanly fractured and smooth at the bottom but was bent at the upper end, and the fracture line was jagged and irregular. "Looks like it was cut by the cable on the lower half, then stretched and bent until it fractured off above," Chaplin noted for the record. He hovered the XMS ten feet away from the open end of the hull and recorded video as he looked around inside. "We can see torpedoes in their hangers. You might be able to loop around one of those. We'd never be able to do it, though. You'll need one of those robotic machines the oil platform folks use to check out their wells."

Chaplin turned the microphone off and said to Tanner, "Let's see if we can roll this thing downhill." He advanced the XMS until it hovered three feet above the ragged metal "Grab it, buddy," he said.

Tanner turned the claw until it was in position to get a good grab on the hull, then clamped and locked it on the protruding rim. "I've got a good grab. Let's lift it up," he said.

Chaplin adjusted buoyancy to give as much lift as possible, then turned the XMS so it was parallel to the fracture plane. He reversed the engines and gave them maximal thrust, trying to roll the bow out of the depression.

The JPC's bow didn't budge an inch. Chaplin drove it in the other direction, trying to get a wobble started. It didn't move. He tried several more times, but the depression was too deep and the bow fragment was too heavy.

"Getting hot in here," Chaplin remarked. "I think it's time to leave."

It was only then that Tanner noticed the bead of sweat running down from his forehead. "How hot is it?" he asked.

"A hundred degrees Fahrenheit and rising. Let go of the rim. We need to get the hell out of here. No AC on this worthless piece of junk."

"We'll have to tell that to the designers. Should be easy to fix," Tanner said, releasing the claw. " 'Course, the number of instances where we have to work around undersea volcanoes might be pretty small."

They backed away and headed up.

Russell Wilkes would have noticed it all and put it together, but neither he nor Susan was present. Both Tanner and Chaplin missed the shimmering of the superheated water surrounding them. They also failed to notice that the depression in which the JPC's bow lay was a recently-formed volcanic crater.

1:10 p.m., Tripler Medical Centeer, Oahu

The medevac chopper circled the rooftop landing zone, then slowly descended until its wheels touched ground. The pilot cut power. Before the blades had stopped rotating, the corpsmen had opened the doors and were transferring the injured occupant's stretcher to a hospital gurney, along with his IV.

Farriott's leg was splinted and wrapped in a blood-soaked dressing. His face was white and his eyes were closed. His grimaces gave testimony to his pain with the movements required to transfer him from the chopper to the gurney, but he displayed no other indication that he was aware of his surroundings or what was happening to him.

In the elevator to the ICU, the hospital corpsman attached an oxygen monitor to his thumb and noted down his rapid pulse and low blood pressure on the air-evac card that was his medical record until he could be admitted to the hospital and enter into the computerized medical records system.

The elevator opened and the orderlies pushed the gurney out of the elevator and into the ICU. There, a team of doctors and nurses surrounded Farriott and worked on him. "He's in shock, one of the doctors said. Type and cross him for three units stat." He increased the IV drip in the meantime and began a systematic evaluation beginning with his airway, making sure his breathing was not encumbered, then listening to his heart and checking the pulse oximeter to make sure he was getting enough oxygen. The doctor then examined him from head to toe, removing the dressings around the wound on his inner thigh. He put on sterile gloves and probed the wound with his index finger. His patient groaned in response, but the doctor probed until he was satisfied. "Femur fracture," he said. "Seems to be clean. Did they give him antibiotics on the ship?"

"Affirmative. IV cephalosporin," said the corpsman after checking the evac card.

"Good. He's not stable enough for surgery yet, and there's no need to rush to the OR since he's had antibiotics. Let's get him stable, then plan on the orthopedic surgeons doing surgery sometime tomorrow afternoon."

They drew blood for electrolytes, complete blood count, clotting studies, and a metabolic array, then moved him to a bed, where they hooked up an EKG monitor and attached the pulse oximeter. Twenty minutes later, the first unit of blood was hung.

The doctor in charge of his care whistled under his breath when he saw Daniel's hematocrit. "We better type and cross him for three more units. He's lost a ton of blood. I think he's going to need all six before we get him stable."

"Somebody get hold of his next of kin," the doctor ordered. "Just tell his wife he's here and she needs to come in."

An hour later, Ellen Farriott buzzed the door of the ICU. One of the nurses unlocked the door and showed her where Daniel lay. Daniel was asleep, his face ashen, with two IV tubes running, including one carrying blood. A urinary catheter ran from under the sheets to a bag hung on the side of the bed. "He's heavily sedated and he's lost a lot of blood," a nurse told her. "We don't expect him to respond much for a couple of days. Believe it or not, he's a lot more stable than he was a couple of hours ago."

"Can I sit down?" Ellen asked, her voice shaky and her eyes wet.

"Sure. Have a seat here," the nurse said, pointing to one of the chairs. "I'll get the doctor. He can tell you more." The nurse stayed until Ellen was safely seated, then exited.

A moment later, a young man in a white coat entered. "I'm Doctor Fitzgerald," he said. "Is this your husband?"

"Yes. I'm Ellen. Ellen Farriott."

"Hi. Your husband's been through a lot. He sustained an open femoral fracture and lost a lot of blood. He was resuscitated, as well as possible out at sea, then air-evaced here. We've been replacing blood and stabilizing him."

"I'm sorry," she answered. "I don't understand some of the terms you used. What exactly is an 'open femoral fracture?' "

"Sorry. The femur is the thigh bone. It's broken, and the bone fragment pushed through the skin. That's what we mean by an 'open' fracture."

"Is he conscious? Will he wake up?"

"We think so. We're keeping him sedated. Otherwise, he would be in a lot of pain. Plus, he was in shock when he got here. That sometimes leads to a short-term delirium. He won't be much company, I'm afraid, until a few days from now."

"How are you going to treat the thigh bone fracture?"

"The orthopedic surgeons will operate on it when he's more stable. Usually, they put what they call an 'intramedullary nail' in it. It's a metal rod that runs down the middle of the bone. The rod has holes in it. They can put screws through those holes to hold it in the bone.

"I see. Is he going to be all right?"

"It's still touch and go, but barring complications, I think he will."

"Thank you. When can I talk to the surgeons?"

"They'll have a counselling session with you just before surgery. You'll have to approve the surgery, as his next of kin. I assume you have power of attorney?"

"Of course. I'm a Navy wife."

"We'll call you. I would guess that the soonest they can do surgery would be late tomorrow afternoon. Frankly, he's lucky to be alive right now. He's been through a lot, and we want him to be strong again before we take him into the OR."

"Thanks for taking care of him."

"It's my job," Doctor Fitzgerald answered. Now, if there are no more questions, I have other patients to see."

"I'm sure I'll have more later, but that's about all the information I can handle right now. Thank you very much," she said.

After he left, Ellen took Daniel's hand, which was cold and unresponsive. She sat for a half-hour, then arose.

"I need to take care of the kids," she said to the nurse.

"Sure. I didn't tell you before, but what happened to your husband is classified. You can't tell your kids what happened to him. Not yet. You can tell them he's injured, but not how he sustained his injury."

Ellen's face took on a disgusted look. "I know," she said. "I've been sworn to secrecy for a long time."

5:20 p.m., Foster Village Subdivision, Honolulu

Ellen first intended to tell the kids, but then decided not to. They would want to see their dad, she reasoned. But they couldn't. Not in the ICU. They'd be horrified if they saw him like that. They'd just have sleepless nights and be miserable. It would be better if she waited until he was over his surgery and out of the ICU. Then, she'd tell them and they'd all go together and bring him balloons and flowers, and he'd be able to talk to them and laugh with them. It would be a happy time, not a scary time. Tomorrow, that was the time to tell them. Not tonight.

She'd bought a roasted chicken from the local grocery, added a few fresh vegetables she knew they'd eat, and heated up some leftover rice. A nutritious and delicious dinner, with very little prep time. And to top it all off, ice cream and sliced strawberries for dessert.

While she rinsed the dishes for the dishwasher, she wondered about Marisa. No one had said anything about Mike. She found that strange and decided to call her up. When Marisa picked up the phone, Ellen said, "Just wondering about our guys. Have you heard anything?"

"Not a thing," Marisa answered. "I'm starting to get worried. We should have heard something by now."

Something terrible must have happened to Mike, Ellen thought. *But I don't want to be the one to tell her. Besides, I don't know anything about him.* "Right. It's frustrating not knowing anything," she said.

"Well, I'll let you know if I hear something," Marisa said.

"Okay. Do good." She hung up and wondered if Marisa would notice that she hadn't reciprocated her promise. She didn't want to lie.

She then thought about Victor. Should she call off tomorrow's consultation? She decided not to.

Daniel's plight made it even more imperative that she break it off with Victor. She'd planned to do it for a long time. She was ready. She'd sign the surgical forms for Daniel in the morning, see Victor one last time, get it done, and then she could return to the hospital with a clear conscience.

Chapter 20

14 February 2020

10:50 a.m., Tripler Medical Centeer, Oahu

Marisa was on a coffee break when the other receptionist delivered a message to her. It said, simply, "Call the ICU. Ask for Tammy." A number followed.

"Do you have any idea what this is all about?" she asked.

"She wouldn't say. Said it's private," the other receptionist said.

Marisa called the number and asked for Tammy. A moment later, she came on the line.

"This is Tammy. Is this Mrs. Polanski?" Tammy asked.

"Yes, it is," Marisa answered.

"Your husband was admitted here. He's in bed 954."

Marisa felt cold sweat break out on her forehead. "How is he? Why's he here?" she asked.

"He's conscious. Stable. We shouldn't talk over the phone, though. I think it's better if you come up and see him. We can talk then."

"I'll be right up." She hung up and turned to the other receptionist. "My husband's in the ICU. I need to go see him. Can you cover?"

"Sure. How is he?"

"I don't know. The nurse wouldn't say. I have to go."

"Take all the time you need. I'll handle the clinic."

"Thanks. I owe you one."

When she got to the ICU, she pressed the door opener on the wall and charged over to the nurse's station. "I'm Mrs. Polanski. My husband is here. Tammy just called me. Can you get her?"

"I'm Tammy," the nurse said. "Let's go into the counseling room. No one's there right now, and we can talk in private."

She led the way out of the ICU, opened the door to the counseling room, and closed it again after Marisa had entered. After they'd seated themselves, she said, "I'm a nurse-practitioner here, and I'll be coordinating your husband's care. Dr. George, the ICU Director, asked me to brief you on your husband's case. What I'm going to tell you is classified. Please keep it to yourself. You can tell your kids your husband was injured, but not how the injury occurred. Just tell them there was an accident and you aren't privy to the details. Okay?"

"Okay. Just tell me whether he's okay."

"He escaped from a submarine that was very deep in the ocean. He has a case of the bends. Initially, he was unconscious. Pure oxygen revived him, but then he was found to have no control over his arms and legs. He was treated on-site in a decompression chamber and his condition improved a lot. He's now awake, but he has some residual paralysis. It affects his left arm and leg. He can't feel or move his left hand. His left leg has spotty sensation loss and some muscle power loss. It looks very much like he had a stroke, but it's due to nitrogen bubbles that formed in his brain, not to interference with the brain's blood supply."

"Will he recover?"

"We think so. But we don't know how complete his recovery will be. He's getting an MRI of his brain late this afternoon. We'll know more after the results of that are back, including whether he needs more treatment in a decompression chamber."

"Can I see him?"

"Yes. I'll take you to him. I'll also give you a list of the doctors who are taking care of him. They'll know more about his condition and prognosis than I do. You should ask them when they're available. but be careful what you tell them. They may not be fully briefed on the classified material. They'll be able to tell you if he needs any further decompression treatment by tomorrow morning." She stood and said, "Follow me."

Tammy led Marisa to bed 954 and opened the door for her. "I'll get the list of doctors for you," she said, then left.

Marisa entered and burst into tears when she saw Mike lying there, an IV dripping into his vein, and monitors beeping with his heartbeat and recording his breathing. She sighed, sat beside the bed and took his right hand in hers.

He was asleep but awakened with her touch. "Hey, Babe," he said.

She noticed that his smile was a little crooked, only half his face moving. "Mike, what the hell happened?"

"The JPC sank. Broke in half while it was being lifted up. Everybody's alive, though. Farriott's got a busted leg. The others escaped before the breakup."

"What happened to you?

"I got caught in the escape chamber. Had to wait until the pressure equalized before I could open the door. When it finally opened, I was a good six or seven hundred feet deep. I went up as quickly as I could, and I think I took that last hundred feet too quickly. I blacked out before I hit the surface and woke up in the decompression chamber of a mini-sub we were using."

"Tammy tells me they're going to do an MRI on you this afternoon."

"Right. They want to see if there are any bubbles left in my brain."

"Bubbles?"

"Yeah. That's what causes the bends. Nitrogen dissolves in the blood stream at depth. When you rise to the surface, your blood bubbles like a beer when you pop the bottle cap. Once formed, the bubbles can expand to ten or twenty times their original size and screw up all sorts of things. If they're in the brain, they can kill you or cause paralysis. Anyway, if they see bubbles on the MRI, they may want to squeeze them down in a decompression chamber again."

She wiped the tears off her face with her hand, having no purse with her, and sighed. "I'm just glad you're alive."

"Me, too. My left arm and leg are screwed up, though. I don't know if I can ever climb ladders again."

"We'll see. If you can't, I'm sure you'll find something else to do."

"It's kind of nice having a numb leg," he said. "My big toe got smashed. Hurt like a son of a bitch coming up, but now it doesn't hurt at all."

Marisa left him a half-hour later, when he went for the MRI. On the way out, Tammy caught her. "Do you know Mrs. Farriott?" Tammy asked.

"Yes. We're friends."

"Her husband's here, too. He's going to surgery this afternoon. We've been looking for her, but we can't seem to find her. Her phone just takes messages."

She's with her boyfriend flashed through Marisa's mind, but she just said, "Maybe her phone's in her purse, where she can't hear it. Keep trying. I'm sure she'll be happy to know her husband's here. She's been really worried about him."

"Oh, she knows he's here," Tammy said. "She saw him yesterday and signed forms this morning."

"Really? She didn't tell me," Marisa said. *So that's what that call was about last night. She knew, but she didn't tell me. Wanted someone else to do the dirty work, I guess.*

11:03 a.m., Pacific Ocean, one quarter mile southeast of Loihi Seamount

Admiral Kennedy fumed in his wardroom. He'd taken a break from the bridge after talking to the Pentagon and issuing the requisite orders. It was out of his hands now. They'd failed, pure and simple. They didn't have the proper equipment to bring the JPC up, and the Pentagon had vetoed the idea of trying to roll the JPC's nose downhill with jury-rigged equipment. They'd opted to think it over, then come back another day with a better plan and the right salvage gear to pull it off.

They also had discounted the possibility that weapons could blow, causing a tsunami. In that, Kennedy had agreed and made his opinion loud and clear with his superiors at the Pentagon. He wondered about Green. How could a Rear Admiral, who should have been raised to think logically, have been seduced into believing in such a fantasy?

The two winch vessels had just been separated and, as soon as the beams holding them together were stowed, they would be heading back to Pearl Harbor. Kennedy was in the lead vessel and was anxious to leave.

Admiral Green had choppered back to Pearl Harbor the day before. Kennedy was glad to see him go. Green was a nuisance, in his mind, someone who worked against him for the whole damned salvage operation. That Green had been right all along didn't redeem him in Kennedy's mind.

He wasn't going to be the fall guy. A screw-up like this could end a career, and he wanted at least one more star on each shoulder, hopefully two. Green was going to take his share of the blame. Kennedy was adamant about that. If he went down, he'd take Green with him. That was only fair.

As he paced in his wardroom, he talked out loud to himself. The doors were closed, and no one would hear, so he let it all hang out, including a string of profanity directed at the stupid winch team that had forced him to give the orders that cut the JPC in half. The commander of that ship would take his share of the crap. The commander of the JPC, Farriott, he'd get him too. Imagine being so dumb that you ran your submarine into a floating dock? Jesus, he thought, is no one in this man's Navy competent anymore?

All right, he conceded, it's not "this man's Navy" anymore. It's "this man and woman and whatever's Navy." That's part of the problem. When real men ran things, there weren't all these screw-ups.

He pulled off his uniform and lay on his bunk in his skivvies. He thought of more pleasant times, mistresses he'd had, nights spent in foreign ports, where the prudish rules that enslave America weren't operative. Of course, you had to be discreet these days, even when you were thousands of miles from home. He enjoyed getting laid, but he didn't want to lose his career for it.

He felt and heard the ship get underway. The rocking of the ship and the steady up and down movements as they plowed through the waves were soothing for him.

He began to relax, finally coming down from the adrenalin rush he'd been on for the entire mission. He took his pulse, and it was still high, over eighty. He took a couple deep, slow breaths and concentrated on calming himself. He took his pulse a moment later and it was down in the seventies. Still not normal, but getting there. He began to doze.

He later described it as a slap from the hand of God. He was dozing in his bunk one moment, and in the next moment, he lay in a heap on the floor. It was as if the entire ship had been lifted a yard and then dropped back down. The emergency sirens began wailing, He jumped to his feet, pulled on his clothes and charged to the bridge.

"What the hell was that?" he yelled when he got there. "Did we hit something?"

"No sir. We didn't hit anything. I think we were blasted with an explosion," the Officer on Deck (OOD) told him. "We're doing damage assessment now. We've got some leaks, and we don't know how severe they are yet. There's some damage to our drive train, too. The propellers are vibrating, and we don't know why."

The intercom rang, and the OOD answered it. He listened, then handed the phone to Admiral Kennedy. "You need to hear this, sir," he said.

"Kennedy. What's up?" the admiral said into the speaker.

"Admiral, this is Lieutenant Handy. I'm in the engine room. We're leaking like a sieve, in multiple locations. A lot of the rivets holding our hull plating together have ruptured. Our folks can't fix them. Both drive axles are bent and shaking their housings. Water is pulling in through the axle housings. In my view, they're not stable and going to shake both drive trains to death if we maintain speed."

"How much water's coming through?" Kennedy asked.

"The lower level's flooded already. At least ten feet of water. Pumps won't do anything against this. We're sinking, sir."

Kennedy was taken aback. He couldn't believe what he was hearing. Losing the JPC was bad enough. But to lose this ship, too, only a day and a half later? It was unthinkable. "Do your best to stop the leak and get the crew out of there safely. Then report to the bridge, Lieutenant," he said.

He turned to the OOD. "I'll need to have confirmation before I can issue an order to abandon ship. Besides, that's the Captain's prerogative. Where's the Captain?"

"Over there, sir," the OOD answered, pointing to starboard. "He was thrown against the bulkhead when the ship jumped. I think he's dead. Maybe a broken neck or a skull fracture. We haven't had a chance to check him out."

Kennedy went to the body lying on the floor. Open eyes stared up at him. The man's face was gray and Kennedy could see no breathing. He felt for a carotid pulse and felt nothing. "He's gone," he said, straightening up.

He noticed the tilt of the deck and its level relative to the sea. Waves were already breaking over her bow. That gave him whatever confirmation he still needed.

"Give the order to abandon ship," he said. As an afterthought, he asked, "Anyone contact your sister ship?"

"Sinking, sir, just like us but faster. They called a Mayday in before we even got a crew down to evaluate our situation. I expect they're all in life rafts by now."

"Very good. Let's get those lifeboats out. You've been through the drill. This one's for keeps, so I hope y'all remember the procedure."

"We do, sir. We've already begun." A moment later, he added, "Sir, there are men drowned below. A half-dozen men are unaccounted for, and two or three floating bodies have been confirmed."

"The floaters can wait. Get the live ones out of there first. Then, if there's time, we can take care of the floaters.

Thirty minutes later, he watched the nose of the ship disappear into the sea. Seventeen men were still unaccounted for. The rest were in lifeboats watching the unthinkable happen.

No one in the lifeboats noted the slight rise in sea level. After all, it was only a few inches high, hidden in the surface chop.

Chapter 21

14 February 2020

11:21 a.m., Pacific Ocean, above Loihi Seamount

The sister ship was still on site when the JPC's bow exploded. Within milliseconds, all the munitions on board the JPC exploded. The ship above was thrown upward ten feet and fell back into the ocean with a ruptured hull. Half the crew died during the next few minutes. A few were lucky enough to board life boats. The rest jumped into the sea.

The men in lifeboats picked up as many of their comrades as possible, but then something horrifying happened. Deep in the ocean, the explosion had created a huge bubble of superheated water turned gaseous despite the enormous pressure at depth. As this bubble rose, it expanded and fragmented, dispersing its heat to the cooler water around it. This hot water also then rose toward the surface. By the time the bubble rose a thousand feet, it was no longer gaseous, but its energy had created a huge mass of water, heated near the boiling point, that rose slowly to the surface. When it hit the surface, the men still floating in the water didn't have a chance.

Down below, the lava flowed. The explosion had blown the top off Loihi and released Pele's fury. Lava poured out of the caldera, half of its side blown away, and shot out of the vents, flowing down on the slopes below, where the shattered remains of the back half of the JPC lay. Within the next two hours, the JPC's remains were covered and melted by a hundred thousand cubic yards of lava.

The bow of the JPC, of course, had vaporized with the explosion.

The shock wave from the explosion of the JPC traveled at the speed of sound in water, nearly fifteen hundred meters per second, and impacted upon the Kilauea undersea lava field twenty-two miles away in less than twenty-six seconds. It imparted pressure of one - hundred-eighty-one foot-pounds of force per square inch to the Kilauea lava field, about eighteen times the pressure needed to shatter a normal window. The impact shook loose the surface gravel and sand, which began to slip downhill. The lava shelf above, now cantilevered above the ocean, broke loose and thundered into the ocean. The material from above, now a mix of black sand and the shattered lava shelf, impacted upon that below, resulting in a massive downhill slide of sand and rock. This solid material, in turn, displaced water, causing a series of waves to form. These waves moved outward at a rate dependent upon the depth of water, but averaging a little over six hundred fifty feet per second. They circled around South Point and headed northward toward Kailua-Kona and westward toward Honolulu, where the first wave would arrive twenty-eight minutes later.

The tsunami sirens began seven minutes after the landslide was recorded on the seismometers–fast, but not fast enough. Very few people had enough warning to evacuate. Most of those who did hear the sirens weren't in a rush. They were used to having sirens sound a warning hours, not minutes, before the possible tsunami. Some turned on the TV or radio immediately, and the emergency warning network saved their lives. Most weren't as lucky

Unlike normal surface waves, these waves had a peak-to-trough breadth of more than a mile, not just thirty or forty feet. In the deep ocean, the waves were barely perceptible as the water tended to move back and forth and not up and down. As the water neared shore, however, the ocean bottom slowed the progress of the leading edge of the first wave, so that the water behind it was forced on top of the slower moving bottom water. By the time the first wave hit shore, the wall of water was fifty-five to eighty feet high, a mile in breadth, and many miles wide. It hit the eastern coast of Oahu first and only minutes later, it hit the southern coast, where Waikiki Beach lies and the population is most dense.

Some of the tourists on the beach at Waikiki saw the water recede, heard the sirens, and put two and two together. The ones who survived ran up Diamond Head Road or to the upper floors of sturdy hotels. The rest were caught in the wave that tore across Waikiki and proceeded more than a mile inland, well past the Ala Wai canal, before the water began to recede. Then the water reversed direction, flowing outward into the face of the next wave and lifting that wave even higher than the first had been. A few people were lucky. The water carried them inland without crashing them against anything, then deposited them on a roof or high in a tree when it receded. Most were not that lucky.

Some of the sturdier hotels in Waikiki held up to the mass of water buffeting them. Others, with a flimsier structure, did not. Most of those within these hotels perished. None of the private homes along the coast survived. They were torn to shreds, unrecognizable flotsam littering a wild sea. What was left of Kalanianaole Highway after the water finally receded was covered with uprooted trees and the roofs, walls, furniture, and appliances of expensive homes. Their occupants were strewn about like collateral damage in a war zone.

The ocean-side houses and condominiums of Kahala, Aina Haina, and Hawaii Kai were converted to a slurry of floating wreckage in Maunalua Bay. Ewa Beach ceased to exist.

On the leeward coast, the waves were not as high, but that didn't keep Waianae, Makaha, and Nanakuli from being destroyed.

11:22 a.m., Kilauea Volcano Observatory, Big Island of Hawaii

Russell was in his office when he felt a slight tremor. It was just a momentary shake. His secretary came in a minute later. "Something big is going on," she said. "You need to look at the seismographs."

He took one look and knew exactly what had happened. "There's been an explosion. It's got to be from Loihi," he said. What he saw next terrified him. "My god. It's triggered a landslide at Kilauea. We need to get the coastlines evacuated. There's going to be a tsunami. Call civil defense and let them know what's happening."

Susan, he thought. *I've got to warn Susan.* He pulled out his cellular and dialed her number. His anxiety rose as her phone rang over and over. He was about to hang up when she answered.

"Thank God I got you. Get to high ground. You have twenty minutes or so. Don't waste any time. A tsunami's going to hit you. Get in your car now and go before the traffic blocks up."

"I didn't drive. I rode my bicycle. I'm at the ocean-side facility, where the *Hululua*'s kept."

"Then either grab a ride with someone or pedal like hell out of there. Get to high ground. The higher, the better."

"I have to warn the others."

"Leave now. You don't have time," he answered. "I have to go now. I've got civil defense on the line. You have about one minute before the sirens go off. Then, there'll be a stampede. I don't want you caught in it."

"Okay. I have to warn my colleagues, though. Then I'll go."

"Please hurry. I don't know them, but I love you. It's you I care about."

"You too. Thanks for the warning." She hung up.

His secretary put a phone to the Civil Defense in his hand. "This is Russell Wilkes, volcanologist at the Hawaii Observatory," he said. "We've detected an explosion at Loihi, the undersea volcano off the Big Island. This has triggered a massive undersea landslide at Kilauea. A tsunami is going to hit Oahu in about twenty minutes. You need to warn people. Those near the shore are going to die. It's too late for the other islands. Hilo and Kona have less than five minutes. But Oahu and Kauai have a little time, maybe twenty minutes. You need to put out a bulletin immediately."

"I don't have the authority to do that," the voice on the other end of the line said.

"Do you have the authority to drown thousands of people, because if you don't get that bulletin out now, that's what you're going to do. Now do your fucking job. I'm not kidding around."

"Profanity won't help, sir. I'll contact the director. He'll probably be calling you soon. I hope you'll treat him with more respect."

"Just issue the damned bulletin and start the tsunami sirens, you incompetent ass," he said. He hung up.

He looked back at the seismographs. A new pattern was emerging. He shook his head from side to side. "They've awakened Madame Pele," he said, speaking to no one in particular. "Loihi was already erupting, but now lava's flowing like water out of a faucet. We've done what we can. Nothing much we can do now but wait to see what happens."

He knew the tsunami was coming, but he couldn't tell how high it would be. A thousand feet? If so, ninety percent of the people in the islands were going to die. He prayed it would be smaller, a lot smaller.

11:25 a.m., UH Oceanside Laboratory, Honolulu

Back on Oahu, Susan ran through the offices, opening doors and yelling, "Earthquake and landslide on the Big Island. There's a tsunami coming. Get to high ground now." She knew everyone heard her. Only a few started running, though. No matter. She'd done what she could to save them. She ran, too, reaching her bike a moment later.

On the level, she could do twenty miles an hour, but not going uphill. She'd make it to the foothills, but she wondered how high she'd be before the wall of water swept over. *I'll have to avoid valleys,* she thought. Valleys would funnel the tsunami and magnify it. Better to head for a promontory. She headed toward Round Top. It was steep. She'd have to use all her biking skills and strength to get high enough, but she had a chance there, unless the tsunami was a thousand feet high, as it might be. But if it were that high, no one on Oahu would survive.

She pedaled as though her life depended on it, which it did. She weaved in and out of traffic, dodging turning cars, taking chances that she would never otherwise take.

She was a mile inland before the tsunami sirens finally wailed. *The next few minutes will be gridlock at the shore*, she thought. She hoped her colleagues had taken her advice. If so, they might have a chance.

She considered riding up to Punchbowl but decided against it. She could get higher, faster, on Round Top, and she knew the way better, since she lived in that neighborhood.

She didn't encounter a traffic jam until she was on Wilder Avenue. Cars were stalled there. No one was moving.

They're all going to drown, she thought.

11:27 a.m., COMSUBPAC, Bldg. 619, Pearl Harbor

Admiral Green had early warning, even before the sirens sounded. He made a quick assessment. The Navy had protocols for dealing with tsunamis. Ships and boats that were able would leave Pearl Harbor. Those that couldn't leave would be at the mercy of the wave.

COMPACFLT Headquarters was in the flood zone. At Green's urging, the Commander-in-Chief ordered an immediate evacuation. Most personnel were able to make it to higher ground before the waves hit. Green was not one of them. He had to help organize the evacuation of others and the security of documents and computers. He did what he could then, at the last minute, ran into the Communications Building two hundred yards away. He ran up the stairs to the top floor of the windowless building. It was strong, with three-foot-thick concrete walls and a solid roof to eliminate eavesdropping and ensure military secrecy. He guessed it might survive the waves. Several others who had chosen the same course of action waited together for the impact. They didn't have long to wait.

When it hit, a sudden increase of pressure popped Green's ears as the water blew through the doors and poured into the building. The lights went out as the water forced itself up the stairway and began to flow over the second floor. Green found himself in pitch blackness, in a knee-deep current that pushed him backward against a wall. He felt a sharp pain in his leg as it encountered the edge of a desk. He flailed in the water with his remaining good leg. He collided with and grabbed hold of a support column, hanging on for dear life as water flowed inward and then receded. Desks tumbled in the escaping water, crashing into other desks and into people flailing in the current. Everything not attached was carried toward the stairs. People who were dragged down the stairs were carried out of the building into the flood.

When the second wave came, there was little left to destroy, but the rubble caught several of those still hanging on in the blackness. They became part of the debris, human flotsam in the flood.

The third wave was much smaller than the second, but it still flooded the first floor. When that wave receded, he and the rest of the survivors waited another half hour before trying to exit the building. Green stumbled through the wreckage in the dark, lit only by the faint glow of light emanating from the double doors at the bottom of the stairs. He fought his way through the rubble on the stairs and emerged through the gaping hole left by the destroyed doors.

He blinked in the glare of sunlight. It took a moment before his eyes adjusted enough that he could appreciate the utter devastation around him. The submarine base was completely destroyed. The two-hundred-foot water tower, where submariners practiced escapes from the depths, was broken off at its base and reduced to a pile of bricks. A destroyer caught in the flood lay on its side in the middle of what had been Nimitz Highway. A submarine rested on its side against the cliff on the in-shore side of the road, its crew now crawling out of its exit port.

Overturned cars were everywhere, many of them still occupied with drowned people. Human bodies, all ages and both sexes, littered the landscape.

He knelt by the side of the road and cried, overcome with the enormity of the devastation. Then, he composed himself and stood up, gasping from the pain in his bruised leg. "Where do we start with this mess?" he said out loud to himself.

Cries for help surrounded him, and he responded automatically. He had no training as a medic, but he knew enough to splint broken bones and put pressure on bleeding open wounds. He limped from one injured person to the next before he recognized that the work was beyond his capabilities. He needed help. He began to organize other uninjured people, particularly the crews of the wrecked submarine and the destroyer that blocked the road.

They gave basic first aid, then pulled injured people and dead bodies off the road. Cleared roads would be necessary. Not all the vehicles on Oahu were destroyed, he reasoned. At some point, these injured people would need to be transported to some place where they could get medical care.

He worked for hours in his immediate vicinity, handling the problem that was before his nose, but increasingly conscious that the solution to this problem was not individual activity but organization. He had to do what he could to organize the crisis response. He realized he didn't know where to go or who to contact. All he knew was that somewhere inland, there had to be something intact. He decided to walk until he found it. Then he could begin the process of rebuilding.

He began walking inland on Puuloa Road, heading toward Tripler Medical Centeer. A massive structure initially built to withstand Japanese bombings during the Second World War, the hospital was high on a hill. A landmark visible from most of Oahu, Tripler was nicknamed "The Pink Palace" because of its coral color. It was closer than Camp Smith, the other military facility high on a hill. He was sure that both facilities would be centers for the organization of relief, but the immediate focus had to be on providing first aid. His skills would be well-used there.

11:28 a.m., Kailua, Island of Oahu

Ellen heard the sirens and ignored them. She'd seen Daniel early in the morning, after dropping off the kids. He was still moribund when she left. From there, she'd driven to Victor's to tell him their affair was over. She'd finally acquired the strength and will to end it, and she'd told him so. Then, he'd smiled and asked, "One more time, just in farewell? A good-bye kiss, so to speak?"

She didn't have the heart to say no, and so she now lay naked beside him, in post-coital bliss, not wanting to leave, but knowing that she must. She had another life to live, another man to love, two children to raise, and the affection she shared with this man threatened everyone else she cared so much about. It threatened her own life, too. Her honor, her place in society, her opinion of herself. And still, she wanted to prolong this bliss one more minute, or two, or three.

It was like an addiction. Wrong. It *was* an addiction, just as self-defeating as alcoholism or heroin. She recognized what it was, she knew it had to stop, and yet she'd just succumbed to "one more for the road."

Already in emotional turmoil from her breakup with Victor, the sirens she heard were an irritant and not a source of concern. She felt no rush to do anything. The kids were at school, well away from the tsunami flood zones. She and Victor were a couple of miles inland, and Kailua's residents had never had significant worries about tsunamis. No tsunami had ever hit Kailua, and there was no reason to think that one ever would. But the sirens had broken the romantic spell. She sat up in bed, shrugged at Victor, kissed him one last time, and said, "I'm sorry. I really am. But I can't do this any longer. I'm ashamed."

"I'm a big boy," he said. "I'll miss you, of course. But I'll survive."

"The damned tsunami sirens are going off again. I'd better leave. I need to pick up my kids in an hour and a half, and now traffic will be a mess."

"It's probably just another false alarm. They get everyone excited, then the tsunami hits and it's one foot high. I wish those folks would get their act together. You're right, though. Some people will get excited. Twenty minutes from now, it might be hard to get out of Kailua, much less over the Pali."

She went to the bathroom to freshen up. When she returned, she leaned down, kissed him on the forehead, then retrieved her panties and bra and put them on.

"Would you please close the lanai door before you leave?" he asked. "Something is making a terrible racket out there."

"I'll see what's going on," she said and stepped out on the lanai, pulling her open blouse around her. There was, indeed, a terrible racket, and it seemed to surround her. She heard screaming and a thundering noise that sounded like surf but was louder and more constant. *What the hell is happening*, she thought. Then she saw the palm trees of Lanikai swaying and disappearing, and the roof of a house disappearing into a wall of water.

"Victor, come quick," she said, the words catching in her throat as she finally saw the enormous wave that was barreling toward them. *Thank God, we're above it*, she thought, but then the wave hit their building and the water splashed upward and knocked her off her feet. It flowed into the apartment, two feet deep. The flow first pulled her into the apartment, then as it receded, it dragged her outward again, toward the lanai. She tried to grab at the sofa, but it too was floating toward the lanai. With horror, she saw it hit the lanai rail and tear it away. A moment later, she was falling and then underwater, flailing in a powerful current that pulled her inland. She was already a quarter mile away when Victor's apartment building collapsed into the maelstrom, burying Victor in the rubble of the building he had himself designed.

11:28 a.m., Tripler Medical Centeer, Oahu

Marisa Polanski was still at Tripler with Mike when the sirens began. During the next few minutes, chaos reigned. Tammy came in and told them, "We're going to be hit by a tsunami very soon. We're preparing for mass casualties, and we'll need to move you out of intensive care in order to free up the room for those who are worse off. Please gather any personal items. We'll move you during the next five minutes or so."

"Shit. It's the JPC," said Mike after she left. "It's blown up and started a landslide."

"I've got to get the kids," Marisa said. She started to get her things together

"Too late. We have less than a half hour before the tsunami hits. You won't even get to their schools.

Stay here. They'll need you alive afterward, particularly with me being crippled up like this."

"We can't just leave them."

"Call them on their phones. Tell them to climb to the top floor and stay away from windows. That's the best you can do. Their schools are pretty far inland. The tsunami won't get to them unless it's huge."

She dialed Missy first. Finally, she picked up.

"Thank God I got you," Marisa said. "There's a tsunami coming in less than half an hour. You need to get up as high as you can and stay away from windows and doors."

"Mom, we've already moved up to the top floor. The school has us all gathered together. They're telling us what to expect right now. I need to listen. Are you okay?"

"I'm at Tripler with Dad. We love you. We'll call again after it's over."

"Love you, too. Say hi to Dad. Bye."

She dialed Rudy next, but got a busy signal. She tried several times but couldn't reach him. "The lines are all jammed up," she told Mike.

Tammy came in with an orderly and moved them to a room on another floor. "They'll take good care of you here. I'll check on you when I get a chance, but I think we're going to be very busy for the next few hours. Maybe for the next few days."

"I can help," said Marisa. "I work in the dental clinic, and I know a lot about crowd control and organization."

"We may need you. I'll let my supervisors know you're here. Right now, let's just get your husband situated." She plugged Mike's bed into the wall socket, then left. Another nurse plugged his monitors in, then checked his IV.

After the nurses left, Marisa sat down but couldn't bear the inaction. She thanked God that her children attended Catholic Schools that were further inland than the schools they would have gone to otherwise. She tried calling Rudy again, but still couldn't get through.

"It drives me nuts that I can't talk to Rudy," she said. "What if something happens? I want him to know we love him. I want to hear his voice again, too."

"Nothing we can do about it," Mike said. "Except pray, maybe. You're better at that than I am. Seems to me that would be a good thing to do."

She knelt beside Mike's bed and prayed they would all be together again soon. When she closed her eyes, a flood of images flowed into her brain, the children at various ages, the discussions they'd had, Missy dancing and Rudy competing. The fun times they had as a family. She thought of their quarters and wondered if they were about to be homeless. She wished she'd had the chance to rescue some of their treasured items but then realized that they wouldn't make a difference. It was the people that were important, not the things. Her prayer was fervent, if undisciplined and incoherent. When it was done, she knew in her heart she had been heard.

She also knew that God didn't answer every prayer. She stood up. The outcome would be in His hands, not hers.

"I'm going to the roof. I have to see what's going on," she told Mike.

"Go. I'm fine," he replied.

She left him and took the elevator to the top floor, where the medical library was. From the rooftop lanai there, she could see half of the Southern shore of Oahu, from the Waianae Range to Diamond Head. The airport was closest to her, appearing just above Aliamanu Crater.

At first, she saw nothing. Then, the water off the airport began to recede, and the reef south of the runway was exposed. Water swirled out of Kewalo basin revealing the mudflats beneath. Slowly, the wave formed. It looked so small out in the ocean, except that it reached as far as she could see from side to side. As it came closer, it peaked and broke. Still, it looked small. There was nothing to give perspective until it broke over the runway.

One moment, the runway was there, and in the next, it was gone. The wave continued, hitting the airport terminal, which also disappeared. She became conscious of the sound then, the thunder of the surf, but eerily different than she had ever heard before, and then a cacophony of snapping as trees broke off at their trunks and disappeared under the water, and the screaming of people, a wailing that took the place of the destroyed tsunami sirens.

She watched as the water flooded the Ewa plain and curled around Aloha Stadium. It flowed over Moanalua Freeway. She watched cars disappear into it, some floating upside down into Moanalua Valley. To her left, the water flowed over Mapunapuna, utterly destroying the industrial district, and carrying masses of rubble with it. The clatter of colliding rubble added to the screams.

Toward downtown and Waikiki, she saw high-rises topple. It was too far away for her to see details, but she saw enough to know how devastating the tsunami was. From where she stood, she could not see her children's schools. Punchbowl Crater blocked her view. She could see the flood over downtown and Waikiki, but she couldn't tell how far it reached inland.

The water receded, dragging rubble out to sea, and a second wave formed, larger than the first. This one broke further out to sea due to the water rushing back into it, and its reach was not as great, though its height was greater. It ensured, however, that whatever the first wave had partially destroyed was churned into oblivion.

The impact of what she saw hit her, and when she thought of how many had surely died, she felt faint.

She dropped to her knees and vomited until she was retching on her empty stomach.

In a daze, she found her way back to Mike.

When she entered Mike's room, she saw his questioning look and shook her head. "Don't make me describe it," she said. "I can't talk about it. It's the worst thing I've ever seen."

She sat down beside him, and his good arm wrapped around her and pulled her toward him. She wept on his shoulder and said, "I pray to God our kids are okay."

11:37 a.m., Makiki district, Honolulu

Susan peddled with all her strength. She nearly collided with a car turning left into her path as she crossed Wilder Avenue, forcing her off the road and onto the sidewalk. She hit the grass and her wheel was twisted from her grasp. Tossed from the bike, she crashed on the sidewalk, scraping the skin off her right knee over a three-inch patch.

"Damn, that hurts," she said aloud as she ran back to her bike. She looked down and blood was flowing down her right leg. She ignored her leg, set the bike upright, twisted the handlebars back to almost straight, and began peddling again. She was at the base of Round Top when the sirens stopped and the roaring began. She knew the flood was coming, but she didn't dare stop to look behind her. She peddled furiously, now going uphill at a rate that seemed glacially slow to her.

Her already exhausted leg muscles cramped and she realized she wasn't going to make progress fast enough on the switchbacks that went up the hill. Of course, she had no idea how high she would have to go. According to Russell Wilkes, the wave could be anywhere up to a thousand feet in height. If it was, she knew, she was going to die.

Very soon, her leg muscles were so exhausted that even the switchbacks were too steep for her to peddle upward. She threw her bicycle down and started to run. Then she abandoned the winding road and began to climb.

It wasn't quite a cliff going upward. Some people had made terraces, and she ran through their backyards and then climbed upward to the next terrace, and then the next. She crossed the switchback road twice and felt she had climbed nearly a hundred feet before she gave it up. She found a place where no houses blocked her view and turned to face the incoming tide.

She watched as the wave toppled buildings, destroyed trees that had survived for hundreds of years, floated cars and trucks, and converted a thriving city to a floating pile of rubble. She watched as people ran down the streets trying to escape, only to be overcome by the wave that crashed over them.

Nothing seemed to stop or slow it. Its unrelenting course led straight to her, a miles-wide wall of water that seemed impossible to stop. She tried to estimate its height but realized that its velocity would carry the wave far uphill. She could only hope it didn't reach up to her. She was too exhausted to go any further upward

A hundred feet below her, she could see her bicycle, and she watched as the wave drowned it. The water reached the next switchback upward and the next but didn't go further. The water receded, taking houses and cars with it, flowing in a massive waterfall of rubble downhill.

She began to climb again, knowing that another wave would come and might be higher than the first. Scientist to the end, she counted the seconds until it came. From that, she could calculate the length of the wave and the volume of water it contained. By that time, she already knew the height of it. Not that it made a damn bit of difference, of course. It was what it was. It couldn't be prevented or mitigated. And she was what she was, an oceanographer, and so she buried her panic with science.

After the second wave, the subsequent waves rapidly declined in height. By the time of the fourth wave, the damage had been done. She started to walk home, but then realized that her home probably no longer existed.

Miraculously, she found her bicycle almost intact on the side of the road at the bottom switchback. There was no way she could ride it however. The roads were strewn with debris. Besides, her muscles were spent. They needed rest. She sat on a curb and rubbed them and pondered what to do next.

She thought of the phone in her pocket and wondered whether it would still work. She dialed Russell's number and put it to her ear. In a minute, she heard his voice.

"Susan, what happened. Are you all right?"

She cried, unable to speak, while he repeated the question again, then again.

He had repeated it four times before she was able to answer. "I'm alive, thanks to you. I just made it. Another five minutes and I would have been caught in it. God, it's awful. Everything's gone."

There was a pause on the line. Then he said, "You're not gone. That's most important to me."

She began to cry again. "All my colleagues, my friends..." She couldn't continue.

"Listen. I want to keep talking to you, but you need to conserve your battery. Chances are, you won't be able to charge it up for a long time. Call me tomorrow if you can, or if you need help. Look for a way to charge your phone. Communications are going to be important. Look for food, too. And fresh water. The problems are just beginning. Don't waste your time talking to me."

"I don't want to hang up. I need you."

"I know, but you'll need me tomorrow, too. Right now, you must take care of yourself. You're smart. Figure out what you're going to need and make sure you have it. Start now."

"I will. I'll call you tomorrow." She hung up. She thought it through. Food, water, shelter, and batteries. That's what I need. She went in search of these, heading for the remains of the nearest grocery store. *Then,* she thought, *I'll see whether my apartment is still standing.*

11:33 p.m., Makalapa Elementary School, Oahu

When the sirens went off, Steven Farriott didn't notice. He was inside a classroom, the windows were closed because the air conditioner was on, and he was actively day-dreaming, having listened to Mr. Chang drone on for far too long about the minutia of eighteenth-century America.

He did notice, though, when the principal came in and talked quietly to Mr. Chang, after which Mr. Chang announced that the class was over, school would be let out early today, and that the children should gather their things and be ready for pickup by their parents during the next ten or fifteen minutes.

The class then was marched in two lines to the loading circle, where parents' cars would usually line up in a long traffic jam, fill with kids, and drive away. This time was different, though. Their teachers accompanied each classroom's children and checked them off as they were picked up by their parents. The teachers didn't allow any of the children to walk home without their parents, as many would have done normally.

Roughly half the children had been loaded into vans, trucks, or sedans when the noise began. A dull roar seemed to come from all around them. The principal barked out an order and the teachers quickly herded the remaining children into the gymnasium, accompanied by all the school's teachers and staff and a few parents who abandoned their cars and ran in with their kids.

They waited there, each child staying with his teacher. Steven looked for Penny but couldn't find her.

The principal activated the PA system, and after a few squeaks from the amplifiers, her voice could be clearly heard. "Children, we've gathered you here because a tsunami, a tidal wave, is hitting Honolulu. This is the safest place for you to be right now. We will keep you informed of any new developments. In the meantime, stay with your teachers. They need to keep track of you so that we can reunite you with your families after this is all over."

Steven sat on the floor next to one of his friends, Larry Murdock. "This is pretty cool," he said. "I've seen tsunamis on TV and the movies, but I've never seen a real one before."

"Me, neither. It's kinda scary. Houses and things get smashed and people get killed. I hope my mom's okay."

"Where do you live?"

"On Radford. Not far away"

"We're a long way from the ocean," Steven said. "I live in Foster Village."

"That's right next to the school, right?"

"Yeah. The entrance to the neighborhood is right across the street."

"So, if your house gets smashed, we'll probably all get smashed, too. Does your mom work? She didn't make it here to pick you up, right?"

"She's an interior designer. She's probably in the city consulting on something. She should be okay. My dad's in a submarine, probably a long way from here. My sister's here, at the school. Probably right in this room. How about your parents?"

"My mom doesn't have a job. She's just a mom. My dad works in one of those office buildings."

"So, they should be okay. They're not near the ocean, right?

"Right."

"Hear that roar? I wish we had a window so we could see what's going on."

"Me, too."

Screams of alarm erupted from the mouths of many children as the lights went out and they were pitched into utter blackness. Some of the children started to cry. The darkness was short-lived, though. Someone turned on a flashlight. Soon, a half-dozen flashlights were illuminating the area.

The ground seemed to rumble, and Steven wondered if there was an earthquake too. Then some of the children started screaming as water flowed under the outer doors and soaked them where they sat. The noise, by that time, was terrific and fear spread contagiously from one to the other until many were on the brink of hysteria. The teachers and staff tried to calm them down, with uneven success. The panic of one teacher was not reassuring to her students, a few of whom were now screaming in terror.

3:28 p.m., Tripler Medical Centeer, Oahu

When Daniel awoke, he was lying on his back, and looking at a white ceiling. The monitors around him told him he was in a hospital, but he couldn't remember what had led to his being there.

He found a button next to his hand and pushed it. Shortly after, a nurse entered, turned off the call switch and said, "So you're awake, Commander. How do you feel?"

"Disoriented. What happened to me?"

"You had successful surgery on your left leg. You're in the recovery room. Your thigh now has a foot-long metal rod and a few screws in it. We're going to get you walking on it as soon as we can. What do you remember?" the nurse asked.

"It's all kind of blurry. I remember being underwater and having tremendous pain as I swam for the surface. I have a vague recollection of being in a helicopter then lying around here for a while. I don't remember that much. I must have been drugged."

"You had a broken left thigh bone. The bone poked through the skin, and you lost a lot of blood. They gave you emergency treatment on board the ship, then air-evaced you to Tripler. We transfused you and got you stable enough for surgery. Then, our orthopedic surgeons fixed your leg. They washed out your wound, then put a rod and screws in your thigh bone.

"You were pretty out of it when you got here, maybe because of the bad air you breathed during your escape," the nurse continued. "Your blood chemistries were all out of whack, and it took a while to get them normal. It's a wonder you survived, what with that and all the blood you lost."

"So now I do PT, and when I can walk, I can go home. Is that correct?"

"That would be the norm, but... I don't know an easy way to tell you this, so I'll just blurt it out. A few hours ago, a tsunami hit Honolulu. It caused massive destruction. You may not have a home anymore. None of us are sure of anything right now. I don't know whether I have a home, either."

"What about my wife and kids?"

"Your wife was here this morning, but she left before the tsunami hit. We haven't been able to contact your wife or kids since. Telephones systems are down. Only some mobile phones work. I haven't been able to reach my husband either. We're all in the same boat, you see."

"I live in Foster Village. That's pretty far inland. I would guess it's okay there."

"The tsunami hit in the late morning. Your kids were probably in school, and your wife could have been anywhere on the island. We could see the tsunami from the windows. The airport was hit severely. Hundreds of injured people who were at the airport are finding their way here. Some walked and others were carried here.

"Is there a telephone I can use to call my wife?"

"Sorry. They're at a premium right now. Land lines don't work, and mobile phones can't be charged up. We're on emergency power, and we need to reserve it for emergency coordination. There's not much more we can do right now.

"Listen, I have to go," she went on. "We have hundreds of people who need care. You're stable, and frankly, you're low on the priority list right now. I'll try to catch you later, when things start to settle down. I'm afraid that until then, you're going to be pretty much on your own."

"Thanks. I appreciate your candor."

"If you need something for the pain, push this button," she said, pointing to a box on the IV pole. "It's regulated so you won't get too much medicine. Don't use it unless you need it, but if you do, it's there."

"Okay, thanks."

She flashed him a smile and rushed off.

He lay his head back on the pillow and closed his eyes. "Unacceptable," he said to himself. Somehow, he had to know where Ellen and the kids were. All the time he had been in submarines, he had known that he was the one most likely to be in danger, not his family. He'd taken it as a given that they'd be there waiting for him when he got off the boat. Now, he had no idea whether they were even alive. He couldn't accept that, particularly not when the danger they faced had been the result of his failure.

He knew what caused the tsunami–his stupidly running his submarine into a floating dock. Then, he'd lost the submarine he commanded. It had been cut in half and sunk on an active volcano, where it must have blown up. His errors had resulted in untold misery for Hawaii residents. His mistakes had cost him his command, almost surely his home, and possibly his family as well. In addition, he was responsible for the death and misery of thousands of innocent people.

But he couldn't think about that right now. He had to know about his family, no matter what the cost, and he wasn't going to find out by babying himself on a hospital ward. He had to get out of bed, walk if he had to, first to his home, his kids' school, wherever. He had to get access to a working phone so he could call Ellen, wherever she was. Then, they could find the kids together.

It'll all begin with the first step, he told himself. He put his good ankle under the ankle of his injured leg. He used his good leg to support his bad one and his belly muscles to lift his legs off the bed while his hands turned him so his legs swung off the bed. Then he slowly relaxed his good leg, allowing his left knee to bend.

Excruciating pain emanated from his thigh. He backed off a couple of degrees and then gradually eased forward until only his buttocks were on the bed. Grabbing hold of the orthopaedic trapeze suspended over the middle of his bed, he lifted his trunk and let both legs slowly descend to the floor.

He waited for the pain to subside, then lifted his buttocks off the bed, progressively putting more weight on his two legs. When he was finally standing, his good leg bore most of the weight. He realized he could never walk until the bad leg could bear his full weight. At least, not without crutches. He gradually shifted weight to the bad one until both legs bore about equal weight. He gritted his teeth as he shifted weight to the broken bone and then took a tentative, small step forward. An involuntary groan escaped from his mouth. He waited until the pain subsided, then shifted his weight to his good leg and tried to take a step with his bad leg. It didn't work and he lost his balance, crashing to the floor.

He lay there, unable to get up again, until one of the nurses noticed him. She and an orderly lifted him up and put him back in bed. The nurse scolded him for trying to walk on his own. It wasn't necessary. He knew it had been a dumb idea.

"Find me some crutches, will you," he said.

"I'll try," she said. "When you try them out, though, wait until one of us is here. Or a physical therapist. We have to show you how to use them. You won't figure it out on your own."

"I promise."

Tomorrow, he told himself, after she left. *I'll be out of here tomorrow.* In the meantime, he had to figure out how to get his hands on a working phone. He lay back on the bed, and his imagination began to run wild. His anxiety level rose until he felt like screaming. He forced himself to calm down, but his heart still pounded and he could feel his muscles tensing. The pain in his leg became intolerable. He pushed the button giving him an intravenous dose of painkiller. The pain and anxiety decreased, and he fell into a fitful sleep.

Chapter 22

February 16, 2020

1:10 PM: Tripler Medical Centeer

Daniel reconnected with Mike Polanski at Tripler in Physical Therapy. Mike couldn't walk and still had poor control of his left hand. Seeing him so disabled dismayed Daniel, but Mike was optimistic. "You should've seen me a few days ago. I couldn't move a damn thing below my neck. Now, I can wiggle my toes and feel my arms. Best yet, I'm starting to be able to control when I pee. The docs got no idea how much I'm going to get back. We'll see about that."

"You heard from your kids?"

"Missy's fine. She was lucky. Her school was demolished. Most of her fellow students were killed, but she was saved by the dad of one of her friends, who drove her uphill. They're in a shelter together now. They're safe. Marisa's with her in the shelter," Mike said. He frowned. "We haven't heard from Rudy. Marisa's having a hard time with it. She's tried to get him on the phone a hundred times. No luck. Missy says his school was wiped out, just like hers. They're only a couple blocks apart. We're praying, but it doesn't look good."

"A lot of phones are out of service. He may still show up." Farriott said. "Ellen's missing, too, but I bet she'll show up here sometime soon. I haven't been able to track down my kids, either."

"Tough. Your kids should be okay, though. They were at Makalapa Elementary, right?"

"Right."

"I hear that area wasn't hit hard. The kids are probably in a shelter somewhere."

"It drives me nuts, being stuck here. I can't even look for them."

"Marisa tells me they're fixing up a computer search network in the shelters," Mike said. "You'll probably have no problem finding them once you get to a shelter."

"I hope so," Daniel said. "You heard anything about the rest of our crew?"

"Don't know. They all made it off the sub, but what happened during the tsunami is anyone's guess. I haven't seen any of them here at Tripler except Lozano, so that's a good sign. Lozano's had some surgery, and he says he's going to need a lot more. Hard to tell. He makes it a lot worse than it is. You know what I mean?"

"I do. Some guys get over it. Others let medical problems take over their lives. That's Lozano," Farriott said. "The rest of the crew are probably cleaning up the mess at Pearl Harbor right now,"

"Unless they got caught in the tsunami, of course."

Farriott sighed. "I hope not. That would be a horror, to get to safety after that ordeal and then drown anyway? I can't deal with that thought."

"Cleaning up should keep them occupied for a while. I'm told Pearl's a disaster zone."

"Half the city's a disaster zone." Farriott's face fell, guilt written all over it.

"Right. There was another guy in the decompression chamber with me before I was air-evaced here. A diver named Sampaga. He's one of the divers who cut the cables to that dock. He didn't make it."

"Too bad," Farriott said. His voice caught in his throat. "Why are so many innocent people hurt or dead when we're still alive? It just isn't fair." He turned to leave, then turned back and held out his hand. "It was an honor to serve with you, Chief."

"Likewise," said Polanski, grasping his hand with as tight a grip as he could muster. He held it, looked Farriott straight in the eye, and said, "It wasn't your fault, Skipper. It was just a damned accident."

"Maybe. We'll see what the Navy determines. They'll have an inquiry, of course."

"You make sure they get me to testify," Mike said. "I'll tell them what's what."

"Thanks," Daniel said. "Good luck with the rehab."

He didn't see Polanski again until Rudy's funeral a month later.

Chapter 23

February 18, 2020

11:15 a.m., Tripler Medical Centeer

Daniel left Tripler on the fourth day after his surgery, but he did not go right home. By then, he could walk with crutches, but the distance he could walk was still very limited. With his limited capacity, it would have been hard to survive at home. Besides, he wanted to find his kids, and the most likely place to find them would be at one of several shelters established in the un-flooded areas of Honolulu.

When the hospital van dropped him off at the nearest shelter, he found that the computer network Mike had mentioned was already up and running. By using that, he was finally able to track down Penny and Steven. They were in a children's shelter not far away. He hitched a ride to their shelter later that day.

When he arrived, he was directed to a gymnasium filled with children of all ages. Hundreds of kids were sitting on mats on the floor. The mood was somber. Some were playing, but there were few smiles, and the noise level was nowhere near what he would expect from that many kids packed together. As he walked down the rows, hopeful eyes raised to his face, then fell with disappointment.

He was going down the third row of children when he felt a searing pain in his left leg and saw two arms wrapped round it. "Daddy," Penny cried, tears running down her face. She held on for dear life, then lifted her arms, asking him to pick her up. He had no choice. He lowered his crutches to the ground, shifted his weight to his good leg, lifted her up, and hugged her tight. He could feel her tears on his face and neck. Steven was next, but he couldn't lift him and Penny at the same time, so he lowered her, then bent down enough to hug Steven.

"Where's Mommy?" Steven asked.

"I don't know," Daniel answered. "I haven't found her yet. I'm still looking."

He thanked God that the kids were safe, but he dreaded the bad news that he expected might come. The computers had two lists now, a list of the alive and a list of the dead. He hadn't been able to find her on either list yet, but as time went on, he knew that the odds became greater that he would find her on the second list.

Chapter 24

22 February 2020

3:32 p.m., Kailua, Island of Oahu

The woman's arm was caught in the crook of a tree so that she hung there, her feet a yard from the ground. She was dressed only in underwear and a torn blouse. She had no identification. The cadaver team climbed a ladder to reach up and unhook her arm, then lowered her to the ground. They placed her supine, photographed her face, scraped the inside of her mouth for DNA, and zipped her into a body bag. They put the body bag into a truck bed with a half-dozen other cadavers and transported it to a collection area for disposal.

Those involved with war are the most experienced and equipped to deal with large numbers of casualties, so the treatment of the wounded and the dead became primarily a military operation, with a lot of help from the Red Cross. The main emphasis was on the wounded, but the dead could not be ignored, either. They had to be gathered, identified, and either buried or cremated quickly to avert a public health crisis.

At first, teams simply gathered the dead and lined them up in rows. Those with identification were toe-tagged and separated from those who had no ID, and their names were placed on a list of identified victims. This list was disseminated on computer links. Many of those listed were later released to relatives for burial or cremation.

The toes of those with no ID were tagged only with a number and the location where they had been found. Facial photographs were taken and catalogued, fingerprints were taken, and buccal smears were saved for DNA analysis. Identification was a slow process. Many were identified using facial recognition. Others had recorded fingerprints. The ones needing DNA matches took the longest, and many of these did not match in any system.

Honolulu Airport re-opened two days after the tsunami. The passenger loading platforms, ticket counters, baggage handling equipment, and parking facilities were destroyed, but the runways were intact, and the military was able to organize effective, if temporary, ground aviation control. Once the airport was open, emergency supplies began to flow in, including drinking water, supplemental food, medical supplies, and thousands of body bags. When zipped in the impermeable body bags, the corpses represented less of a public health risk and the odor was alleviated, but the problem was not solved. Burial in mass graves began on the fifth day.

By the time Daniel identified Ellen from her photographs, she had already been buried, with over two hundred others, at the newest landfill in Kailua. When the family was mobile again, long after the flood, he and the kids went to that place and had a private memorial service for her, just the three of them shedding tears together. Each in turn said loving words about her, heartfelt and sad. Daniel then read some passages from the Bible and asked God to look after her in heaven. When they left, Daniel felt there should be some form of marker, some permanent recognition of her existence. But there was none, and as far as he knew, there never would be, at least not in that location.

By then, he and the two kids had moved back to Foster Village. When they arrived, their home was mostly intact, though the flood had been a foot deep in the house. All the furniture had to be moved out in the sun to dry. The floorboards were soaked with mud and needed cleaning. Fortunately, they had area rugs and not carpets. Daniel threw the rugs away and bought new ones at the Navy Exchange when that re-opened.

Steven's friend, Larry Murdock, and his family came to stay with them temporarily, as the Murdock family's home had been destroyed. After a month, the Murdocks left for the mainland, to stay with relatives.

Larry's dad was invaluable in helping to salvage the Farriott family's household goods, particularly until Daniel's leg was healed enough for him to walk without crutches.

They had no electricity, but Daniel did have a Coleman lantern, five gallons of propane and a gas barbecue, so they could cook and see at night. With no electricity, the refrigerator wouldn't work, but the water had not leaked past its seals, and the air was still cool inside, as no one had opened its doors since before the flood. Most of the food within it was still edible, and eighty percent of the food in the freezer was still frozen. They also had a cupboard full of canned and boxed food. He'd always kept a ten-gallon bottle of water in his garage in case of emergency, and now was the time to use it. They also had iodine tablets and a water filter for camping, so they could collect rain water and purify it when they needed it. They had enough for two weeks, at least, Daniel judged. They lived off what they had until supplies from the mainland were in sufficient quantity to support the population.

Daniel was particularly pleased (and surprised) to find that their car still worked. Since it had automatic transmission, he could drive, even with his injured leg. Not far, of course, since they couldn't buy gasoline, but they could at least use the car for transportation when their bicycles wouldn't suffice.

Daniel was on three months' medical convalescent leave, but a courier from the Navy brought him official notice of a military tribunal involving the loss of the JPC, set for a month after his return to duty. He was ordered to appear as a witness on Monday, April 22, 2020 at 0800. He was advised that he could have a military attorney present at the inquiry and he could select one from a list provided as an addendum.

They're going to bury me, he thought. *I'm dead meat.*

Epilogue

June 20, 2029

3:30 p.m., Halekulani Hotel, Waikiki, Honolulu

The upper deck of the renovated Halekulani Hotel was decorated with a thousand golden origami cranes made by the bridesmaids and with a thousand silver stars made by the groom's sister.

Two hundred guests heard the wedding vows as the young couple pledged eternal love to each other. After being declared husband and wife, Ensign David McFarlane, USN, kissed his new wife, Yvonne (Missy) McFarlane, and the couple then exited through a gauntlet of guests blowing soap bubbles.

It was an all-white wedding, with the groom, the groom's men, and the groom's father in their Dress White Navy uniforms, the bride in a beautiful white dress, and the bridesmaids in sleek white silk cheongsams.

Daniel Farriott was at Table 4 for the reception, sitting with his wife of two years, former Navy Commander Wendy Peyton and two of their three children. Now retired from the Navy and working for a civilian defense contractor, he wore civilian clothing, an aloha shirt and light slacks. Wendy, Penny, and Penny's half-sister, Mary Ellen also wore aloha attire.

Also at table 4 were retired Rear Admiral Jacob Green and his wife, also dressed in civilian clothes. Daniel had crossed paths with Admiral Green many times since the tsunami, and they had become close friends over the years. Admiral Green had supported him during the grueling inquiry, then after no malfeasance had been found, suggested to Daniel in private that he leave the Navy anyway. "They're not going to give you another command," he'd said. "It makes no difference that you didn't do anything wrong." It had been good advice.

Daniel's reminiscing was interrupted by an attractive, distinguished-looking woman at Wendy's side. "Are these seats taken?" she asked. "We're assigned to this table."

"They're all yours," Wendy said, and the woman put her purse down at the seat next to Wendy's. The man with her, who had a full beard, long hair tied in a ponytail, and appeared to be uncomfortable in his aloha shirt, smiled at the table and put his wine glass in front of the next plate.

"I'm Susan Cho, and this is my husband Russell Wilkes," the woman said.

Both Daniel and Admiral Green rose. Admiral Green said, "It's a pleasure to see you two again. It's been almost a decade, hasn't it?"

"Admiral Green? I didn't recognize you without your uniform," Susan said. "It's nice to see you."

"I'm Daniel Farriott," Daniel said. "We've never met, but you and I had several interesting conversations underwater. I owe you a lot."

"Oh, my gosh. You were the submarine commander, weren't you?"

"Right. This is my wife, Wendy. She was the XO on the JPC."

"It's a pleasure to meet you both. Imagine. After all these years."

"It seems that Mike Polanski engineered a reunion for us, the devious bastard," Admiral Green said, chuckling. "When did you two get married?"

"Eight years ago. It would have been sooner, but we were both very busy, particularly after I became Chair of the Oceanography Department at Manoa."

"When did that happen?" Green asked.

"Right away but it didn't mean anything, really. There was a vacancy because the former Chair was killed in the flood. Then, there was the chaos of reconstruction, when titles became insignificant, and I became an interim Chair with no power. The University got around to choosing a permanent Chair a year or so later, and I was selected. That's when the real work began. I served five years, then resigned as Chair, although I'm still a Professor. I hated the administrative part. I'm much happier doing field research. Russell and I live on the Big Island now. We've made a whole career out of studying Loihi together. We're also busy raising three kids." Susan sat down next to Wendy.

"We have three, too. Mary Ellen is five," Wendy said, pointing to her daughter. "The others aren't kids anymore. They're twenty-one and eighteen. Steven, the oldest, is at Yale, and Penny, here, is at Punahou. She'll be attending Stanford next year."

"Two naval officers as parents, and no kids in the navy?" Susan asked.

Wendy shook her head and smiled. "Steven was offered a place at Annapolis but turned it down. I think he's better off where he is. Penny's more interested in fine arts. She wants to be a writer."

"Ours are too young to know what they want yet, but they're whizzes at science and math. They may be scientists too, but who knows, right? I didn't choose my career until I was in college."

"Daniel and I are enjoying second careers. He's a Naval retiree, and I'm in the Navy reserves, so we're both subject to being called up in an emergency, but we're not on active duty. We remember the Navy days with fondness, but we're glad we moved on."

"What do you do now?" Susan asked.

"Naval engineering, as a civilian," Daniel said. "I can't tell you much more than that. It's classified."

"I'm a law student," Wendy said.

"And an advocate for women in the military," Daniel said. "Did you know she was the first American woman to command a nuclear submarine? She gets calls all the time to speak to groups ranging from girl scouts to political advocacy groups."

"Wow. You and I have a lot to talk about, then. I do deep exploration in mini-submarines."

Wendy's expression grew somber. "Yes, I know. We should have lunch together. But maybe we should talk about something else right now." She glanced at Daniel. "It can be a touchy subject."

Susan nodded. She understood. She turned to Admiral Green. "I understand you're going to do some teaching," she said.

"I plead guilty," he said, with a laugh. "If you were still Chair of the Oceanography Department, you would be my boss."

She laughed back. "Don't tempt me. I might sign up for another term."

Green turned to Russell Wilkes and asked, "How about you? Are you still studying volcanoes?"

"Susan and I are joined at the hip," he said. "We've become world experts on undersea volcanoes. There are a lot of them, you know. We wander around the world studying them. I check out their geology, and she works on their associated biodiversity. Did you know she's discovered and named more than thirty new species? It's been an amazing collaboration."

Their conversation was interrupted by the tinkle of a spoon against a wine-glass. Mike Polanski was standing at Table 1, a glass in his hand. "We're going to drink some toasts, so could you all charge your glasses. You teetotalers can drink water, but I want everyone to participate. When you're ready, please stand up." He waited until he saw everyone was standing.

"Some of you might have noticed that the groom here is all in white and he's got butter bars on his shoulder, which means he's in the Navy and he's an officer. You all know what that means? It means, for the rest of my life, my son-in-law's going to outrank me? Ain't that the pits?"

He waited for the laughter to die down. "Most of you have some relationship to the Navy, and old Navy guys have a tradition of toasts that are given at formal events. So, we're going to do those toasts. There's going to be several, so don't gulp it all down at once. Save a drop for the last one."

He raised his glass. "To the United States of America," he said. They all took a sip.

"To the Commander-in-Chief," he said. Another sip.

"To the United States Navy," he said. Another sip.

He paused then. "You all may know that the last boat I served on was the John Pina Craven, what some people called the JPC. A lot of the folks here were on that last voyage of the JPC. It sunk when Loihi blew up. Many of us are survivors of that day, mostly due to our fantastic officers, who saved us when everything went to hell. They were helped by a bunch of people who gave their all to get us home. Without them, my Missy here wouldn't have a dad to give her away."

"Most of these folks are seated at Table 4, and I'd like to make one last toast. And I'd like to thank them for getting the whole crew home." He raised his glass. "To the JPC, Commander Daniel Farriott, it's fine officers and crew, and the people who risked their own necks to keep us alive." He drank his glass dry, then sat down.

He noticed that everyone else remained standing. He slapped his forehead, stood up again and said, "I forgot I'm not in the Navy anymore. If I was, my toasts would be done. But I got to make one more toast, and no, it's not to this guy here," he said, pointing to the groom. "The best man will make s toast to him later. But I got to make my toast to my lady, Marisa, who stuck with me all the time I was underwater, held my family together, and raised my kids to be the incredible people they are today."

He filled his glass again, held it up and said, "To Marisa, my queen."

She stood, they kissed, and the room exploded with applause.

Acknowledgements

For three decades, I lived within two miles of the submarine base at Pearl Harbor. As a surgeon working at Tripler Medical Centeer, Honolulu, I cared for the brave Navy men and women who worked at Pearl Harbor and their families. I formed an immense respect for these dedicated professionals, who did a job that I would have found to be incredibly difficult. Their dedication and their patriotism was amazing.

My first tour of an American nuclear submarine, a Seawolf class attack submarine, was in the 1970's, during the Vietnam War. In this time of separation of military services, the event of an Army officer stepping into an active Navy nuclear submarine was notable enough that a picture of my climbing through the hatch was published in an article in the Army Times. I later was privileged to tour a ballistic missile submarine, a boomer, and more recently, a modern submarine, the USS Santa Fe. I spoke to many of its crew and its commanding officer, CDR Jake Foret, and learned a great deal from them regarding the physical and psychological realities of being confined for months at a time in submarines far below the surface of the ocean. I thank them for their willingness to share, their service to our country, and their professionalism.

I also became a good friend of John Piña Craven, Chief Scientist of the Navy Special Projects Office and Project Manager of the Polaris submarine project. Dr. Craven was one of the most intelligent and innovative men I've ever met. Dr. Craven, in my opinion, was one of the unsung heroes of the Cold War. The attempted salvage of a sunken Russian nuclear submarine, an operation in which Dr. Craven was intimately involved, is described in three books cited below. Dr. Craven also was an early pioneer in the development of deep water submersibles and led the Navy's efforts to develop rescue vehicles for submarines in distress.

The capabilities of American nuclear submarines are highly classified. I have not used, nor do I have access to classified material, nor have I received or sought secret information from any source. The capabilities of the JPC in my novel are derived from speculation based upon public information available to anyone on the internet. Similarly, the details of salvage of nuclear submarines are derived from published material, with some updating on my part to reflect my own knowledges of advances in material properties, deep ocean physics, robotics, and computer science. Similar assumptions were made regarding communications with the JPC, temperature control aboard the vessel, the composition of the hull, and numerous other details.

When relevant technology is classified, a fiction writer can speculate about the truth without fear of being contradicted, particularly when the events depicted are in the future, involving submarines that are not yet built. Nevertheless, I have done my best to ensure that the events depicted in this novel are compatible with existing science and engineering. If not real, they are at least realistic.

Loihi Seamount is real. It is an active volcano east of the Big Island of Hawaii. Scientists from the University of Hawaii and the University of California, San Diego have used submersibles to explore it on many occasions. Details regarding it are available on the internet from the oceanography departments of these Universities, several sources being cited below.

The danger of an undersea landslide of lava accumulated from the Kilauea Volcano—the so-called Hilina Slump—and its potential for causing a tsunami have been well-reported in Hawaii's local media. Details regarding this threat are also easily found on the internet.

I have many people to thank with regard to this book. My mentor and friend, William Bernhardt, gave invaluable advice regarding the manuscript and the design of the cover. My editor, Jacqueline Ben-Zekry, provided a superb analysis of the book, with numerous helpful suggestions for improvement. I am very thankful to her for her professionalism and insight. Similarly, Nevin Nelson and my lovely wife, Howena, read all my books prior to publication, catching the vast majority of my numerous misspellings, plot problems, and typos, and they both have the strength to tell me when I have gone seriously wrong. I rely on their advice and objective appraisal. Without it, my books would be much diminished.

My fellow members of Sisters in Crime, Hawaii, and the Hawaii Writers Association give me moral support, help in marketing, and a friendly but useful sounding board on all my projects, including this one. I particularly want to thank Gail Baugniet and Laurie Hanan, two excellent writers who have earned my respect for their honesty, my admiration for their skills, and my friendship for their humanity.

Pertinent references from published works and the internet are below:

Loihi

http://www.schmidtocean.org/story/show/2225

https://en.wikipedia.org/wiki/Lōʻihi_Seamount

https://www.soest.hawaii.edu/GG/HCV/loihi.html

http://ocean.nationalgeographic.com/ocean/photos/deep-sea-creatures/#/deep-sea01-frill-shark_18161_600x450.jpg

Underwater explosions

https://en.wikipedia.org/wiki/Underwater_explosion

http://scholar.google.com/scholar_url?url=http://www.dtic.mil/get-tr doc/pdf%3FAD%3DAD0268905&hl=en&sa=X&scisig=AAGBfm1TtXNqpJPkkCuMp_nmjPSPmu6Vrw&nossl=1&oi=scholarr

https://en.wikipedia.org/wiki/Shock_factor

Submarine rescue & salvage

The Silent War: The Cold War Battle Beneath the Sea, by John Piña Craven, 2001, Simon & Schuster

Blind Man's Bluff: The Untold Story of American Submarine Espionage, by Sherry Sontag and Christopher Drew, 1998, Public Affairs

Project Azorian: The CIA and the Raising of the K-129, by Norman Polmar and Michael White, 2010, Audible

www.navy.mil/navydata/fact_display.asp?cid=4100&ct=4&tid=400

www.navy.mil/search/display.asp?story_id=40147

https://en.wikipedia.org/wiki/Submarine_Rescue_Diving_Recompression_System

Submarine technology

https://en.wikipedia.org/wiki/Seawolf-class_submarine

https://en.wikipedia.org/wiki/Virginia-class_submarine

http://www.navy.mil/navydata/fact_display.asp?cid=2200&tid=1300&ct=2

Tsunamis & Hilina Slump

General Oceanography: An Introduction, by Gunter Diedrich, 1963, Interscience

https://www.sciencedaily.com/releases/2003/12/031209080659.htm

https://pubs.usgs.gov/ds/2006/171/data/cruise-reports/2001/html/24.htm

Diving Physiology

Diving and Subaquatic Medicine, 4th Edition, by Carl Edmonds, Christopher Lowry, John Pennefather, & Robyn Walker, 2005, Hodder-Arnold

Watch for:

The Titanium Rib

by Alain Gunn

Pediatric surgeon Melvin Smith did not know how to save his patient, an infant with a deformity of his rib cage from birth. In desperation, he sought the assistance of a pediatric orthopedic surgeon, Robert Campbell. Their subsequent collaboration led to the development of the titanium rib, a device that has saved the lives of countless children world-wide, resulted in the definition of a new disease, revolutionized the care of small children with curvature of the spine, and led to changes in federal policy that encourage and assist the development of similar surgical devices in the future.

The Titanium Rib is a novelization of the twenty-year struggle of these two dedicated surgeons to change the technology and concepts of the time, in order to relieve the inability of certain disabled children to do the most basic activity of life--breathing. Publication is projected for November 2018.

Made in the USA
Columbia, SC
10 September 2024

42048848R10205